Lament of Badblood

LEGEND OF APOCALYPS

ARTHUR BARILLAS

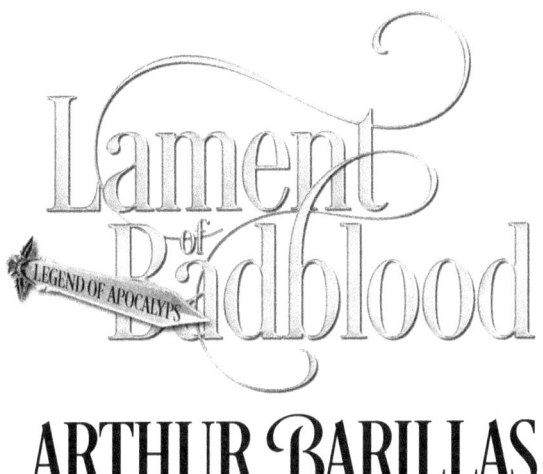

ARTHUR BARILLAS

ISBN Paperback book 978-1-77400-068-7
ISBN Electronic book 978-1-77400-069-4
ISBN Hardcover book 978-1-77400-070-0

To God above all else and his only son, Jesus Christ.
To his Blessed Mother, the Virgin Mary.

To my loving wife Cristina, who never
abandons me in pursuing my dreams.
To my daughter Grace Nicole. May this book show
you that love and forgiveness are the only options.
To my son Gerardo. Always cherish that marvelous
gift given to you and share it with the world.
To my daughter Isabella. May this book series
inspire you to be brave, just like your mom.

To my best friend, Rebeca, for
being my number-one fan.
To Danny, because in writing and reading, we
explore new worlds and new emotions.

To my editor, Sandra, and publisher, Gwen,
thank you for simply being awesome and always
being there for me and my book series. No words
can describe all that you've done for me.

"A woman's worth is not measured by her accomplishments or possessions, but by the love she gives and the lives she touches."
–St. Katharine Drexel.

PROLOGUE

Mexico City, CDMX, Mexico; Feb 7, 12:30 a.m.

UNEASINESS OVERWHELMED SIXTEEN-YEAR-OLD DEMON hunter Anna Rodriguez as she gazed at the back entrance of the run-down dance club. Its deteriorated and rotten decor gave out the perfect vibe for demons, vampires, and other undead creatures. The girl felt out of place for this particular incursion, though, watching from afar as two of her older sister demon hunters walked up to the club, confident the large six-foot-three bouncer would grant them access. *It should be me going in,* the teenager thought, removing strands of dark brown hair from her eyes.

"I hate this plan," the girl said over her intercom to her Guardian and brother, who heard her loud and clear. "Sending them in without communication, leaving us outside."

"Easy," Luis Rodriguez replied. "Mercedes and Blanca are good, being eighteen and all. They can handle it. If something goes wrong, we have the panic button."

"Feeling left out, *pitufa?*" Maria chimed in.

Anna gritted her teeth, hearing the demeaning nickname the older Mexican demon hunters had given her. The five-foot girl looked up toward the opposite six-story building where Maria was perched on the roof with her black compound bow. Her long dark brown hair had been tied in a bun above her head. Her black denim jacket, white blouse, and black jeans gave the older teenager an excellent look for hunting the undead. Even from a distance, Anna could distinguish the girl's sly smirk staring down at her.

Anna shook her head. It had been over eighteen months since the Guardians had chosen her to lead the demon hunters from the region. She was the youngest of that particular Gathering and had proven her worth. She tried to ignore the verbal badgering, seeing Mercedes and Blanca reaching the entrance while she firmly grasped her trusty automatic crossbow—a gift from Elizabeth Somiere and the rest of the Assembly for being part of that event. The air-pressurized weapon had a clip with twelve arrows, ready to fire. The young demon hunter looked down at her black Converse shoes, reminiscing on that joyful memory she treasured, being with her sister demon hunters and engaging in an all-out battle as equals.

Anna refocused on Mercedes and Blanca, who had now reached the back door and talked to the bouncer. The five-foot-five demon hunters had bright smiles on their faces. Their outfits screamed that they were ready for a night out—short dresses and nice heels for dancing. But hidden within them was the power to fight any undead creature that dared challenge them. Anna could hear Mercedes giggle while playing with her long, curly brown hair. Blanca removed the strands of black hair from her face before touching the bouncer on the arm.

"You catch that, Maria?" Anna asked.

"I'm not blind, *pitufa*," Maria replied. "Do I take him out?"

"Negative," Anna responded. "We wait for the signal."

"You're the boss," the seventeen-year-old demon hunter said as she aimed her bow straight into the bouncer's heart. "Did you catch the other two on the second-floor windows?"

"I'm aware," Anna said. "Crappy lookouts for this particular nest."

Anna's impatience was getting to her as she watched the eighteen-year-old demon hunters giggle, and the bouncer let them inside the club. Then something caught the demon hunter's eye, seeing a black limousine roll along the street, with a man in his early thirties visible in one of the windows. Anna saw the man smirk at the bouncer and nod. The limousine then sped off. Something inside Anna snapped like a twig. "It's a trap," Anna whispered on her communicator.

"What?!" Luis exclaimed.

Anna sprang into action and started running toward the club. "Maria!" Anna commanded. "Take the shot! Now!"

Maria tensed her bow and released a single arrow. She grabbed two more projectiles from her quiver and fired them off as well.

Anna heard the projectiles snap. An arrow thrust right into the bouncer's heart, turning the vampire to ash as he screamed. Two more arrows went through the open windows, while Anna called for Mercedes and Blanca with her mind. *Anna, please help us!* Their dread-filled thoughts screamed at the young demon hunter, feeling her fear compounded with Maria's.

"Maria!" Anna screamed. "Get your butt down here!"

Anna was a few feet from the club door when it burst open, sending pieces of wood and metal everywhere. The demon hunter looked in horror at a five-foot-one, gray-skinned bald demon with sharp fangs and claws. Its red eyes looked straight at Anna, piercing her soul as it screeched a war cry.

"Anna!" Luis called out. "What is it?"

"It's an Uroks-Nah demon," Anna stuttered. She could feel her entire body shaking in dread, seeing the beast growl at her as its body contorted. The bones from its back cracked and popped out unnaturally; drool streamed from the beast's jaw. Soon, the monster growled at the demon hunter as gray batwings spurted from its back, extending outward six feet on each side. The young demon hunter pulled out her crossbow and fired several arrows, aiming for its chest, which the beast deflected with its wings as it jumped up and took flight.

"Maria!" Anna called out, seeing the deadly trajectory the demon had taken. "Look out!"

Maria fired three more arrows at the incoming beast while it was airborne. The demon dodged and wove in the air as if it were second nature, flying straight into the dark-haired demon hunter, causing her to drop her compound bow. Maria grunted in pain as the beast tackled her on the rooftop.

"Get off me!" Maria screamed at the monster as she wrestled it, tossing and turning. She punched the beast in the face, which only further angered it as it growled and slashed Maria with its claws across her belly and chest. Maria screamed in agony as she used her legs to push the beast away from her. The demon hunter stood up, pulling a stake from her jeans pocket and running toward the beast, tackling it across the chest. The Uroks-Nah wrapped Maria with its wings as both demon hunter and demon flipped over the edge of the building, dropping six stories onto the concrete.

Anna closed her teary eyes and looked away, hearing concrete and flesh pound each other. She opened them back up and saw no movement from the impact zone.

The sixteen-year-old demon hunter whipped her eyes in the direction of sounds of commotion inside the club. She ran at full speed, entering the building and gasping in horror at the scene that greeted her. Six Uroks-Nah demons stood crouched over the lifeless bodies of Mercedes and Blanca. Their dead eyes stared back coldly at Anna as the demons feasted on their demon-hunter blood.

"Anna!" Luis screamed over her intercom. "Get out of there!"

Anna pulled out her crossbow and fired the remaining bolts, emptying the clip. The demons growled at the girl as the arrows hit their hearts, causing the beasts to combust in ashes and dirt. The black and gray powder covered Blanca's and Mercedes' bodies as Anna sobbed on her knees.

A growl from inside the club brought the demon

hunter back to reality. She saw five pairs of red eyes in the darkness. The growls intensified as dark silhouettes stepped into the moonlight, revealing themselves to be even more Uroks-Nah demons. The beasts screeched at Anna as the demon hunter looked at her crossbow, realizing she was out of ammunition.

The girl felt a hand pull her out of the club. She turned around and saw Maria half-running, half-staggering, leading her to the exit. "I got her!" Maria said, her voice sounding hoarse.

"Get to the temple!" Luis instructed. "They can't get by the barrier! I will meet you there!"

Anna followed Maria out of the club as both demon hunters started running. Anna could see Maria was severely hurt, seeing open wounds across her stomach and back. The older demon hunter had her right hand covering her throat while her left hand dragged Anna across the deserted dark streets and alleys of the Mexican capital. Closed street shops around them compounded with a claustrophobic ambiance as they escaped. "Didn't they teach you in the Gathering that you run in the presence of a Urok-Nah demon?" Maria asked rhetorically. Particles of blood came out of her mouth as she spoke.

"Mercedes and Blanca are dead," Anna stated. "We were set up."

"Damned right," Maria said as she turned left. She could hear the demons running right behind them. "You have to find out who did this!"

Anna looked back and saw the five Uroks-Nah trailing behind them. Even though they were the most formidable demons to dispatch, their running speed was one of their main weaknesses. Still, with Maria's injuries, they were gaining on them.

Maria turned right again, and The Basilica of Our Lady of Guadalupe temple was just one hundred meters away. The final obstacle was the white metal steel fence that protected the ancient structure. Just then, Maria's head started feeling fuzzy and her knees buckled. She looked down her body and saw she was losing a lot of blood. The demon hunter fell to her knees.

Anna, seeing her sister fall, did not miss a beat. As if she had a second wind, she lifted the taller demon hunter, putting her in a firefighter carry position on her back. The shorter demon hunter started sprinting toward the temple. She could feel the demons on her heels, but did not dare turn around and look back. The metal fence drew closer and closer. The young demon hunter turned her body around and jumped full force, smashing the left side of her body on the metal fence, breaking the steel barrier. She and Maria crashed hard on the ground beside the holy water grotto.

Anna heard unnatural howls of pain. She looked up and saw the five demons contorting in agony as an invisible force trapped them within the temple's perimeter. Soon, all five burst into flames and turned to dust.

Anna turned toward Maria and gasped, seeing her sister's injured body for the first time. The beast had bitten a big piece of flesh from the demon hunter's throat and collarbone, causing massive blood loss. Her face and arms were bruised, with streaks of red and purple caused by the fall. Her chest and stomach had large open wounds where the Urok-Nah had clawed her.

"I'm sorry, Anna," Maria managed to say, having difficulty articulating. "I'm sorry how I treated you."

"Hang in there, Maria!" Anna pleaded, crawling toward the injured demon hunter and embracing her, trying to put pressure on the large open wounds. "Hang in there! Luis is coming!"

"I'm done," Maria said as her body relaxed. "My last battle was with an Uroks-Nah. There is no better way to go, and I go right at the foot of the Temple of Our Lady."

"Don't say that!" Anna exclaimed. "Don't you give up!"

"Find them," Maria whispered as her eyes slowly closed. "Find the one responsible for this...."

Maria's body went limp in Anna's arms. "No!" Anna exclaimed as she burst into tears. "Maria! Please don't do this! Maria!"

The sixteen-year-old demon hunter looked up and saw her older brother running up to her. The young six-foot-two, twenty-four-year-old Guardian knelt next to his kid sister and held her tight as she buried her face into his chest and inconsolably wept.

CHAPTER I

St. Helena, California, USA; Feb 7, 2:00 a.m.

GRACE WU SPRINTED FULL-SPEED through the cemetery, feeling the three vampires trailing behind and gaining on her. She smiled as she jumped over a chest tomb and zig-zagged around three tombstones, hoping the vampires were agile enough to keep up as she made her way to the central mausoleum of the hallowed grounds. The imposing marble structure loomed in front of her, with a wall of tall bushes creating an enclosed area for her, and the demons with no way out. The demon hunter ran inside, jumping over a trip wire at the entrance. She stopped and turned to see two male and one female vampires, their red eyes piercing her dark ones with drool streaming from their fangs.

"Wrong turn, little girl," the tallest vampire said as the mausoleum door shut behind him. He was approximately six-feet-one and had dark, curly hair. His attire was relatively new: a red and white button-up Hawaiian shirt, dark blue blazer, and matching dress pants. "It seems you ran out of space to run."

"And you ran out of space in your closet," the seventeen-year-old girl retorted. "Did your mom pick that outfit for you?"

The vampire looked surprised at the girl's lack of fear. He examined her from head to toe, trying to sense something different. Her silky shoulder-length black hair was loose and well kept, with a red trench coat covering a loose white blouse, dark trousers, and white Adidas trainers. "Who are you?" the vampire asked.

"Someone from Hawaii," Grace retorted. "That shirt you're wearing is seriously offending me right now."

"Come on, Charlie," the female vampire urged. "What are we waiting for? I'm hungry."

This small crew of vampires was apparently new in town, with their attire not quite matching the local batch. The female vampire wore a yellow flowery tropical dress, a jean jacket, and flat sandals that went well with her brown hair and yellow nail polish. The third vampire wore a similar green Hawaiian shirt, with brown cargo pants and loafers. Grace giggled a bit at the demon's comments. "When did you guys arrive?" Grace asked.

"Shut up!" the tall vampire exclaimed. "You should be scared of us. We're vampires."

"Is that what you are?" Grace exclaimed, acting surprised. "I thought you were part of an acting troupe from Hollywood."

"Enough!" the other male vampire said as he approached her. "You're trapped here, with nowhere to go."

"See, that's where you're wrong. I am not trapped here with you." The demon hunter pulled out a stake from her red trench coat, bringing fear to the vampires' eyes. "You're trapped in here with me."

"Demon hunter!" the female vampire shrieked as she tried to escape.

Grace darted toward the tallest vampire, plunging her stake into the demon's chest. The fiend didn't have time to think before his body exploded into ash and dust. The seventeen-year-old girl jumped and spun in the air, kicking the second male vampire twice in the face with a butterfly kick. The demon staggered back just as Grace flung her only remaining stake at the female vampire, impaling her wooden weapon in the vampire's back. The female monster squealed before exploding into ash.

The third vampire stood up, only to see the young girl stroll toward her stake and clean it off. She then turned and glared at him with her piercing black eyes. The vampire looked around, seeing there was nowhere to run or hide as she approached him. "Please!" he begged. "I'll leave town!"

Grace frowned before rushing him and plunged her stake into his heart, turning the vampire to dust and ash. The young girl cleaned her clothes and proceeded to exit the marble structure. As the demon hunter opened the door, she felt a cool breeze caress her face. She looked at the star-filled, clear night sky while pondering the vampire's last words. It was the first time a vampire had begged for his life, but that was not what troubled her.

Grace closed her eyes, remembering her nightmares of the master vampire Neil glaring at her, while her parents lay dead at his feet. The word *'please'* rang in her mind. She was unsure whether she uttered it and begged, or if it was part of her nightmare. She opened her eyes and pulled out her cell phone—five missed calls. Four of them were from her Guardian, Elizabeth. The last and most recent one was from her boyfriend Bryan, who had dialed just two minutes earlier.

The dark-haired girl deleted Elizabeth's calls and called back her boyfriend.

"Hey," Bryan answered. "You're still outside?"

"I'm almost done," Grace responded as she approached the cemetery's exit. "A small pack of vampires from out of town showed up. I took care of them."

"You okay?" Bryan asked, his voice filled with concern.

"Just normal bloodsuckers," Grace said, smiling a bit. Even though Bryan knew she had the superhuman strength to fight the undead and other night creatures, he couldn't help worrying for her every night. "I'm fine."

"Did you talk to Izzy and Nikki before they left?" Bryan asked.

Grace scowled at the question. "There wasn't time," the demon hunter lied to her boyfriend. "Nikki's dad pulled some strings to get a private flight to Mexico. It all happened so fast I didn't get the chance."

"I understand," Bryan said. "You feel okay about staying here all by yourself?"

"I'm fine," Grace replied as she exited the cemetery and made her way up the main street. "And I'm not alone. You're here. I couldn't leave even if I wanted to."

Bryan laughed. "That's good to hear," her boyfriend responded, trying to lighten up the mood. "It's late. It would be best if you ran back to Elizabeth. DM me when you get home."

"Yes, sir," Grace joked at the so-called order her boyfriend had given her.

"Love you," Bryan said.

"Love you too, teddy bear." Grace smiled.

The demon hunter hung up and stood alone on the deserted street for a moment. Ever since she knew about her gift and calling, her primary focus had been to become the best demon hunter on earth. Having a boyfriend had never occurred to her when she was younger. She wondered what her parents would have thought if they had known. As she continued walking down the main street, memories of her training with her mom and dad flooded back.

*

GRACE RUSHED HER FATHER, *Xianquan Wu, trying to grab onto his legs. But the older, dark-haired man just dodged and moved out of the way, tapping her back with a kendo stick. At the tender age of ten, her demon-hunter strength had just begun manifesting.*

Grace looked up at the man, who had a serious look on his face, but his eyes were full of life and emotion. The little girl turned toward the right, seeing her mother supervising the training exercise from one of the wooden oak chairs in the library. Her eyes reflected a soft warmth of pride as she looked at her daughter.

Grace felt a tap on her shoulder from the wooden kendo stick. "Don't lose focus," Xianquan scolded softly. "A lapse in your attention could determine victory or defeat in battle."

Grace rushed at her father again, rage filling her energy as he quickly sidestepped and tripped her daughter, causing her to fall flat on her face. "Control your emotions. Rage is not the only fuel you need in battle."

"Play close attention to what your father says," Grace's mother, Anhe Wu, said. "The more you learn here, the less you will need to learn out there."

"What is wrong with rage?" Grace said, standing up and rushing her father again.

Xianquan did not dodge this time. He crouched and swept Grace's legs from under her, causing the little girl to fall on the carpeted floor with a thud. "Rage is like a ravening storm," her father said. "It is destructive in power, but with no control."

Grace sat on the carpet and looked at her mother. "How do I control it?"

"Focus on your breathing," Anhe replied. "You can't let it control you."

"Fear is the source of all rage," Xianquan said, helping his daughter stand up. "What do you fear?"

Grace looked at her bare feet as she made fists with her toes on the navy carpet. "I'm afraid this is a mistake. I'm no demon hunter."

Xianquan kneeled before his daughter and looked into her eyes. "Don't ever think that," he said. "You have the gift. You are chosen for this."

"Love and truth push out fear," Anhe said as she stood up from her chair and walked beside her husband. "That is the source of your strength."

Xianquan looked at his wife adoringly. "A warrior's true strength is the person fighting alongside you."

"So give honor and respect to them," Anhe said. "And it will be returned to you."

Grace nodded at her parents' instructions when

she caught her father turning pale. Without warning, Xianquan started coughing as he turned around, and Anhe gave him a glass of water. She turned toward Grace. "Training is over," her mother said. "Start doing your schoolwork."

*

GRACE WAS BROUGHT BACK to reality as she saw that Elizabeth had called her twice. She frowned as she read the text messages. *I know you're upset—no reason for the silent treatment. Get back to the Jeep. Patrol is over.*

Grace sighed and typed back. *OMW.*

The demon hunter continued walking up the main street while looking through the contacts on her cell phone. She could feel Izzy and Elizabeth trying to reach out to her with their minds, but the dark-haired demon hunter blocked their thoughts. She found the number of her old Guardian and dialed his number.

"I wondered when I would hear back from you," Mashahiro responded.

"Did you find anything else from my father's records?" Grace asked.

"I've gone over them three times now, Grace. There's nothing new."

Grace looked up and saw her blonde Guardian leaning against her black Jeep with crossed arms. The blonde woman had her hair tied in a neat ponytail with a nice gray turtleneck blouse, a long dark skirt, and a black jacket. Grace always admired Elizabeth's fashion style, feeling slightly envious of her simplicity. "Send me all the information," Grace said to her old Guardian. "I will look at the data myself."

"Grace," Mashahiro called out. "There's nothing. Trust your father and mother. They would never keep anything from you. You know that."

Grace looked up and saw that Elizabeth was looking at her. "Send me everything, Mashahiro," the demon hunter ordered. "I just hope you're not keeping anything from me." The girl hung up and walked toward the Jeep's passenger side.

"Anything?" Elizabeth asked as she opened the door on the driver's side.

"Small pack of vampires from out of town," Grace stated, now sitting in the passenger seat. "Took care of them before they could do some damage."

Elizabeth nodded, starting the engine of her vehicle and driving back home. "I know you're upset," the blonde woman said.

"It doesn't matter," Grace replied, staring out the window and ignoring her Guardian's attempts to have a normal conversation.

Elizabeth nodded and continued driving. "When demon hunters shared their thoughts, I tried my hardest not to pry," Elizabeth said with a sad smile. "Now that you girls have learned to block each other out, I kind of feel guilty for trying."

"I know," Grace said, pointing at the side of her head. "I could feel you and Izzy trying. The best part of controlling the gift is learning who to block."

"Would it make a difference if I said I'm sorry?" Elizabeth asked.

"You don't understand," Grace murmured.

"I understand that you're angry," Elizabeth said. "I understand you're obsessed with finding answers about Neil and why he killed your parents."

"And you won't help!" Grace yelled back, turning her attention to the older woman, frustrated at the lack of effort on her part to get justice for her parents.

"The answers are not there," Elizabeth calmly responded. "We're working on it."

"You and the Guardians have been working on it for almost four years, and you've got nothing. It took an ancient vampire to stir the investigation, and you're still nowhere."

"Your father was a great Guardian and great friend of Sean's," Elizabeth said, remaining calm. "He was methodic and precise, leaving nothing to chance."

"What's that supposed to mean?" Grace asked bitterly, sensing her rage starting to overwhelm her. "You sound just like Sabine, speaking in riddles."

Elizabeth ignored the insult of being compared to an ancient vampire as she drove up the hill toward their home. "It means that if he left a hint of everything that happened, the clue wouldn't reveal itself until he considered it wise to do so."

Once the Jeep was parked, Grace opened the door. She looked back at Elizabeth with fire in her eyes. "I'm here until I graduate high school," she hissed. "Once I graduate, you, your daughter, and I are done." Saying that, Grace stormed inside the house.

Elizabeth sighed as she sat back in her Jeep and closed her eyes. Her cell phone beeped several times, causing the blonde demon hunter to look at the device. The first message was from her husband, Sean. *We're in the air. Nikki's flying the plane.*

Elizabeth smiled, knowing Colonel Rogers was

letting his daughter pilot their ride to Mexico.

The other text messages were from Grace's old Guardian, Mashahiro Nagayama. *She will not give up.*

Elizabeth sighed again as she continued reading. *I sent her all the files The Guardians have. Maybe her set of eyes can shed some light.*

Elizabeth replied. *I hope she can help us. I'm worried she may think we've hidden this from her.*

Mashahiro responded. *I'll talk to her.*

Elizabeth smiled a bit. *Do you have any recommendations on dealing with your protegee?*

Mashahiro's response was simple. *Patience.*

CHAPTER II

Toluca, State of Mexico, Mexico; Feb 7, 4:30 a.m.

ISABELLA O'BRIEN STIRRED IN her uncomfortable plane seat and looked around the small cabin. Her father, Sean O'Brien, sat beside her in what seemed to be a deep sleep, his leather jacket wrapped firmly around his torso. In front of him, her other Guardian and friend, John Simmons, was reading on his computer tablet. The twenty-one-year-old man hardly ever slept, believing he could hide his condition from everyone. His genius intellect had a huge pitfall—he couldn't shut off the constant bombardment of thoughts, ideas, and memories that plagued his mind. Theories and unproven conjunctures were the silent companions that continuously screamed, rendering him unable to have a peaceful slumber.

Izzy gazed into the small plane's cockpit, watching her friend and sister, demon hunter Nikki Rogers, pilot the aircraft as if it were second nature. Beside Nikki was her father, Colonel Rogers. The older man whispered instructions to his daughter, gently but firmly guiding her through the air. It was the first time Izzy had the privilege of meeting the man Nikki spoke about frequently. He was everything the red-headed demon hunter had described and as a result, she'd come to admire him.

Izzy looked out of the tiny plane window and saw that they would probably be landing soon. As if Nikki had read her mind, her voice came over the aircraft's loudspeaker. "Wake up, team," Nikki chimed. "Buckle up those seat belts, because we're about to land."

Sean barely stirred, while John put away his tablet and looked out the window. The younger Guardian adjusted his reading glasses and rolled down the sleeves of his white dress shirt. Izzy noticed he had been fidgeting almost the entire trip. Isabella was aware of her Guardian's uneasiness, since he was returning to where the love of his life and fellow demon hunter Angela had fallen. Few knew about the relationship, and Izzy was one of those few John had confided in.

A few minutes later, the plane landed safely at Toluca International Airport outside the capital. "Thanks for flying Air Rogers," Nikki said as she parked the aircraft at one of the private terminals.

Sean stirred awake and looked at his daughter. "We're still a two-hour drive away," the older man said. "Try to get some sleep."

Izzy nodded, adjusting her leather jacket. She grabbed her gear and followed Sean and John out of the aircraft. Outside, an older gentleman in his late sixties waited for them. His military crew cut and bombardier jacket were a solid indicator that he was

Colonel Rogers's contact. "Lieutenant Anthony Wells," he introduced himself to Sean, Izzy, and John.

"Nice to meet you, sir," Sean shook his hand. "Sean O'Brien. This is my daughter Isabella, and my colleague John Simmons."

"It's a pleasure," Tony replied, looking up and seeing Nikki and Colonel Rogers step outside.

"Uncle Tony!" Nikki squealed as she ran and gave the older man a big hug.

"I can't believe you're little Nikki," Tony said. "You're all grown up. You look just like your mom."

"Doesn't she?" Colonel Rogers said as he embraced his brother-in-law. "She has her looks and spirit."

"Got your flight ready for JTF-Bravo," Tony said. "Plane is ready when you're ready."

"Excellent," Colonel Rogers said. "My daughter and friends here will be in Mexico for a few days. Please provide an aircraft for Nikki to fly back to California when she requests it."

"Will do," Tony said. He then turned toward Sean. "Your ride is waiting over there," the older man said as he pointed at the black polarized SUV at the end of the airfield.

"Thank you," Sean said, turning toward Colonel Rogers. "Thank you again for this favor."

"No," Colonel Rogers said. "Thank you for letting me spend these two weeks with my daughter. With school work and her 'extracurricular' activities, I am glad she had the time."

"I'll catch up," Nikki said to her team as they walked to the SUV.

"Alone at last," Colonel Rogers said to his daughter

as he cleared red hair strands from her face to see her blue eyes.

"Thanks for spending time with me," Nikki said, adjusting her eyeglasses. "How long will you be deployed at Soto Cano?"

"At least six months," her father replied. "I'll let you know if there are developments."

"Please do," Nikki said.

Colonel Rogers paused and looked at Izzy, who was walking away. "I noticed you and your sisters are unusually silent around each other."

Nikki looked down, trying to avoid the subject. "It's complicated."

"It's not complicated when you depend on each other and fight those creatures," Colonel Rogers said. "Remember that you are a team. One chink in your armor, and you will all fall."

"I got it covered, Dad," Nikki said, looking at Izzy, who was staring back at her as she walked to the SUV.

"I assume it has something to do with Isabella," Colonel Rogers said as he waved at the brown-haired girl.

"Dad," Nikki said. "I don't want to talk about it."

"And I don't want you to get hurt," Colonel Rogers said. "I don't want anyone to get hurt. You have a better chance if you clear the air before entering any battle engagement."

"We've survived so far," Nikki mumbled under her breath, adjusting her black bomber jacket and avoiding eye contact with her father.

"Careful with that passive-aggressiveness, airwoman," Colonel Rogers scolded softly. "You know very well it doesn't suit you."

Nikki looked up at her father and stared into his eyes. "I'll get on it, Colonel,"

Colonel Rogers looked at his daughter, trying to read her expression and failing to do so. "Okay," he relented. "I've got to go now. I'll call you when I arrive. Please be careful. Take care of yourself and your wing women."

"I always do," Nikki said, hugging her father. Colonel Rogers picked up his duffle bag and started walking toward a tiny hangar with Tony. "Dad," Nikki called out. Colonel Rogers turned back and looked at his daughter. "I'll clear the air."

Colonel Rogers smiled and nodded as he continued walking toward his plane. The red-headed demon hunter sighed, seeing her father walk toward his next mission. She looked down at her black boots and pondered her next step for a moment. She had given her father her word. She couldn't back down from it.

Nikki picked up her duffle bag and headed toward the black SUV. The front door opened as she approached the vehicle, and a beautiful young woman stepped out. The woman was in her mid-twenties, around five feet three inches, with medium-length dark brown hair and a somber demeanor. She wore light gray training pants and a light blue hoodie that read "Monterrey Institute Of Technology And Higher Education." "Welcome back to Mexico, John," she greeted the twenty-one-year-old Guardian.

John drew a sad smile and gave the young woman a fraternal hug. He then turned toward his team. "This is Victoria Rodriguez," John said, making the introductions. "She and her twin brother, Luis

Rodriguez, are head Guardians of the region. Victoria, this is Sean, his daughter Izzy, and Nikki. I'm sure you're familiar with them."

"I am," Victoria said, shaking their hands. "I wish our meet-and-greet came under better circumstances. Let's go so we can beat traffic."

The team boarded the SUV in silence. John took the front passenger seat while Nikki and Izzy sat in the back, with Sean separating them. Sean looked at Izzy, who was visibly hurt, while Nikki looked out the window, deep in thought. He said nothing and listened to John and Victoria talk while the brown-haired woman started the engine and drove out of the airport.

"Where's Luis?" John asked, fearing the answer.

"Three demon hunters died, John," Victoria responded. "Where do you think he is?"

"Sorry," John said. "Stupid question."

"For being a genius, you sure miss the obvious," Victoria snapped at the young Guardian. She looked at him and saw the hurt in his eyes. The memory of Angela flashed before her mind. Victoria sighed and continued driving. "I'm sorry. You know better than anyone how it is when this happens."

"Do we have any leads?" Sean interrupted.

"None that we know so far," Victoria said, looking in the rearview mirror. She noticed the icy bond between Izzy and Nikki. "It's only been a few hours. Everything is fresh right now."

"The surviving Guardians are handling preparations?" John asked.

"Like clockwork," Victoria replied. "We have contacts with the local police sealing the area until we take a closer look. We're spinning this as if it's local criminal activity. Luis is breaking the news to three families as we speak. That means you may not see him until this afternoon."

"How's Anna?" Izzy asked, breaking the demon hunter's icy silence.

Victoria looked at the rearview mirror and saw a profound sadness in Izzy's green eyes. "I wish I could say she's handling this like a pro. But the deaths are getting to her. With Maria, Mercedes, and Blanca gone, seven demon hunters have died under her watch. I saw it in her eyes. Tonight's deaths shattered the little confidence she had left."

"You girls need to talk to her," Sean told Nikki and Izzy. The red-headed demon hunter looked at Izzy and nodded at Sean. "We'll take care of her," Nikki said.

Sean turned back to Victoria. "Could this be a warning before someone makes a move to open the Hell Spot in Mexico?"

Victoria looked at Sean, and then at John with a confident smile. "Sean doesn't know, does he?"

Sean looked confused as John turned toward him. "The last time the hell spot in Mexico opened was around the early fifteenth century," the young Guardian stated. "This brought devastation across the land, unlike anything described in ancient Toltec, Aztec, and Mayan stone glyphs. The hell spot closed, but the dark creatures infected the region and propagated south. The Temple of Lady of Guadalupe serves now as a protective seal over the area, extending up to Southern California and reaching just North of Brazil."

"The Bunker of our Lady," Victoria stated as she

drove the vehicle through the dark road. Few cars shared the road as they traveled to the country's capital. "That hell spot will never open as long as The Temple stands. Our contacts in the underworld are aware of the situation. No dark creature can get close to the temple without being incinerated."

"If the Temple is such a big barrier, how did a nest of demons pop up so close?" Sean asked.

"Even though the Hell Spot can't be opened," Victoria stated as she looked in the rearview mirror at the older Guardian, "the dark essence still attracts demons from far and wide. Why they chose that particular nest is a mystery to us. But we're certain they're not trying to open the Hell Spot."

"What's the assignment for the demon hunters in the region?" Izzy asked.

"Crowd control," John replied, looking back at them. "The demon hunters from Mexico are the last line of defense, so powerful demons don't move north, just as you are responsible for monsters not moving south. A group of Demon hunters controls Guatemala City, Izalco, and Juticalpa. When a demon passes those checkpoints, the Demon hunters from Mexico take care of them."

"Which doesn't make sense," Victoria interrupted. "This has been the normal demon behavior for decades now."

"The pattern changed in the last three years," Sean commented.

Victoria looked at the older Guardian. "How did you know?"

"I read the reports," Sean said as he looked at

John. Izzy also looked at John, who sat back in the passenger seat.

"Angela was the last line of defense," John said. "She caught the pattern change. Demons were moving without the demon hunters detecting them, as if some outside entity protected them from our nets."

Nikki looked at John. "You figured it out?"

"I had help," John said as he looked at Victoria. "Victoria and Luis were instrumental in all of this. With their electrical and mechanical engineering background, we figured out and pinpointed the central nest. We did some reconnaissance of a small abandoned warehouse outside the DF. Three dozen demons were lined up in a battle formation. All sorts of species, vampires, lycans, zombies, incubi, succubi, rage demons, and all manners of shape or form, working as a single unit."

"What happened?" Nikki asked.

John closed his eyes as he tried to find the words. *You have to let me go.* "Angela unleashed her demon hunter power on all of them," John said, looking back at Nikki.

"A forbidden demon hunter technique that she had recently discovered," Victoria said. "She stopped the horde, but it claimed her life."

There was a brief silence in the car after that. "Based on the reports you've written, it seems the same pattern is repeating itself," John said, looking at Victoria.

"That's Luis's theory," Victoria said. "But it's more vicious this time. Whatever is controlling these demon gatherings is testing this newfound power."

"They're using demon hunters as target practice," Izzy concluded.

Victoria smiled and looked at John. "John told me you were smart."

"So we help Anna find the culprit in all of this and take them out," Nikki said.

"That's the plan," Victoria said as she continued driving. "Try to get some rest." She turned toward John. "That means all of you."

"You know me too well," John said with a sad smile.

Mexico City, CDMX, Mexico; Feb 7, 2:30 p.m.

IZZY STRUCK THE WING Chun dummy with deadly accuracy and force. The wooden structure strained at the impacts the demon hunter made as she moved from side to side. Izzy frowned, continuing her workout. Because time was a factor in the situation, they'd hurriedly departed California, and she only packed the essentials, leaving her trusty violin behind. She hated traveling without it, especially under the current circumstances. She had tried to get some sleep, but her instinct had woken her up, and she needed to relieve the tension. She put on her black Adidas top and workout pants and headed down to the gym in the basement.

The brown-haired seventeen-year-old removed her grappling gloves and grabbed her English textbook. Even though they had asked permission to miss school because of the emergency trip, they had to play catch-up when they returned. A beeping sound came from her cell phone. Her lips drew a smile, seeing a text from her boyfriend, Stephen.

I sent you today's lessons and assignments, Stephen texted. *How are things?*

Brutal, Izzy responded.

I'm sorry, Stephen texted. *How are things with you and Nikki? Grace looked pissed at school today. She barely said a word to Bryan, me, or Jaimie.*

I'm working on it, Izzy replied. *It's not a good time for all of us. Gotta go. Text you tonight.*

Love you, Stephen texted.

Izzy smiled a bit. *Love you too.*

She put her phone down and grabbed her English textbook, trying to distract herself from everything that had transpired just that day. Two hours after landing, Victoria had driven them to their base of operations and family business, a three-star hotel called The Ocelot. The female Guardian had explained that the small establishment was a perfect front, especially with demon hunters and Guardians coming and going from the region. Anna's parents ran the place, fully knowing what their children did. The hotel was a small two-floor building with a dozen rooms and a small swimming pool in the back. Some rooms were off-limits and served as office and lab space for Luis and Victoria. The best part of the hotel was the secret lower level. It had a spacious gym, with numerous demon-hunting weapons such as compound bows and crossbows, battle axes, and short and long swords.

But the mood in the hotel was somber. The Guardians of the fallen demon hunters were staying in the hotel. Everyone had spent the entire morning on digital calls with parents, breaking the devastating news. Sean instructed her and Nikki to go to their respective rooms and get some rest while the Guardians handled the emotional load. After several hours of sleep, Izzy needed to blow off some steam in the gym. But it wasn't working.

"Are you done with that?" Nikki asked from the gym entrance.

Izzy looked up from her book and saw the red-headed seventeen-year-old pointing to the Wing Chun dummy. Izzy silently nodded as Nikki walked toward the wooden figure. The girl trained in colorful gear that afternoon, using loose, bright purple workout pants with a yellow over-the-head hoodie. Her purple-framed glasses hid the intensity in her blue eyes.

There was an awkward silence as Izzy saw Nikki start her training routine, smashing the dummy hard with her fists and legs.

"Can we talk while you train?" Izzy asked, looking at the ground.

"There's only so much 'I'm sorry' I can bear, O'Brien," Nikki replied while striking the wooden dummy.

"Would it help if I repeated it?"

"Not likely," Nikki replied as she punched hard into the wood, straining it almost to the breaking point. "But, we have a job to do. Anna needs us. That's the only reason I agreed to come with you."

Izzy was getting angry now. "I am sick and tired of begging," Izzy retorted with her slightly elevated tone, bringing out a surprised smile from Nikki. "I did what I considered right and would do it again. I don't feel sorry at all for protecting Grace."

Nikki turned around and squared up against Izzy, who stood up. "It was her choice," Nikki stated. "She trusted us to watch her back, and you failed to do so."

"I did what I did because I was watching her back," Izzy replied, not backing down. "She was making the wrong choice, and you know it. She almost got you killed."

"Am I interrupting something?" a young voice asked from the door.

Both girls turned around and saw sixteen-year-old Anna Rodriguez about to enter the room. Anna was dressed in workout attire with a gray hoodie, black pants, and black tennis shoes. The dark-haired and dark-eyed five-foot demon hunter looked dead tired, as if she hadn't slept in days.

"Just a small disagreement," Izzy said dryly, sitting back on the bench while looking at Nikki.

"It didn't sound like it," Anna said, stepping into the gym. She focused her thoughts, trying to peer into Nikki and Izzy's minds. She could still feel their essence as demon hunters, but their thoughts seemed locked away from her.

"I'm sorry, Anna," Izzy said, looking at the petite demon hunter. "We've developed a new skill in blocking our thoughts from other demon hunters. It's a privacy thing."

"I understand," Anna said, remembering the screams of her fellow sisters piercing her mind. It felt as if the beasts were tearing at her flesh. "That would have been helpful last night."

Izzy winced at the comment as she turned toward Nikki, who now had a sympathetic look. "How are you holding up?" the red-headed demon hunter asked.

Anna sighed. Her eyes were bloodshot from crying. "Still processing," she managed to say. "I was just with Luis and Victoria while they broke the news to Mercedes', Blanca's, and Maria's parents."

Izzy frowned. That was the Guardian's job, but if Anna was there, it was because she was the Demon Hunter lead in the Mexico Hell Spot. She was sure the Guardian objected, but Anna must have insisted. "We're here for you," the brown-haired demon hunter said.

"Thanks," Anna said. "You'll help me with my last assignment. After I find the ones responsible for these deaths, I quit."

Nikki and Izzy shared a look. They didn't have to read each other's thoughts to know they disagreed. But they were in no position to say anything, let alone judge Anna's decision. They understood the Guardians had given her a choice, and she took it. "Where do we begin?" Nikki asked. "It's your last assignment, so you have the lead."

Anna was about to protest, but Izzy interrupted her. "You know the region better than us. We're here for you. Where do we start?"

Anna frowned. Luis and Victoria had shared the rift between the demon hunters from St. Helena. She knew this could affect the outcome of her mission, but right now that didn't matter. What mattered was the promise she had made to Maria. "There's an entity that seems to be controlling demons to do their bidding," the demon hunter said. "We've got a lead from one of our underworld contacts of a demon nest in an abandoned nightclub. We did some reconnaissance and saw low-level slave demons enter the premises but never leave. We knew we had to act after some vampires dragged their living human prey inside, never to come out."

"It was the correct play," Izzy said, looking at Nikki and putting their differences aside. "Human lives were being sacrificed."

"But since nothing came out, there was no way of knowing it was a nest of Uroks-Nah," Nikki concluded.

"I wonder why you couldn't feel the numbers inside the building," Izzy noted.

"That thought has been driving me crazy," Anna said. "Based on our information, we made the call that Mercedes and Blanca would go in to check it out. It never crossed our minds that this kind of demon could be controlled, let alone an entire nest be there without us feeling their dark essence."

"How do you know they were controlled by something, or someone?" Izzy asked.

"The demon patterns," Anna replied. "The vampires have a consciousness that feeds their demon-controlled free will, but now they battle as if they're in a trance, with calculated moves. The slave demons and Uroks-Nah normally have separate, erratic, and unpredictable attacks. But now they seem to battle in a single coordinated pattern."

"What's our next step?" Nikki asked.

Anna nodded while she walked toward the Wing Chun dummy. She placed her hand on one of the arms. "Two demon hunters are coming in tonight from Guatemala and El Salvador to provide support," Anna grimaced at the idea. "I'm not a fan of risking more demon hunters on this."

"We'll end this," Izzy said, standing up. "And you will lead us through it."

Anna looked at Nikki, who nodded in agreement.

"Thanks for coming," the demon hunter from Mexico said as tears started streaming down her eyes. "I can't do this alone."

Nikki and Izzy hugged Anna as the young demon hunter sobbed. Izzy turned toward Nikki, and the red-headed demon hunter nodded. *Whoever is responsible for the deaths of our sisters will pay.*

CHAPTER III

St. Helena, California, USA: Feb 7, 10:00 p.m.

GRACE WALKED THE CEMETERY with her instincts on high alert. She could feel the darkness in town recoil in fear from her very essence. She could feel the powerful energy of hatred hurled at her from every corner of the graveyard. But the demons and vampires did not dare show themselves, knowing their fate if they did.

The demon hunter walked toward a fresh grave on the east side of the hallowed grounds. She knelt beside it, aware the undead beast would soon rise. Elizabeth had mentioned the victim over dinner, a middle-aged man who went missing over a month ago. The police found his body with two pairs of holes in his neck and wrists. With the help of a virtual back door installed in the coroner's office computer, they discovered the dead body had traces of blood in his digestive system. The report stated that someone had made the victim drink blood. Now, it was a waiting game.

Grace felt a familiar tingling sensation on her neck

and spine. She turned around and saw a black and white wolf appear from the shadows. Grace smiled a bit and relaxed. "Your master told you to keep an eye on me?" she asked the animal.

The wolf sat beside her and looked straight ahead with its deep blue eyes, while Grace stared at the gravestone and tried not to read its name. It was easier for her to realize that the human was long gone and that a vampire had taken its place. Suddenly, Aidan's ears perked up, and he positioned himself in attack mode, growling at the fresh soil. Grace slowly stood up just as a pale hand popped out. The growling sound from the undead brought a sense of ease as the demon hunter's instincts kicked in. The vampire slowly pulled himself out of the grave with its bald head popping up; as soon as Grace saw those blazing red eyes, she remembered the events that had transpired just a few days earlier.

East of Carson City, Nevada, USA; Feb 3, 11:00 p.m.

GRACE SLASHED HORIZONTALLY WITH *her short sword, gashing the Sedit demon in front of her right across the belly. Her rage was now the driving force of her power, seeing the beast growl in agony as it stepped back with its hooved legs, using its harpoon arms for support. The five-foot dark-red-skinned monster snarled at the girl, trying to straighten up as much as possible with its hump on its back. Its pointy-snouty mouth dripped drool from its sharp fangs as it shook its head and pointed down with its horns, ready to attack.*

Grace braced herself, staring at the beast with tunnel vision as it lunged at her. The demon hunter side-stepped and sliced down on the back of its neck with her blade, detaching its head from the red-skinned frame, causing the beast to collapse lifelessly on the cave floor. The raven-haired demon hunter looked up and saw Nikki and Izzy independently dealing with two Sedit demons.

Grace couldn't focus on them now. She turned her attention toward the leader of the Sedit pack. The powerful Kukudh extended his arms, emitting grayish-blue energy from his black armor-covered body. His face looked like the skin had been peeled off, and only muscle tissue remained. Two large horns popped vertically and curved ever so slightly, giving the demon an extra foot of height to his impressive six-foot-one frame.

Grace squared off against Kukudh defiantly, "Where is Neil?" she asked. "Tell me, and I will kill you quickly!"

"Insolent child!" the demon retorted. "You dare bark orders at—" The beast did not have time to finish the sentence as Grace hurled a small dagger at his face. The tip of the consecrated blade embedded itself in Kukudh's eye, causing him to howl in pain as the weapon burned inside his eye socket.

Grace was already on the move, kicking with both feet on Kukudh's torso. Her Adidas trainers dented the metal chest plate, knocking the demon flat on his back. Before he could stand back up, the black-haired demon hunter straddled him, ripping the metal armor from his chest and punching hard on the face and upper body. Her fists drove insane power, causing the beast to spit out blood from the damage.

Nikki stepped forward and slashed up and down with her long sword before her pair of Sedit demons could react. The beasts growled, attacking with their harpoon arms, which Nikki deflected, maneuvering their extremities to the side and gashing both of them on the chest with her weapon. Black blood squirted out of their wounds, staining Nikki's shirt.

The red-headed demon hunter turned and saw Izzy now dealing with two of her own Sedit demons, who were now at her sides. She then saw a third monster appear behind Isabella and bring down both harpoon arms, ready to impale them in her back. "Izzy! Watch out!" Nikki exclaimed, throwing her consecrated dagger with all her might. The blade struck right in the Sedit's throat, bringing his attack to an immediate halt.

Izzy turned and slashed hard with her short sword across the beast's temple. Half of his head flew to the side as the Sedit demon crumpled lifelessly to the floor. Izzy saw one of the Sedit demons thrust his harpoon arm at her from the corner of her eye. The brown-haired demon hunter cartwheeled to the side as the harpoon passed beside her. She saw the other Sedit had made the same move simultaneously. Both of the Sedit demons inadvertently stabbed themselves in the chest and screeched in pain. Izzy swung her blade and decapitated both monsters with one swift motion.

Nikki screamed in pain as a fourth Sedit demon slashed her belly with his harpoon. Nikki staggered back, clutching the wound with her left hand while pointing her sword with her right as the monster approached her. The other two Sedit demons stood up, and now the demon hunter faced three beasts before her. "Want to talk about this?" Nikki innocently asked as she grimaced from the stinging pain in her stomach. The beasts growled at her with a cry of war. "I take that as no."

Izzy jumped before her sister and twirled her sword from left to right. "You okay?" Izzy asked as she slashed at the first Sedit, severing the harpoon arm from his body. The brown-haired demon hunter then stabbed the beast right in the center of the chest.

"Just a flesh wound," Nikki said as she grabbed the severed harpoon from the ground and flung it at one of the remaining Sedit beasts. The javelin weapon pierced the creature in the chest as it flew back a couple of feet. Only one Sedit remained.

Both Izzy and Nikki looked at each other before swinging their weapons. The brown-haired girl swung up while the redhead swung down. The beast had nowhere to go as his body was cut to pieces, spurting black blood all over.

Izzy focused her attention on Nikki, inspecting her wound. It wasn't deep, but the three-inch gash looked ugly as hell. "I'm fine, O'Brien," Nikki said, calming her sister down.

Izzy, however, looked angry. The brown-haired girl turned toward Grace, who was still pummeling Kukudh. Her blood-stained hands kept on punching without any sign of her stopping. "Grace!" she called out, running toward her sister. "That's enough!"

As Izzy approached the Hawaiian demon hunter, she saw the demon's blood on her shirt, face, and hands. "I told him that if he didn't tell me where Neil was, I would bash his brains in," Grace said, standing up. "He refused."

"I can see that," Izzy said, staring at Kukudh's brains splattered all over the ground as Nikki joined them. "Did you get anything out of him?"

"Just another lead," Grace said, staring at the roof of the desert cave. She couldn't feel the Master vampire near.

Wherever he was, he was long gone. "He's heading north to Vancouver."

"Great," Nikki chirped. "I've never been to Canada." The blue-eyed demon hunter looked at Izzy, who was unimpressed.

"That's the fifth lead that gets us to a dead end," Izzy said. "How do you know he will be there?"

"I just know it!" Grace snapped back at her sister.

"And while you do this, you'll leave us hanging out to dry to fend for ourselves?" Izzy asked, crossing her arms.

"I thought you could handle it," Grace shrugged. "I don't see Nikki complaining."

"We could've used your help for a second there," Nikki admitted as she pointed at the dead demons.

"What the hell?" Grace exclaimed. "I thought you wanted to help me—find Neil and find out why he killed my parents."

"Yes," Izzy said. "And we've been doing that. And while we do that, we'd like to be alive to hear the answers."

"I wasn't doing this bitching and whining when I helped you with Athena and Dante," Grace retorted as she squared up to Izzy.

Nikki knew this was escalating quickly. "You volunteered!" Izzy exclaimed. "Like I have! For five excursions out of St. Helena without telling Mom and Dad! And we're nowhere close to finding this guy!"

"So you're bailing on me?" Grace asked. "I thought you cared."

"I care that we all live," Izzy said. "Not get killed while you get the answers that always elude you."

"Look," Grace said, pausing for a moment. "I'm sorry I left you while I handled Kukudh. If I hadn't stopped him, *this would be all for nothing. He was about to teleport out of this cave."*

Izzy shook her head. "Nikki got hurt," the brown-haired demon hunter said. "You could've gotten hurt."

"Hey," Nikki said, stepping in between her two sisters. "It's just a flesh wound." The redhead turned toward Izzy. "We promised Grace we would help her get the answers she needs." She then turned toward Grace. "We're with you."

Grace and Nikki looked at Izzy, who was now staring at her van sneakers. "I'm sorry," the green-eyed demon hunter whispered.

Grace and Nikki looked at each other and then turned toward the cave entrance, where Elizabeth stood with her arms crossed. Grace twirled back at Izzy. "You ratted me out?" the dark-eyed demon hunter asked her sister.

Izzy continued looking at the ground, searching for something to say. Nothing came out.

St. Helena, California, USA; Feb 7, 10:05 p.m.

GRACE DODGED THE VAMPIRE'S feeble attacks, moving from side to side when she saw an opening, and smashed her fist into the ghoul's face. The demon staggered back to receive a front kick in the chest, bringing him down. The dark-haired demon hunter plunged her stake, turning the vampire to ash and dust.

The young girl stood up and dusted off her coat when she felt a presence nearby. She turned toward Aidan, who sprinted into the shadows. Only his eyes were visible in the darkness while he waited. "Traitor," Grace whispered at the animal as she turned toward the source of the presence, seeing her blonde Guardian walk out from behind a large marble mausoleum.

"Great technique," Elizabeth noted as she inspected the ash and dust near the fresh grave.

"My teachers all say that," she responded dryly.

"Did you read the documents sent by Mashahiro?" Elizabeth asked.

Grace sighed, trying not to show surprise. *Of course, Mashahiro told Elizabeth,* the demon hunter thought to herself.

"We've spent six months reviewing those documents," Elizabeth said. "Four Guardians and two demon hunters. We couldn't find the connection between your father and Neil."

"Why didn't you tell me you were investigating this?" Grace asked.

Elizabeth stood up and looked at the sky, searching for the best possible answer before turning back toward the young girl. "Would you have accepted that we've got nothing?"

Grace thought for a second before answering. "I still don't accept it."

"What would've happened if you had the knowledge that Sabine provided when you encountered Neil back in Ireland?"

"I would have answers now," Grace said, realizing Elizabeth's point.

"You would be dead, Grace," Elizabeth said. "You've admitted before, this vampire has a one-up on you."

"Not with the motivation that I have now," Grace retorted. "I'd make him talk before killing him."

Elizabeth shook her head and turned her back to the dark-haired girl, trying not to show her exasperation. *I am not getting through to her.* The blonde Guardian turned again to Grace and was about to say something when a familiar disturbance tugged within her heart. She looked at Grace, seeing that the girl had also felt it.

"Expecting company?" Grace asked, standing beside her Guardian, sensing five demon hunters surrounding them.

"Not this one," Elizabeth said. Grace turned toward her Guardian, sensing a slight tension in the air. The always calm and collected Guardian and demon hunter seemed slightly rattled by the change in the ambiance.

Grace turned her attention back to the primary energy source when a dark silhouette popped up from the shadows. It was a dark-skinned older woman who wasn't over thirty years old, dressed in black pants, combat boots, and a bomber jacket with a white logo on the left. The emblem was a circle that drew the word HELA within its lines.

Another woman appeared behind the demon hunter and Guardian. This one was a blonde, blue-eyed who seemed to be in her late thirties. Three more women appeared on their sides and front. Two of them seemed to be in their early twenties, with one having light brown skin, piercing black eyes, and black hair, while the second had long, curly brown hair with green eyes. The last girl dressed in the same outfit as her friends, but her face and head remained hidden behind a mask and hoodie. They were all demon hunters. Grace could sense their energy.

"Long time no see, Liz," a woman said behind the hooded girl. Grace could feel this newcomer was the leader of the little squad. She had distinct features: fight-foot-seven with short, dyed purple-pinkish hair shaved to the side, dressed like the rest, except her bomber jacket was open, revealing a black tank top. Her pale white skin had a large black tattoo spreading from her stomach to the side of her chest and up to her neck. The drawing started at the base as a vine with flowers, but when it reached the end, it was a dragon's head.

"Sylvie?" Elizabeth asked, somewhat surprised.

"The one and only," Sylvie said, flaunting as she approached Elizabeth.

"You died," Elizabeth stated, putting the pieces together in her head. "Your Guardian died trying to save you."

"That's what she thought," Sylvie smirked as she walked around Grace and measured her. "Poor Francesca. I didn't think she cared that much." The demon hunter smiled and turned her attention toward Elizabeth, shrugging. "C'est la vie."

Grace noticed Elizabeth's demeanor change from surprise to anger in just a few seconds. Her face reflected that she had figured it all out. "You run Hela Corp?"

"You've heard of us?" It was now Sylvie's turn to sound surprised.

Elizabeth nodded as she looked at the other five demon hunters. "We heard whispers and rumors," the blonde Guardian said. "I couldn't imagine demon hunters would need to fake their deaths to do this."

"That has always been your problem, Liz," Sylvie said as she sat on a gravestone. "Your sense of duty has always blinded you from seeing the bigger picture."

"What do you want?" Elizabeth asked. "I am sure

you've not made yourself known to me just for kicks."

"Hela Corp business," Sylvie said, shrugging. "Let's say there is a huge bounty, and we're here to collect it. Girls, do your thing."

The two younger demon hunters approached Grace, while the older women focused on Elizabeth. "We don't have to do this," the blonde Guardian said to the rogue demon hunters.

"I think we do," the hooded girl said without moving from her place. Grace noted an intense accent in her calm, young voice. She seemed to be from Eastern Europe.

Grace noted that the young twenty-year-old with black hair pulled silver chains from her side, while the curly-haired girl grabbed her shoulders. Grace reacted instinctively, pushing her arm to the side and hitting the curly girl's face with an open-palm strike. The twenty-year-old staggered, taking two steps back, groaning in pain, but Grace didn't stop. She smashed her left elbow three times, followed by a front kick to the chest, pushing the rogue demon hunter away.

The black-haired demon hunter tried to wrap Grace in her chains but missed as the seventeen-year-old stepped back. The brown-skinned girl attempted to do a foot sweep, but Grace anticipated the maneuver, moving her leg slightly to the side and using her foot to trip her opponent, causing her to fall to one knee. Grace moved fast, stepping on her rival's thigh and smashing her knee across her face.

The curly-haired demon hunter recovered and tried to punch Grace, but she was too fast, grabbing the girl's arm and knocking her off balance. Grace kicked the girl twice on the chest before releasing her, spinning in the air, and extending her knee, smashing the brown-haired girl on the chest and bringing her down.

Elizabeth fended off her two rogue demon hunters. She moved to the side as the blue-eyed woman tried to wrap the chains around her. The blonde Guardian dodged to the right and struck the woman in the chest with her right fist. She then grappled the woman, smashing her knee twice in her abdomen before extending her leg and kicking the dark-skinned woman in the solar plexus.

Sylvie frowned, seeing her demon hunters getting demolished by Elizabeth and Grace. She turned toward the hooded girl and nodded with an evil smile. "Do your thing, Leah," the purple-pinkish-haired demon hunter said. "Don't play. Just get it done."

Grace turned toward the hooded figure, who was already airborne. Grace grunted in pain as Leah's knee smashed against her chest. She rolled back and got to her feet just as Leah removed her mask and hoodie. Grace gasped, recognizing Isabella's face. But it couldn't be her. Even though the body and face seemed identical, this girl had long blonde hair and blue eyes. She didn't get a chance to react because the rogue demon hunter started a vicious attack—left and right haymakers faster than Grace had ever seen. Each time the black-haired demon hunter blocked, it hurt her arms. Leah had raw power behind every blow as she pushed Grace back. An uppercut penetrated Grace's defenses, causing her to grunt in pain as her head snapped back. She instinctively blocked the second attack, but Leah kicked the young demon hunter in the chest. Grace grunted as she fell on her back.

Elizabeth's face was horrified at what was happening. It was only a split-second, but that was all the demon hunters needed. The curly-haired demon hunter wrapped the chains around Elizabeth's neck. Immediately, as she gasped for air, the Guardian felt like something had taken her demon hunter strength from her. The other twenty-year-old demon hunter wrapped Elizabeth's arms and legs with the second set of chains while the older demon hunters started punching and kicking her down.

Grace gasped, seeing her Guardian being taken out by four demon hunters. She stood up and tried to attack Leah, but the girl had another fighting style Grace failed to recognize. Grace punched down and kicked to the side, but the blonde, blue-eyed beauty anticipated every move. "Weak like Isabella," Leah said in her deep Slavic accent.

Grace screamed, knowing she had to defeat Leah to save Elizabeth. She fired a haymaker, which the rogue demon hunter blocked effortlessly and retorted with a punch of her own. She struck Grace square in the face, followed by a quick succession of blows to the chest and stomach. Leah then jumped and hit Grace on the left temple with a hammer punch. Grace collapsed on the floor, seeing stars, and dazed, tried to stand up, but her body felt sluggish as chains wrapped around her.

"You promised Isabella!" Leah exclaimed, looking at Sylvie with rage on her face.

"That's her sister," Sylvie calmly said as she looked at her chained and defeated opponents.

Elizabeth tried to move, but the magic on the

chains had taken full effect. The rogue demon hunters lifted the blonde Guardian to her knees as Sylvie approached her.

"I never imagined this would happen!" Sylvie exclaimed. "Elizabeth Somiere bowing down to me."

Elizabeth said nothing as she looked at Leah with dread on her face. She couldn't find the words to say anything.

Sylvie noted Elizabeth's gaze and walked toward Leah. "Feeling confused, Liz? Don't worry. I made up for everything where you failed as a mother—in spades."

Leah looked down at Grace as she smashed her knee across the girl's temple. The demon hunter crumpled on the grass, unconscious. Leah then turned toward Elizabeth with an evil smile on her face. "Does it hurt, Mommy? I haven't even started."

Sylvie punched Elizabeth across the face, knocking her out. She turned toward her demon hunters. "We've got forty-eight hours," the purple-pinkish-haired woman said. "You know what to do."

The demon hunters nodded as they dragged the chained bodies of Elizabeth and Grace, all while Aidan watched what had transpired from the shadows.

CHAPTER IV

Mexico City, CDMX, Mexico: Feb 7, 10:30 p.m.

ISABELLA FELT HER STOMACH turn in ways she had never felt before. She turned toward Nikki, who returned her concerned look in her blue eyes. They both knew something was wrong and turned their attention to Anna, who knelt on the floor where her sisters had fallen the night before. Next to her stood her brother, Luis. He was six-foot-two, with a receding hairline, and was built like a refrigerator. The twenty-four-year-old Guardian was nothing like Anna or his twin sister Victoria. He reminded Izzy of John in many ways, especially how he dressed, in a button-up red dress shirt, jeans, and black shoes.

John stood to the side while observing his surroundings in the beaten-down nightclub. The police had drawn the body outlines where they'd found the lifeless bodies of the demon hunters. Next to them, the Guardian noticed piles of gold and black ash equally distributed on the floor.

John turned toward Izzy, who had a sick look on her face. "Izzy?" the dark-haired Guardian called. "Is everything okay?"

"I'm not sure," the seventeen-year-old demon hunter responded. "I can't feel Mom or Grace. I felt their essence, and then they were gone."

John looked at Nikki, who nodded a confirmation, feeling the same thing.

"Is everything okay?" Luis asked as John texted on his cell phone.

"Just covering the bases in St. Helena," John said. "Do you see anything out of the ordinary here?"

Luis nodded and looked at Nikki and Izzy. "Do you girls see it?"

Izzy and Nikki walked closer to Anna and examined the ashes. "The ash is not fully black," Nikki said, noticing John flinching at the comment and momentarily looking at Luis.

"Right," Anna said, standing up and looking at her brother. "Someone infused the bodies of the Uroks-Nah with something. Whatever it is, it left a trail."

"And our first lead," Luis said, picking up a sample of the ash and putting it inside a plastic bag while looking at John. He then turned toward the demon hunters. "Anything else your demon-hunter eyes see?"

Izzy looked at the room, noting discarded broken tables and chairs piled to the side. The back of the room had piles of bones with flesh still clinging to them. The bones were primarily human, but other animals had been used to feed the demons. The green-eyed demon hunter then turned toward Anna. "You killed six of them?"

Anna turned toward Izzy, and Nikki nodded a bit. "Once I saw Mercedes and Blanca, I emptied the clip on all of them. They were young and weak, but drinking from demon hunters; it was just a matter of time before they unleashed all their potential."

"Then five more were in the back," Nikki noted. "Probably eating the scraps the stronger ones had left." The red-headed demon hunter turned toward John, who acknowledged her comments while tucking away his cell phone.

Nikki and Izzy headed to the back of the room where the nest had conglomerated. They were careful not to disturb anything as they looked at the base wall and saw a pentagram star carved with an upside-down cross right in the middle. The smell of fresh human blood in the carving burned their nostrils as they recoiled in disgust.

"Did you find something?" John asked the demon hunters as Izzy pulled out her cell phone and took a picture of the base floor.

"Does this look familiar to you?" the brown-haired demon hunter asked as she sent the picture to her Guardian.

John looked at the picture and frowned. "Human blood?" he asked. Both Nikki and Izzy nodded at the question. "This would explain why Anna and the other demon hunters did not feel the dark essence when they approached the building."

"What is it?" Anna asked.

"It's a corruption emblem," John explained. "It works like the cleansing rite we use to clear a home that has invited vampires inside them. Only this one works the opposite way. It blocks the dark essence, like a spiritual cell phone jammer."

Izzy stood next to Anna. "That means there was no way of knowing what forces you and your team faced.

Anna nodded, continuing to look around. The revelation did little to ease the pain she felt.

Nikki continued looking around and turned toward Anna. "You said that the Uroks-Nah vampire spread wings, like a bat?"

Anna nodded at both her sisters. "I wouldn't believe it if I hadn't seen it with my own eyes."

"Demon evolution," Luis said while packing the ashes in plastic envelopes and looking at John. "Not the first time we've seen this. Just not at this level."

"What do you mean?" Izzy asked, looking at Luis and then at John.

Luis finished packing the ashes he found, placed them inside the plastic bag, and tossed them to John, who caught the bag. "Do you want to bring your demon hunters up to speed so we can finally hunt down these bastards?"

Izzy and Nikki looked confused as they focused their attention on John. Isabella walked toward her Guardian, putting the pieces together. "Tell us what happened three years ago."

John nodded as Luis stood up and stood next to Anna. "The leads grew cold last time," John said. "We found the same behavior, but with lower-level demons in an old warehouse outside the capital. All the clues led to that platoon of demons. But they were different. They had slightly evolved from their original form. We figured the leader would be among them, but Angela couldn't pinpoint them. The demons were about to storm out. That is when Angela stopped them."

"And you gave up after that!" Luis snapped at John.

Izzy, Nikki, and Anna were surprised at Luis's change in demeanor. "Angela wasn't the only demon hunter who died during that operation! We lost three good girls! Remember?"

John shook his head. "I wanted to believe Angela's sacrifice was worth it. I wanted to believe that she stopped them right then and there."

Luis calmed down and looked up at the ceiling. "Maybe she did," Luis relented. "For three years, my sisters and I have been looking for the mastermind behind this—the one pulling the strings and controlling these demons as the puppet master for the undead. He is breeding them and making them evolve for their bidding, just like last time. I ask you—are you ready to finish what we started?"

John looked up at Luis and nodded just as Sean and Victoria entered the building. "We've got a problem," Sean stated.

"Did you reach out to Mom?" Izzy asked.

"I did," Sean replied. "No response." Sean knew that the bond between Izzy and Elizabeth was strong, but somehow he could never hide his surprise when the young girl was one or two steps ahead of him.

"We lost connection with Grace as well," Nikki said, looking at Izzy.

"But they're not dead?" Victoria asked.

"No," Izzy stated, wincing a bit, remembering the death of her best friend. "That feels different than this. This one feels as if they're sleeping."

"Could it be just that?" Luis asked.

"Not during patrol time," Sean said. "Elizabeth is uptight about her schedule."

"That is not the only bad news," Victoria said. "Marcela and Vanessa are having issues at the southern border. They can't get into Mexico."

"How long?" Anna asked.

"Most likely three days," Victoria said. "Until then, we're on our own."

Sean looked at Izzy, Nikki, and John. "I'll head back to St. Helena," the senior Guardian said. "You all stay here and help solve this until Marcela and Vanessa arrive. I'll let you know if I need you to fly back."

Izzy looked at Nikki, who returned the look as both demon hunters nodded. The seventeen-year-old then stepped toward her father and hugged him. "Please be careful."

"I'll do my best," Sean said, kissing his daughter's head. "If I run into problems, you fly up there and get us out of the jam."

"Will do," Nikki said. Sean said goodbye to Anna and the other Guardians, and left the building.

John turned toward Luis and Victoria. "Do we have any contacts in the underworld?"

"We can try Zulma," Anna said. "She's a reliable source."

"Who's Zulma?" Nikki asked.

"She's the owner of a cantina not far from here," Luis replied.

"Why is it always bars or nightclubs?" Victoria asked out loud.

"Anything open beyond midnight," Izzy replied. "Demons work those kinds of hours."

"It will be full of human customers right now," Anna said. "But we may get lucky."

The small squad of Guardians and demon hunters exited the closed-down club and started their silent walk fifteen minutes north. The Mexican nightlife was barely starting, with young men and women storming the streets and crowding local clubs and bars. Small taco stands were full of patrons, with rapid-fire orders in Spanish being yelled all around—typical night scene, with impending doom behind the unsuspecting humans, of the darkness that hid behind the veil.

Anna guided her small party around the corner, and they were greeted by a line of people dressed to party all night. They soon reached a medium-sized club called "La Azotea." The line extended for two blocks as the Guardians and demon hunters walked past it.

Izzy looked up at the second floor, which had only a large tent on a rooftop, with many young people dancing and laughing. A large, heavy, brown-skinned man in a gray suit that seemed too small for him guarded the entrance. His large hands held a clipboard as he questioned the flood of guests.

Anna walked up to him with little emotion in her voice. "Hey, *Giganton*," the five-foot demon hunter called up to the six-foot-three beast of a man. "Tell Zulma that Anna is here to see her."

The bouncer looked down at the child and sneered. "I assume you have an ID to enter this place," the man said, in the most demeaning tone he could muster. "If not, I believe it's past your bedtime."

Izzy and Nikki looked at each other as they felt Anna's rage. But the young demon hunter kept her composure as she glanced at the security camera and pointed at the bouncer. "He asked for it," she yelled before kicking hard behind the bouncer's right knee. The knee made a popping sound as the man screamed in pain, crumpling to the floor. With the brute on his knees and at eye level with Anna, the demon hunter slapped both of the man's ears.

Nikki and Izzy smiled, knowing that Anna was holding back as the man fell to his side, holding the side of his head with one hand and his busted knee with the other. The crowd started murmuring at the scene just as the club door opened, and a forty-year-old, five-foot-nine woman stepped out. The lady was elegant in her own right, with long brownish-blonde hair, a floral polka-dot blouse, black leggings, and strappy stiletto heels. "Anna Rodriguez!" the woman exclaimed. "Manuel has only been three days here with me!"

"Should have warned him I might show up," Anna said confidently as three lackeys wearing black pants and dress shirts with bow ties emerged from the club and helped Manuel inside. "He asked for my ID."

"It's the law, Anna! You and your Guardians know very well that to blend in, you must stick to the rules of the living," Zulma said, picking up the clipboard from the ground and frowning at the line to her club.

Anna looked back at Luis and Victoria, who just shrugged. She then turned toward her sisters, Izzy and Nikki, and saw a look of approval in their eyes. "I apologize," Anna said, accepting responsibility. "Send us Manuel's medical bill. The Guardians are good for it."

Zulma looked at the party for the first time, glancing at the young demon hunters and then at the

Guardians. "Fresh meat?" the bar owner commented. "You can't keep your squad of demon hunters alive for a few weeks, I see."

Izzy and Nikki glared at the woman, but Anna was unfazed by the comment. "Yeah," Anna said, looking at her sisters. "Brought big guns for this type of incursion. These girls can do some real damage. With their help, I can close down your club for three weeks if you don't help me."

It was Zulma's turn to frown as Luis and Victoria crossed their arms. "Fine," Zulma said. "What do you need to know?"

"Irregularities," Anna said. "Something out of the ordinary."

Zulma looked around as one of her minions came from the club, and she handed the clipboard to him. "There is something that has been brewing for the past few weeks."

"Do tell," Anna said.

"A demon I hadn't seen before showed up three weeks ago," Zulma stated. "His name is Alastair. He showed up around two hours past midnight. He talked to some of my nonconventional patrons and they walked out with him. I never saw those customers again. Since he showed up, my nightly clientele has been diminishing considerably."

"Is this true? Or do you need us to help you find your missing patrons?" Victoria asked.

"Hey!" Zulma said. "Anna asked about something rare happening, and that's happening."

"Where do we find this... Alastair?" Nikki asked.

"Back door of the club," Zulma said. "That's the 'other' entrance for my other clientele. He usually stakes it out at night before my customers arrive and leads them elsewhere."

"Do you know if he's there right now?" Izzy asked. "If so, what does he look like?"

Zulma looked at the three demon hunters. "He's always the first one here before the others arrive. You'll recognize him when you spot him."

"Okay," Anna stated as she led her small party to the side of the building. "Thanks for your help, Zulma."

John stayed behind with Victoria as she signed a check and gave it to Zulma. "We keep our word," Victoria said.

The walk toward the alley was a silent one, as the noise from the busy street and the nightlife slowly faded. When the demon hunters reached the dark alley, all three felt a unique tingling in their gut. Izzy turned toward John. "Stay back!" the brown-haired demon hunter ordered as Nikki and Anna continued walking into the alley. The evil presence was near. They were not alone.

The red-headed demon hunter took the lead, slowly making her way further into the enclosed space. She turned back toward Izzy and pointed to the right side, while she signaled Anna to continue on her left. The demon hunters could feel a dark presence inside the alley, almost oppressing the air surrounding them. Nikki continued moving toward the red brick wall in front of her.

The girl stared at the wall closely when two translucent arms grabbed her shoulders. "I got you!" the monster growled, his yellow eyes glowing like two oval orbs from the red brick.

Nikki sneered at the comment. "Are you sure?" the girl said as she grabbed the monster's arms and pulled him from the wall. The beast growled in surprise at the strength of the demon hunter as he was being hurled toward the floor.

Izzy looked at the beast Nikki wrestled for the first time. His entire body seemed to change colors, matching its environment like a chameleon. Green, thick liquid squirted out from where the mouth would be as the red-haired girl jumped and stomped down on where the beast's chest would have been.

The monster growled in pain, standing up in a rage and flinging Nikki to the side. The girl grunted in pain as her back collided with the brick wall. She shook out the cobwebs, seeing only a silhouette of the demon squaring off against Anna, who had a short sword pulled out. The young girl swung at the monster, but it dodged and squirmed out of each attack. The demon fired two hard punches, connecting with Anna's stomach, causing the demon hunter to step back while swinging her blade across the beast's chest. The fiend screeched in pain as green ooze spurted from his chest, forcing him to step back as well.

Izzy was already airborne, seeing her target stained in its own blood. She fired a hard kick to the side of the head, bringing the demon down.

The chameleon-like monster growled and regrouped, crouching and jumping with an uppercut, connecting with Izzy's jaw. The demon did not relent, connecting with a left-and-right combination, striking Izzy hard on the stomach and chest, finishing with a kick to the face. The brown-headed demon hunter collapsed on one knee, feeling dazed. The creature packed power behind each blow he connected.

"Demon hunter blood!" the demon exclaimed, extending his claws and readying to bring them down on Isabella. "I shall enjoy feasting on your bones."

Nikki screamed, pulling two daggers from her pants pockets. She jumped and stabbed the demon in the back, on his shoulder blades. The beast roared, arching its back, but it was too late. Nikki removed her blades, crouching and slicing at the monster's Achilles tendons.

The demon growled, falling on his knees, but not before grabbing Nikki's head and smashing it against the ground, causing the demon hunter to scream as her glasses broke with the impact. The daggers slipped from the redhead's fingers as a massive headache overwhelmed her.

Nikki grimaced as she saw the demon shed its chameleon camouflage, revealing a gray and green lizard-type monster with bright yellow eyes. "Why don't you just die?!" the demon screamed at the girl.

"We haven't been properly introduced," Nikki half-joked in spite of the pain in her head. "Alastair, I presume."

The beast was bewildered at the demon hunter's response when he felt a searing pain in his right arm. He howled in agony, seeing his severed limb fall to the side. He looked up and saw sixteen-year-old Anna twirl her short sword while kicking him in the chest. Alastair fell on his back just as Izzy jumped and jammed a dagger into the demon's left hand, pinning him to the ground.

Alastair screamed in pain, unable to escape. Izzy stood up and pulled a glass canister of holy water from her pocket. "Wait!" the demon screamed. "Get that away from me!"

"We want answers," Izzy said as she stood over the defeated demon. "Why are you stocking up on so many demons?"

"I'm just the piper," Alastair pleaded. "He's the one who wants them. He's the one who controls them."

"Who?" Anna demanded. "Give me his name!"

"A vampire in a wheelchair," Alastair said. "His name is Siegfried!" Izzy and Nikki looked at each other, recognizing the name.

"Where is he?" Anna asked as she plunged her short sword into Alastair's thigh.

The demon screamed in pain as Anna twisted the blade and then removed it. "Abandoned building right outside of town," Alastair confessed. "In front of 'Los Tres Amigos' cantina."

Anna swiped her blade right across the demon's throat, causing green blood to spurt out. Nikki and Izzy looked at Anna, who seemed stone-cold and determined. "Now we're getting somewhere," Anna whispered.

Izzy motioned for the Guardians to approach as she looked at Nikki, who was picking up her broken glasses. "You okay?" Izzy asked her sister.

Nikki nodded and smiled at Isabella. "I'm fine. How about you? Ready to meet an old friend?"

Izzy nodded just as Luis, Victoria, and John joined them. "I assume you got a lead?" John asked the girls while staring at the dead lizard demon.

"Siegfried," Izzy said out loud. "He seems to be in town."

Luis, Victoria, and Anna looked confused. "You know him?" Victoria asked.

"We've had the pleasure," Nikki replied. "Confined the vampire to a wheelchair for the rest of his immortal life, from what I hear."

John turned toward Anna, Luis, and Victoria. "He's an enforcer vampire," John explained. "He was part of a pack of vampires that attempted to assault the castle."

"The same vampire that captured you?" Anna asked.

Izzy nodded, remembering that fateful night. "Siegfried never gave the impression that he could lead," the demon hunter commented as she looked at John. "He seemed more like a follower."

"I guess we'll figure it out when we find him," John replied. "The night is young."

Lake Tahoe, Nevada, USA: Feb 8, 4:05 a.m.

GRACE STIRRED SLOWLY AS her eyes fluttered. She regretted it instantly, as a crippling headache caused her to wince in pain. The seventeen-year-old demon hunter felt disoriented as she sat up, trying to figure out where she was. She looked around and noticed she was in a large bedroom, with plush furnishings and expensive artwork. A comfortable bed with silky sheets and a plush comforter surrounded her. The wooden nightstand on her right side had a small lamp and a glass of water.

Grace slowly stood up but a wave of dizziness hit her, causing her to sit back down. Memories of the fight flooded her mind. The teenager tried to focus past the conflicting thoughts and called out for her sisters, Izzy and Nikki, with her mind, but something was blocking her telepathic connection. It wasn't them stopping her—it was something else.

Grace tried standing up again and grimaced as her body protested, feeling sore all over. She slowly walked to an open door on the other side of the room, hoping it was the bathroom, feeling relieved when she found that it was. Turning on the water faucet, she splashed water on her face, remembering everything about the rogue demon hunters she fought. They were good, but their skill set felt inferior to hers and Elizabeth's—all except Izzy's twin.

After drying her face, Grace returned to the bedroom, feeling the essence of a demon hunter approaching. As the room door unlocked and opened, the dark-skinned, dark-eyed demon hunter entered. "We saw you were awake," the older woman said as she lifted her hand in a sign of no aggression and pointed to the upper corner of the room. Grace noticed a security camera focused on the bed.

"Where am I?" Grace asked, looking out the bedroom window for the first time and admiring the dark water of a lake outside with the snow-covered mountains in the background.

"You're in our base of operations in Lake Tahoe," the rogue demon hunter said.

"Nevada," Grace concluded as she remembered a demon hunter and her Guardians disappearing mysteriously the year before.

"Smart girl," the older demon hunter said. "I sensed you've managed to block the demon hunter's telepathic connection from us. That's an excellent skill asset. It wouldn't be of any use to you here either way. Sylvie figured out a way to block that from the compound. As long as you're here, you won't be able to reach out to your sisters, and they can't find you."

"Clever," Grace said as she inspected the room and weighed her odds of escaping. "I prefer the Guardians' recruiting methods over yours, though. They don't involve kidnapping."

The rogue demon hunter looked surprised. "Sylvie mentioned you were different from Nikki and Izzy. How did you figure it out?"

"Well, I'm not dead," Grace said, looking closer at the closed, reinforced window. "And if you needed me for a more nefarious purpose, you wouldn't put me in five-star accommodations."

"Sylvie knows how to scout talent," the demon hunter said. "My name is Roxanne. I can use the direct approach since you know why you're here. Hela Corp can use a demon hunter with your experience."

"I already have a job," Grace said, looking back at Roxanne while crossing her arms.

"From what we've heard, they're not treating you right," Roxanne said as she stepped closer to the Hawaiian demon hunter. "While you 'protect' the innocent, your parents' killer is still out there."

"I will find Neil in due time," Grace said, composing herself on the sensitive subject. She was surprised at how well-informed Hela Corp was of her activities. Still, the seventeen-year-old pierced Roxanne with her dark eyes.

"Really?" Roxanne asked incredulously. "With Elizabeth and the rest of her Guardian tightening that leash of theirs on you, I don't think you will. And they won't let you. With Hela Corp, you would have all our resources for personal gain."

Grace relished the idea as she tried to calm her racing heart. She was weary of searching for Neil without the help of the Guardians. She'd hunted this beast for too long, only to come up empty-handed. "My answer is no," Grace said.

Roxanne nodded, taking a step back.

"Understandable," the rogue demon hunter said. "Sylvie figured you would say something like that. It's hard to shake off all the lies Elizabeth and the Guardians have fed you all this time. Still, the offer stands."

As Roxanne reached the door, she looked back at Grace. "Hela Corp grounds are open to you. There are no guards or fences, just a mystical shield that doesn't let demon hunters communicate telepathically, and, of course, the harsh weather conditions out there. Take your time. Explore our facility. Get to know us and see if we're worthy of your talents."

"What happens if I refuse?" Grace asked.

"Then you will join Elizabeth and her fate," Roxanne said, walking out and leaving the bedroom door open.

Grace pondered for a few seconds as she headed toward the reinforced window. She pushed with all her strength, but the glass would not budge. The girl looked at her hand and felt her demon-hunter strength was still there. *It's not me,* she thought to herself. *It's this place.*

Grace walked out of the bedroom into a plush furnished hallway with a brick-red carpeted floor. Doors were closed on both the left and the right side, with a couple of cameras monitoring the area. An open door caught her eye as she walked down the hallway. Inside was a sterile white room with several white beds. Grace could see four girls lying on the beds, bandaged up, with artificial respirators plugged into them. Machines were beeping to the sound of their weak heartbeats. A woman in her late thirties in a lab coat was writing things on a clipboard when Grace entered the room.

"You're the recruit?" the woman asked Grace as she looked up from what she was doing.

"That is what I keep hearing," Grace said, noting that the woman was an ordinary human being with no demon-hunter powers. "What happened to these girls?"

"This is what happens when you try to capture an Arzkang demon alive," the woman said.

After remembering her studies in demonology, Grace shuddered at the type of demon they were trying to capture, most likely because of the source of wealth the beast offered.

"Were they successful?" Grace asked.

"The team was," the woman said with a casual demeanor. "But in this line of work, there are always casualties."

Grace's blood boiled, witnessing the treatment of her fellow demon hunters. "Indeed," Grace said through her gritting teeth as she stepped out of the room and back into the hallway. The demon hunter took a deep breath and tried to collect herself as she continued down the hall.

A sizeable curved wooden staircase came into view as Grace looked down and saw the first floor of a large mansion.

The first floor appeared to be a base of operations, with half a dozen women in their mid-twenties to mid-thirties sitting at computer desks, looking at large monitors. Roxanne walked among them with a computer tablet in her hands, giving out instructions. As Grace made her way down, she noticed all the women were wearing the signature black jackets with the Hela Corp logo on them. The girl peered at the monitors and saw multiple security feeds, plus a list of girls of different ages and locations in North America.

"Recruiting never stops," Roxanne said, noting Grace's interest in the computer monitors. "We need to clear up all the bullshit the Guardians feed the poor girls."

"I'm sorry," Grace said. "What lies are you talking about?"

"The fact that demon hunters have a choice," Roxanne said without missing a beat. "While they manipulate our emotions to put our bodies on the line for these 'nameless innocents.'"

"They give the illusion of choice," a demon hunter said without looking away from the computer monitor. "They force you to risk your life, friends, and family in a never-ending war."

"So, what do you do with the gift?" Grace asked.

"Whatever we want," Roxanne said, extending her arms. "We have full control. We do what we want when we want. We answer to no one."

Roxanne's words seemed to echo in Grace's mind as she looked at the end of the room and saw the blonde, blue-eyed demon hunter striking a wooden dummy hard, while half a dozen demon hunters sat around her, watching her train. Grace slowly walked toward her, sensing Leah's energy. She was indeed powerful compared to the other demon hunters in the room. Her essence was almost identical to Izzy's, with subtle differences that few would notice.

The instant Leah sensed Grace behind her, she pulled a silver dagger from the back of her training pants and flung it at the Hawaiian demon hunter, aiming for her head. Grace's instinct saw the action in slow motion as the blade approached her face. Without flinching, she snatched the knife out of the air, right before it reached its intended target. Grace's dark eyes pierced into Leah's blue ones, unable to read her thoughts.

"Good catch," Leah said. Her deep Slavic accent reminded Grace of the demon hunters from Russia she had met at The Gathering. "Is that the end of your skill set?"

"Do you want to find out?" Grace said, stepping forward, ignoring her body's pain after the last fight.

Leah did not miss a beat, walking toward the dark-haired hunter. "Let me finish what I started, so Izzy's pain becomes more unbearable."

Roxanne intervened at that moment, standing between the two demon hunters. "You have Sylvie's orders!" the older demon hunter said. Grace could have sworn there was a nervousness in her voice. "Grace is to join us. She's not to be touched."

Leah sneered and went back to the training area. "Sylvie is a fool," the blonde demon hunter said as she started striking the wooden dummy again.

Grace looked at Roxanne, noting her tense muscles.

"Does she believe what Sylvie preaches?" Grace asked.

Roxanne glared at Grace. "Leah believes in her freedom to do as she pleases."

"And yet, you need to control her," Grace said. "Where does her freedom point to?"

"She's just like you," Roxanne said, guiding Grace away from the training area. "She seeks revenge; we're the tool she needs to achieve it."

Grace measured every demon hunter in the large room as she listened to Roxanne. She could feel they were not at her level, but the number difference would be a factor. And then there was Leah. Grace turned back and saw the blue-eyed girl returning the icy stare. *No need to read her mind.* Grace thought to herself. *She hates Izzy with every ounce of her being.*

As they returned to the computer desks, Grace noted the security feed in one of the monitors. Cameras switched, peering into different areas of the complex. All the bedrooms had security, and they all seemed to be empty. Another camera showed what appeared to be the cellar of the complex, where several demons, vampires, and other night creatures were chained to the white walls. Grace saw the Arzkang demon locked in what seemed like a reinforced cell. The seven-foot white-furred behemoth banged on the thick glass that contained it. Its pure white fur was stained with dirt and dried-up blood. "It seems that the Arzkang beast gave you a lot of trouble," Grace said. "Why capture it?"

"There was a bounty on it," Roxanne responded. "Every bounty collected increases our power."

Grace nodded, not asking whether the four demon hunters in the infirmary upstairs were calculated in the risks taken. There was a final switch on the camera, and Grace saw what seemed to be an octagonal ring with chains around it. Empty seats surrounded the ring. The young demon hunter saw her Guardian, Elizabeth, chained to the far end of the wall. Soon, the security feed flickered, and the signal circled back to the bedrooms.

"How long would it take to find Neil with your resources?" Grace asked Roxanne.

Roxanne smiled at the request and snapped her fingers. A demon hunter typed a few commands on the computer, and a map of Nevada with a beeping dot appeared. "A gift of good will from Hela Corp to you, Grace Wu," Roxanne said. "He's on his way."

CHAPTER V

Lake Tahoe, Nevada, USA: Feb 8, 4:30 a.m.

ELIZABETH LET A SOFT groan escape her lips as she stirred awake. The sound of clanking chains reached her ears as she opened her eyes. She looked around, assessing her location, and saw an octagonal ring with chains surrounding it. The older demon hunter and Guardian turned her attention to the metal shackles keeping her arms and legs anchored to the wall and floor in a sitting position.

There was a blaring roar that echoed inside the chamber. Elizabeth was alert, recognizing an Arzkang was close. She relaxed a little, realizing the beast was one level below her. *You've truly lost your way, Sylvie, bringing an Arzkang demon in here*, Elizabeth thought to herself.

Elizabeth tried to pull free from the chains holding her prisoner but was surprised the metal didn't budge. Normally, her demon-hunter strength would be enough to break free, but something was different. She inspected the chains and saw engraved language on them. *Clever, Sylvie,* Elizabeth thought to herself as she stopped pulling. The blonde woman tried to use her mind to call Grace, but something was blocking her thoughts. She then tried reaching out to her daughter and Nikki, with the same result. *Very clever, Sylvie,* Elizabeth thought as she managed to pull her hand closer to the top button of her red trench coat. She pressed hard on it twice and took a breath of relief.

Elizabeth measured the chains and noticed they gave her enough slack to stand up. She ignored the thought and sat with her legs crossed while she closed her eyes, trying to control the anxiety in her mind. Knowing the rogue demon hunter, the purple-pinkish-haired woman wouldn't resist gloating. Elizabeth didn't have to wait long. The familiar aura of Sylvie made her way down the stairs on the far side of the cellar.

"Finally, you woke up," Sylvie said as she approached the blonde demon hunter.

"You could improve the accommodations," Elizabeth responded, looking up at Sylvie. "I mean, I try to give five-star lodging to my guests."

"Grace is a guest," Sylvie replied. "You're a prisoner. Consider yourself lucky, or I would lock you up with our demon collection on the lower level so they can feast on your bones. But I wouldn't make any money on that."

"I heard the Arzkang," Elizabeth said. "Capturing it alive must have cost you an arm and a leg. Well, maybe not *your* arm and leg."

"My girls are aware of the risks," Sylvie said.

Elizabeth looked behind Sylvie, noticing the octagon with the chains again. "A demon-fighting pit," Elizabeth concluded, seeing the plush armchairs surrounding the ring. "That was always your problem, Sylvie. No imagination."

Sylvie scowled at the remark, but composed herself as she approached the blonde Guardian. "Always the smart-ass with the quick quips," Sylvie said. "Not even a little curious about why you're here."

"Not really, no," Elizabeth said. "I'm sure it's a money-making scheme of some sort. I always read Francesca's reports on you. Always the material girl, and not the good kind."

"Well, Francesca is no longer here, is she?" Sylvie said with a sneer, turning her back on Elizabeth.

"I guess she isn't," Elizabeth said. "Your Guardian cared for you. And you betrayed her."

"Stop lying!" Sylvie yelled at the blonde woman. "I'm sick and tired of your lies. Francesca didn't care! Nor the Guardians! You didn't care when demons stormed my home and killed my mom and brother! "

"If I remember correctly, you were moonlighting as an enforcer for a local gang, making extra money, not realizing that would compromise your identity to the underworld," Elizabeth said.

Sylvie rushed Elizabeth in rage, slapping her across the face. Elizabeth immediately felt dizzy from the strike. Without her demon-hunter powers, the slap felt like a brick across her face. "That wasn't my fault!" Sylvie screamed. "The demon hunters abandoned me! The Guardians left me!"

Elizabeth shook off the cobwebs and looked at Sylvie's dark, hatred-filled eyes. "No matter what I say, I won't convince you otherwise," Elizabeth managed to say as she moved her jaw, ensuring it still worked. "Killing Francesca was the point of no return for you."

Sylvie stepped back and walked toward the Octagon. "I didn't kill her," Sylvie whispered. "I just chose not to save her. Isn't that what you preach? The girls with the gift making choices on our own."

"I guess I'm just an idealist who hopes they make the correct choice," Elizabeth said.

"And according to you, what is the correct choice?" Sylvie asked, turning back toward the blonde woman.

"The choice that lets me sleep well at night," Elizabeth said.

"Do you sleep well knowing of all the girls who have died while you were in charge?" Sylvie asked defiantly. "Of all the families shattered because you put innocent girls in harm's way, while men sleep tightly in their beds?"

"Better than knowing I could have done something and did nothing," Elizabeth replied. "That's my choice, which I've always preached."

"Right?" Sylvie scoffed. "The same speech where you implicitly call us selfish and evil if we don't use our powers the way you want us to use them."

"I don't remember using those words," Elizabeth calmly replied.

"You didn't need to," Sylvie said. "It doesn't matter. What matters is that girls are now free of your sect-like brainwash."

"So they can join yours?" Elizabeth asked.

"My girls are free!" Sylvie exclaimed. "They can do with their powers what they like. I gave them the freedom you denied them for so long."

"Congratulations," Elizabeth said, clearly bored from the conversation.

Sylvie was getting angry at Elizabeth's condescending demeanor, but then a crooked smile formed on her lips. "I know you're not scared of me or whatever plan I have. But your carefree attitude has limits. And before I squeeze every ounce of money your body can provide for me in that octagon, you will beg me for death."

"Glad that will bring you good sleep," Elizabeth said.

"You will see," Sylvie said as she walked back up the cellar stairs.

Elizabeth crossed her legs and closed her eyes. She had to keep her cool, even though her mind was racing. There was a single chink in her emotional armor that lingered in her thoughts, and Elizabeth knew full well Sylvie would exploit it. She needed to be strong for the next part.

Hurry up, Sean, Elizabeth called out to her husband. *I can't face her without you.*

Saint Helena, California, USA; Feb 8, 4:20 a.m.

SEAN WATCHED FROM THE shadows of the nearby alleyway as the police bustled about near the cemetery entrance, securing the area and gathering evidence. The Guardian was careful not to draw attention to himself, knowing the authorities' procedures fully. Sean paid close attention to the head detective, who stepped back from the crime scene and pulled out his cell phone.

Sean let the phone ring twice before pulling it from his trench coat pocket, recognizing the detective's number. "Bryce," Sean said over the phone.

"Where the hell are you?" Bryce asked.

"On a family trip in Mexico," Sean said. "Why do you ask?"

"Is your wife with you?" Bryce asked.

"No," Sean answered.

"It's not much of a family trip without the wife," Bryce said. "I need you to come in and identify two female bodies."

The idea that those bodies could belong to Elizabeth and Grace crept inside Sean's heart, but only for a second. Elizabeth was alive. He could feel her—that sensation that he had difficulty explaining, but was forever present. "You think one of the bodies is my wife?" Sean asked

"Did I stutter?" Bryce snapped back. "Not only that, but I'm sure one of the foster girls who lives with you is here as well."

"Okay," Sean said. "I will come to the station as soon as I arrive."

"Look, Sean," Bryce said. "I know you're innocent in all this. I know what you and the women you live with do at night. And these bodies in the middle of the cemetery, where only you and your girls are always around, do not make you look good. I look the other way because you keep the town safe from stuff I can't explain. But I have a boss to answer to."

Sean thought for a moment. "Do your job, Bryce," the older man said. "I can assure you... if my wife or one of my girls were one of those dead bodies, you would have me beside them, covered in the blood of the monster that killed them."

Sean hung up and hid in the shadows while reducing the brightness of his cell phone. He looked up a particular application and clicked on it. "Come on, Liz," Sean whispered to himself, hoping his wife had activated the tracker in her jacket. "Where are you?" The app loaded a map, and after what seemed like an eternity, a small red dot appeared near Lake Tahoe. "Good girl," Sean whispered to himself, copying the coordinates.

The Guardian put away his cell phone when he heard a slight growl from deep in the alley. He turned around only to see a pair of blue eyes in the shadows. "Oh," Sean said. "It's you."

Aidan stepped out of the shadows and looked directly into Sean's eyes. "Okay," Sean said. "I'm sure you saw what happened. These are extraordinary circumstances under which we're allies, you and I. Walk with me."

Sean stepped out of the alley and started to walk back toward his SUV, which was parked a few blocks away. Questions bounced back and forth in his mind on who would be stupid or brave enough to kidnap a high-ranking Guardian or a senior demon hunter. Either way, it wouldn't have been easy. Whoever they were had the skill and the resources to pull the feat off. That meant underestimating the culprits would be foolish.

Sean took a moment to control his conflicting feelings. He needed to keep his head cool and control his rage. The idea that someone targeted his wife and one of his demon hunters made his blood boil. But if he let his emotions run wild, he could make stupid mistakes. He took a deep breath and tried to process the situation logically. He had the coordinates. His wife was alive, and that meant Grace was alive, too.

The dark-haired man turned back and looked at Aidan, who strolled behind him, keeping a prudent distance. The wolf had been a stable ally to Izzy and the rest of the demon hunters for the past couple of years. Still, the senior Guardian could not willingly trust the animal, and Aidan knew it.

As Sean reached his vehicle, pondering how he would journey to Lake Tahoe with a wolf in the back seat, a pair of headlights turned on not far behind him. Sean looked up and saw a black stretch limousine approach. Soon, the dark vehicle parked at his side, and the passenger window revealed a dark-skinned young woman in her early twenties, dressed in a black suit with her long, silky black hair tied in a ponytail.

"Mr. O'Brien," the young woman said. "My employer would like a word with you."

Sean felt a tug on his insides, sensing a familiarity with the young woman. He looked at the back of the limousine, feeling a dark essence coming from within. A soft growl came from his right side; Aidan had taken up an attack position, ready to strike. "Calm down," Sean said, extending his hands at the animal.

The senior Guardian reached the back of the black vehicle and opened the door, revealing an empty seat. The man crawled inside and was shocked to see the familiar face of Sabine, the vampire. "Thank you, Sean, for giving me this audience."

"I have to admire your ego in coming back here," Sean said, cautious of the encounter with the elder vampire. "It's not every day the person who tore out my life essence casually invites me into her car."

"Now, Sean," Sabine said. "It was a means to an end. Besides, your girls came through for you and restored you to your brooding self."

"You caught me at a bad time," Sean said as he exited the vehicle.

"Searching for your wife and one of your demon hunters?" Sabine asked as she poured a glass of wine into a crystal glass. Sean growled, looking at the ancient vampire, who had a mischievous smile on her face. "I pay good money to be informed, and when a rogue group of demon hunters targets a high-ranking Guardian and demon hunter, I can't just stand in the wings."

Sean tried to control his rage as he sat back inside the limousine. "This doesn't come without a price. What do you want?"

"An exchange," Sabine replied.

Sean looked puzzled, staring at Sabine with curiosity in his dark brown eyes. The Ancient vampire took a drink from her glass before continuing. "This group that has brought disarray to you is also causing disorder on my side. They have taken a friend of mine, and I need him back alive."

"Rogue demon hunters capturing an ancient vampire?" Sean said, nodding as he tried to put the puzzle pieces together. "How was Neil captured?"

"We're not invincible; we are the ancient ones, Sean," Sabine said, putting down her crystal glass. "They came in numbers. They are beyond the service age; they were older and well-equipped—like a special Guardian task force."

"That doesn't sound like us," Sean pondered for a

minute. "But I may know who is behind these women."

"I'm sure you and your fellow Guardians have been aware of this rogue organization for years. You have avoided engaging them, hoping the problem would go away on its own. Unfortunately, they've made their first move. Lucky for you, they've pissed me off, so I am reluctantly on your side in this engagement."

Sean measured his options. Sabine smiled, looking at him and reading his thoughts while pouring another glass of wine. "Don't think it over too much, Sean," Sabine said. "While the rest of your team is in Mexico, I'm your best option."

Sean smiled as he whistled a call. Aidan pounced inside the limousine and sat beside him while growling at Sabine. Sabine sighed, putting down her glass again. "I give you my word, Sean. It's beneficial for me and the world for you and your team to do your job. As it's beneficial for you to get Neil out of this alive."

Sean nodded and closed the limousine door. "We're heading to Lake Tahoe," the Guardian said.

Sabine smiled as she looked at her driver. "Lake Tahoe, Sam."

Samantha nodded, putting the limousine in drive and pulling out.

Sabine looked at Sean and the wolf in front of her. "I thought you hated that animal," the vampire said.

"Not as much as you. And we both have an understanding right now," Sean said. "If you don't mind me asking, how is it that you are always so well-informed?"

"Trade secrets, Sean," Sabine said. "But this rough group is a little sloppy in this particular case." The ancient one pulled a folded picture from her red jacket pocket and handed it to the Guardian. Sean opened it and frowned, seeing the class picture of the Gathering. A red circle was drawn over Izzy, Grace, Nikki, and Elizabeth. "Where did you get this?" Sean asked as he flipped the photo, revealing a logo that read HELA Corp.

"One of the demon hunters that took Neil dropped it," Sabine said.

"How did you figure out they're demon hunters?" Sean asked, putting the picture away.

Sabine scoffed at the question. "I've known demon hunters for over two thousand years," the vampire replied. "They were a dead giveaway."

"Okay," Sean said with a nod. "Can I have a guarantee that you won't stab me in the back like last time?"

Sabine smiled. "I already got what I needed from you," the dark-haired beauty said. "I would assume that helping with UrthaMal would give me a little leeway with you guys."

Sean nodded as he looked at Aidan. "What do you think?" Sean asked the wolf. The animal just continued growling at Sabine.

"Okay, fine," Sabine said to the wolf. "I'm sorry for hurting your master and you last time I was here. But look on the bright side. The girls are stronger because of it."

Sean pulled out his cell phone and frowned as Sabine continued speaking to Aidan. *The girls will not be happy about this*, Sean thought to himself.

CHAPTER VI

Mexico City, CDMX, Mexico; Feb 8, 5:00 a.m.

JOHN LOOKED OUTSIDE THE SUV window as his mind raged on the possible variables of the incursion they would face. It all seemed so similar to last time, as if he was repeatedly reliving the exact moment. To the young Guardian, this was his curse.

"You have to let me go," Angela said to him.

"Give me time," he said. "Give me five minutes. Let me think of something. There's another way."

Angela cupped his face in her hands, making him meet her gaze. There were tears in both their eyes as they looked at each other. "It's the only way. You know that no one else can do this but me."

He grabbed Angela's hands, kissing them. The dark-haired demon hunter held his face in her hands, drawing him close until their lips kissed tenderly. Her eyes closed, savoring the sensation of his lips on hers. She poured all her love and longing into the kiss, knowing it would be their last time together. The kiss lingered, a bittersweet reminder of their love and the painful separation that awaited them. Eventually, they pulled away, tears glistening in Angela's eyes as she looked into his. "I love you," she whispered, her voice choked with emotion, before running inside the dark warehouse.

John shook his head, shaking away the painful memory as he turned toward the brown-haired demon hunter beside him.

"Are you okay?" Izzy asked her Guardian. "You've been more reflective than your usual self."

"Memories flooding back," John said, drawing a sad smile. "I spent five years here with my parents."

Izzy nodded, deciding to pry just a little. "You've told me a lot about Angela. The journals you wrote about her were very enlightening. How did she die?"

John thought for a moment. "I usually write facts and not theory," John replied. "For some time, Angela had been trying to access the essence of her demon hunter power. She believed that by doing so, she would channel the energy to become faster and stronger. Days before the incursion, she told me that she almost had it, but while performing the technique, it left her drained."

"Nikki, Grace, and I have felt ourselves accessing new levels of power," Izzy noted.

"I've seen it," John said. "Remember that this was before you cleansed the demon hunter line with Apocalyps. Angela was trying this on her own. She told me she focused on her core, pulling down all the energy within. And when the time was right, she would release it, destroying the undead inside the blast zone."

"She turned her body into a bomb," Nikki said from

the seat in front of them as the SUV made a right at the next intersection.

"That was my guess," John said.

"I'm sorry, John," Izzy said, grabbing her Guardian's hands and offering comfort.

John smiled at her as a beeping sound came from Izzy's phone.

The demon hunter pulled out the device from her jacket pocket and frowned as she read her father's text while sitting beside her Guardian in the back of the SUV. There was a sense of relief knowing her father was on the way to Nevada and that he had located her mother and Grace. But she regretted not being there with him on this expedition. Izzy looked at Anna's face and contemplated what the sixteen-year-old had gone through in the past few weeks—the pain of witnessing her sisters' death in battle, with her being the sole survivor.

Izzy put away her phone and looked at John. "Dad found a lead on my mom and Grace."

"He did?" John asked. "Where are they?"

"It seems these rogue demon hunters captured them and took them to Nevada."

"Hela Corp?" John asked, almost fearing the answer.

"Yes," Izzy said. "Who are they?"

John looked out the window of the SUV as the vehicle made its way through the capital's deserted streets. "It is what you said," John said. "A group of demon hunters who act independently, not regulated by The Guardians."

"Are they bad?" Izzy asked.

"They do what they want," John replied. "The Guardians don't get involved unless innocents are in danger, and most of the time, they're not. Hela Corp is a freelance group. They act as bounty hunters for the undead, using their powers for personal gain only."

"They make money off their powers?" Nikki asked.

"Many interested parties are looking for a demon skull, a werewolf rug, or a hell gargoyle wing. Hela Corp acts on the demand for its services and is remunerated."

"Why take my mom and Grace?" Izzy asked.

"Grace, most likely recruiting," John responded. "Hela Corp is continually expanding its ranks, and capturing one of the best demon hunters on the planet would be a considerable gain."

Izzy thought for a moment about all her sister had gone through. Based on her father's text about Hela Corp taking Neil, Izzy figured the price Grace had requested for her services. Izzy shook the thought away. *Grace would never turn her back on the Guardians or her sisters. Not even for Neil. Would she?*

Izzy looked at John. "Why take my mom? That would put this organization in the Guardian's crosshairs."

"Elizabeth must have a huge bounty on her head," John said. "Hela Corp must have thought the risk was worth it. Is your father on his way?"

"He's got a lead," Izzy replied. "He's checking it out, scouting the place. That will be our next stop after we finish here."

Anna turned toward Izzy, who sat right next to Nikki. "I will go up with you," the young demon hunter said.

"There was no doubt in my mind you would," Izzy said as she looked toward Nikki, who sat next to Anna. Izzy gently knocked into her mind, asking to come in. To her surprise, Nikki let her.

The red-headed demon hunter turned her attention toward Izzy and shared a single thought. *Grace wouldn't betray us.*

Izzy nodded toward her sister, as Luis drove up the road with Victoria as his copilot. Both Guardians paid close attention to the conversation in the back of the vehicle, but remained silent.

Nikki took in the sights as she looked at the deserted streets through the window beside her. The last conversation she had with her father lingered in her mind. She also replayed the last words she had exchanged with Izzy. She needed to make this right, but couldn't figure out how. She turned back toward her sister, who was staring through the window. Nikki wanted to talk to her using their telepathic connection and clear the air, but this wasn't the moment. The redhead took a deep breath. Her heart felt torn. Deep down, she knew Izzy was right. But that would leave Grace alone with her demon haunting her. She couldn't do that to her.

John turned on the tablet in his hand and studied the plans for the building he would send the demon hunters into. Using two possible entrances that led to the second floor via the emergency exits on each side of the building was the best way to try and catch whatever was inside by surprise. But there were too many variables. The building would likely have a talisman that would impede the girls' ability to detect the monsters inside. They would be going in blind. *Just like last time*, John thought to himself. John looked at the vehicle's ceiling and then turned his attention back to Izzy, who had a small golden crucifix hanging around her neck. John's mind clicked as his eyes widened with an idea. "That could work," John whispered out loud, catching Izzy's attention at his side.

"You got something?" Izzy asked.

"I've given us a fighting chance," John said as he scrolled through his tablet. "Luis! Victoria! Can you contact your parents and get an image of the lady down here?"

Victoria looked at John through the rearview mirror with a knowing look while she pulled her phone out. "Lady of fire?" she asked.

"Lady of fire!" John exclaimed as he confirmed the plans of the building.

A few minutes later, demon hunters and Guardians arrived at their destination. They inspected the building as Izzy, Nikki, and Anna got out. It looked like an ordinary gray three-story building, with a metal emergency ladder to the side that led to the roof. The front of the building had a double-glass reinforced door that led into a dark hallway. The windows in the front of the building were polarized, protecting whoever was inside from the harsh sunlight.

Luis, Victoria, and John got out and headed toward the back, opening the vehicle trunk. "You want to call the shots?" John asked his fellow Guardians.

Victoria and Luis shook their heads. "This is your show," Luis said as he pulled a small white box from the back of the car. "We follow your lead," the tall Guardian said as the demon hunters joined them and handed them white earpieces. He then pulled out a larger box, revealing short swords, daggers, and stakes. The large crate also contained small canisters of holy water and a large crucifix.

John grabbed the crucifix and looked up at the building, seeing a large water tank installed on the roof. He could see a small gray electronic panel on the side of it. "Perfect," John said.

Victoria pulled out a smaller crate and opened it, revealing three pairs of black fingerless gauntlets that were five inches long. Nikki grabbed a pair and inspected them. "Magnesium alloy?" the red-headed demon hunter asked.

"Prototypes," Victoria said as she grabbed a pair and handed it to Anna. She then grabbed another pair and pointed at the wrist portion with a small orifice. "A take on Sean's weapon," Victoria said to Izzy. "The entire wristband holds a dozen blessed four-inch wooden projectiles. Hold with your index and thumb to fire. The gauntlet reloads the projectiles until the dozen are gone."

Izzy smiled, recognizing her father's design as she slipped her pair onto her wrists. "How hard are they?" she asked.

Victoria smiled. "It will leave a mark when you hit a demon with it. It can also shield you from bladed weapons."

Anna aimed her gauntlet, feeling the new weapon in her hands. "What's the plan?" the younger demon hunter asked.

John nodded as he pulled up his tablet and showed the building plans to the demon hunters. "There are three entrances," the Guardian explained. "The first one is the emergency metal stairs that lead to the roof. Izzy will go up and deposit this crucifix inside the water tank."

Izzy took the crucifix and examined the building's roof, interpreting John's plan. "You will hack into the emergency sprinkler system?" she asked her Guardian.

"Already did," John replied. He then turned toward Nikki. "Nikki will enter the side entrance. Whatever you see, turn it to ash."

"What about the alarm system?" the red-headed demon hunter asked.

"I'll disable it," Luis said. "You'll be set."

"What about me?" Anna asked.

John looked at Luis and Victoria. Anna's older siblings only nodded. "You will go through the front entrance," John said. "Once the alarm system is out, I will activate the sprinkler system inside. That will be the signal for Nikki and Izzy to enter the building. You will open the front doors and kill the horde coming out."

"And how will I do that?" Anna asked with a bit of doubt in her voice.

Just as Anna asked the question, a car parked right behind them. Anna saw her father behind the wheel, a five-foot statue of Mother Mary of Guadalupe riding in the passenger seat. Anna looked at her Guardians. "Lady of Fire," she said, knowing what was expected of her.

"Once Anna takes care of the main horde, you will all go inside and clear out the building," John instructed the three demon hunters. "It will be only you against Sigfried and whatever he managed to salvage."

Izzy looked at Anna and Nikki. "Sounds like a plan. Let's do it!"

John saw the faces of the demon hunters with their confidence high. The young Guardian couldn't help but reminisce on that fateful day. *I just needed five more minutes,* John thought to himself.

Izzy darted toward the emergency staircase and made her way up. She opened her mind toward Nikki and Anna, ensuring the telepathic connection held. She felt relieved, sensing her sisters connect back with her. *We're working,* Nikki said to Izzy's mind. *We got this.* Izzy looked down and saw Nikki smile back at her as she sprinted to the side of the building.

Nikki looked up at her sister. *Izzy,* she called out with her mind.

Izzy looked down at Nikki, but her thoughts were jumbled with too much emotion. *We'll talk later,* Izzy thought back. The brown-haired demon hunter turned toward Anna, standing in front of the building, staring directly at the entrance. Izzy could see Luis and his dad put the five-foot statue of Mother Mary of Guadalupe right behind the demon hunter.

Izzy reached the roof of the building and saw the rooftop entrance a few feet away. The demon hunter headed toward the large water tanks and opened the small door, seeing it was packed to the brim. Izzy pulled out the crucifix from the back of her pants and looked at the consecrated object. Izzy looked at the water and started praying in Latin. *"Exorcizo te, creatura aquæ, in nomine Dei Patris omnipotentis, et in nomine Jesu Christi, Filii ejus Domini nostri, et in virtute Spiritus Sancti."* The demon hunter continued performing the blessing rite and dropped the crucifix inside the water tank. She also opened one of her vials of holy water and mixed it with the tank's water for good measure. "Tank is ready," Izzy called out to her earpiece.

Anna looked up at her counterpart on the roof and nodded, while Victoria approached her younger sister with a piece of cloth and a small container of oil. Anna grabbed the piece of fabric and wrapped it around her left hand. She then drenched it with the oil from the container in Victoria's hands. The young girl then looked up at her sister with a fierce look.

"You got this, Anna," Victoria said. "We got your back."

Anna nodded and stood before the image of Lady Mary. "In position," the young demon hunter said to her earpiece.

"I am ready to breach," Nikki said over the intercom.

John looked up the roof and nodded at Izzy. He then looked at Luis. "Disable the security system," John ordered.

Luis nodded and typed instructions on his tablet. As he looked up, he saw the building lights flicker for a few seconds, and then the emergency lights lit up. John pressed enter on his tablet, and he could hear the sound of running water hissing from inside the building, followed by animals howling and screeching. "Izzy and Nikki. Breach and move in," John ordered.

Anna looked directly at the entrance of the building as the screeching was becoming louder and louder. She pulled out a lighter from her pocket and lit the cloth wrapping in her hand as she crouched right in front of the statue of Lady Mary.

Suddenly, the glass door exploded, and demons, vampires, and other creatures of the night screeched and howled as the holy water burned on their flesh. Before they could react, Anna lifted the fire-lit cloth before the statue's face. A white light flashed from the figure as rays streamed from it, striking the beasts coming out. As the beams of light touched their bodies, the demons screeched in agony before exploding into dust.

Anna moved her arm from side to side, aiming the rays of light through the entrance of the building, destroying any undead creature that tried to venture outside. After a few seconds, the only thing left was the putrid smell of sulfur.

Anna stood up and looked at her Guardians, nodding. She then sprinted inside the building. The young girl reached with her mind, sensing both Nikki and Izzy fighting what was left of the demons inside.

*

NIKKI STORMED INSIDE THE darkened hallway, pushing past three vampires that still had smoke emitting from their bodies. They looked more like zombies than anything else she encountered, with their flesh partially burned off. The beasts tried to overwhelm the red-headed demon hunter with their numbers, but Nikki just plunged her wooden stake into their hearts, putting them out of their misery. She then pulled out her short sword and continued to enter the building. She could feel Izzy and Anna struggling inside, but they were also moving forward, to the center of the structure.

A painful flash in Nikki's mind suddenly pushed the girl to the side wall. Nikki grimaced in pain, seeing a blonde version of Isabella beat down Grace in a graveyard. The scene replayed over and over again, giving Nikki a throbbing headache. *Tell my sister I got something that belongs to her,* a voice echoed in her mind as if a girl was whispering directly in her ear.

Nikki regrouped just as three red rage demons with reddish-brown skin almost peeled off to the bone by the holy water stormed toward her. The demon hunter slashed upward, diagonally, and horizontally, causing the consecrated blade to pierce through the already damaged flesh of the monsters. She did a final three-hundred-and-sixty-degree swipe with her short sword, decapitating the beasts. The demon hunter leaned against the wall and focused on the voice talking to her. *You got the wrong demon hunter,* Nikki thought.

I got the right one, the voice replied. *I find indirect attacks on Izzy hurt her more than the direct approach.*

We'll visit you soon, Nikki replied as she pushed the foreign girl away, focusing her mind on the task at hand and reconnecting with Anna and Izzy. The red-headed demon hunter reached a balcony at the end of the hall. She looked down and saw a large lobby a level below, with half an inch of holy water flooding the entire floor. Black and golden ash with black bones floated in the puddle of water. In the center of the room, a single being stood floating a foot above the floor, covered in a long, impermeable black hood.

Nikki made her way to the stairs, seeing Izzy and Anna appear from the opposite side of the room. Soon, the three demon hunters were in front of the being floating in the center of the room.

Isabella looked at the dark-hooded figure closely. A metal mask covered his face while the being floated, seemingly unaware of the girl's presence. Isabella looked at Nikki and then at Anna, who nodded, reading her thoughts. The demon hunter pulled a stake and threw it at the being, aiming for the heart. The being flicked it away with his right arm.

"We destroyed your little army, Sigfried," Izzy said. "You're all alone now."

"Little Isabella," Sigfried replied, lifting his head and removing his iron mask. Isabella, Anna, and Nikki were unfazed seeing the black-haired vampire. "Such a pleasant surprise for you to come and meet me in person."

"You forced me to bring the big guns," Anna said, walking closer to the master vampire. "You'd think that leaving a trail of dead demon hunters would not put you in the eye of the storm."

"Yes," Sigfried replied without moving, looking at the petite demon hunters. "I was wondering how many I would need to kill before I brought forth the best demon hunters in the world coming after me. As someone told me, Mexico is where to come and kill demon hunters. Sadly, Grace is not here with you, too."

Izzy and Nikki looked at each other, somewhat confused, bringing a smile to Sigfried's face. The master vampire looked at Anna. "It's okay, Anna. Two of three is enough for me."

Anna looked confused as Sigfried removed the large black cloak from his body, revealing his six-foot-four muscular frame. He was bare-chested with only a pair of dark pants and dark dress shoes as he floated gracefully over the puddle of holy water beneath him. A black chain with a dark blue orb hung around his neck. The vampire extended a long arm, using invisible energy to start choking Anna.

Anna gasped as the air left her. She tried to grab her throat, but there was nothing to grasp as the invisible energy slowly squeezed, blocking her airway. To Nikki's and Izzy's horror, Sigfried lifted Anna's body two feet from the floor.

The two demon hunters acted fast and rushed the master vampire when two large five-foot bat wings erupted from his back, stopping both girls in their tracks. Sigfried flapped his wings together, causing an invisible wave and sending the two demon hunters flying into the wall behind them. Nikki and Izzy grunted in pain as their bodies cracked the concrete wall behind them.

Nikki looked at Izzy, bewildered at what she was seeing. "Is this the same vampire?" the redheaded demon hunter questioned.

"He is," Izzy replied. "With upgrades."

Sigfried smiled, seeing the demon hunters tremble at the power, sensing their doubt and fear. "I've waited a long time for this," the master vampire said. He flung Anna toward both demon hunters, who caught the girl, and all three crashed against the wall. The master vampire rose a few feet from the floor, revealing a fifteen-foot-long, thick, snake-like tail attached to his behind. The tail moved as if it had life of its own across the holy water, smoke streaming from it. The vampire seemed unfazed that the consecrated liquid was burning his reptilian extremity. "I am going to enjoy watching you die by my hands," Sigfried said as his face morphed and his eyes turned red. "My clan will finally have its revenge."

Sigfried lunged at the demon hunters like a cobra,

reaching them in seconds. Anna and Nikki managed to dodge out of the way, but the vampire struck Izzy across the face with the back of his fist, sending the girl sprawling across the floor, sliding in the holy water.

Isabella shook off the cobwebs, sensing the vampire had packed a wallop behind his strike. She looked up, seeing the vampire upon her. The demon hunter kicked herself back up and jumped, trying to kick the beast in the chest, but the vampire was too fast. Moving to the side, the beast struck Izzy squarely across the chest, sending her flying back. Izzy felt the wind knocked out of her as she crashed back on the floor.

Isabella was amazed at the sheer power Siegfried displayed. She saw Anna and Nikki try to attack from behind, but the vampire's snake tail knocked both demon hunters to the side.

That moment allowed Izzy to get up and fire three bolts from her wrist gauntlets, aiming for Sigfried's eyes. The vampire used his bat wings to shield himself and block the projectiles. "Your attempts are futile!" Sigfried said as he lunged at Izzy. The demon hunter moved out of the way just as the vampire crashed into the opposite side of the wall, breaking the concrete in the process.

"Izzy!" John exclaimed through the intercom. "Talk to me! What do you see?"

"Sigfried is not a normal vampire!" Izzy exclaimed as the demon whipped at her with his tail. The demon hunter moved to the left, trying to find an opening, but it seemed the vampire had eyes everywhere. Isabella saw Nikki try to use her short sword, but Sigfried knocked it out of her hand and punched the red-headed demon hunter to the side.

"Did you clear the building?" John asked.

"What?" Izzy asked, not understanding what her Guardian was asking. She fired three more bolts at Sigfried's back. The bat wings caught the projectiles as if they were nothing.

Sigfried turned toward Isabella and flapped his wings at her. Izzy was ready this time and lifted her arms, standing her ground. The sonic wave passed right through her, leaving her ears ringing. She turned toward the vampire with defiance in her eyes. "Artificial upgrades make you tough? Still the same lackey, though, playing second fiddle to someone bigger than him."

Sigfried growled at Izzy and powered toward her, firing right and left haymakers that the young demon hunter barely managed to block. She felt her arms being tested, as if the vampire was using iron fists to strike her. Her wrist gauntlets took the harsh punishment, not giving in to the sheer power the demon unleashed.

Sigfried smiled at Izzy's resilience. He extended his wings and moved back swiftly, bringing his snake tail to the forefront. He unleashed his python-like extremity and wrapped it around Izzy, constricting her body. Izzy gasped as she felt her bones cracking under the pressure the reptilian extremity was causing.

Anna screamed, seeing Sigfried wrap his snake tail around Izzy and start constricting her. The sixteen-year-old girl jumped and climbed onto Sigfried's chest, wrapping her legs around his bare torso. The demon hunter started smashing her fist into his face, unleashing her fury on the demon. As Anna let loose her power, flashbacks of Anna's fellow demon hunters fallen in battle flashed before her mind.

Sigfried screamed in pain and rage as he grabbed the little demon hunter from his torso and flung her hard against the floor. The tiled floor cracked under the impact as Anna screamed in pain. "Pathetic insect!" Sigfried screamed at the little girl. "You dare strike me?"

Anna looked up at Sigfried and out of the corner of her eye she saw Nikki jump. Sigfried grabbed Nikki by the throat with an invisible force while she was mid-air. Anna looked on in fear, seeing Nikki dangle helplessly from the sheer psychic power of this vampire. The sixteen-year-old saw Izzy struggle to release herself from the constricting force of the tail, almost turning blue from the lack of air.

Seeing all three demon hunters at his mercy, Sigfried turned his attention to little Anna. "Thank you, Anna," the vampire said. "You've brought me my great prize."

"Why here?" Anna asked. "Why my city?"

"The why," Sigfried pondered, looking at the ceiling. "Good question. I can answer that. My consultant has always used this city since opening the hell spot is impossible—perfect conditions where monsters and demons can be experimented on without attracting attention. For years, your city has been a test area. And now the tests have come to fruition, when I kill three of the best demon hunters on the planet."

Sigfried lunged at the young girl when he screamed in pain as the sound of searing flesh was audible across the room. The vampire saw two men and a young woman looking down from the staircase. The Guardians threw glass vials of holy water at Sigfried. The vampire used his bat wings to cover himself. "Insignificant ants!" the demon bellowed. He flapped his wings hard, sending a shockwave upward, pushing Luis, Victoria, and John against the wall behind them.

Izzy grimaced in pain and fear, seeing Sigfried fling her Guardian as if he were a rag doll. She then looked at Nikki, who returned the stare, powerless to release herself from Sigfried's grip.

Nikki saw Izzy's intentions with horror in her eyes. *Don't do this!* She thought out to her sister.

Isabella closed her eyes as Sigfried's tail tightened his grip around her body, causing excruciating pain. Izzy looked deep down within herself, focusing her energy on a single point within her being. She felt the energy accumulate as she saw her parents, sister demon hunters, and Guardian John all in her mind. The idea of this vampire hurting them caused her to snap within. Izzy screamed hard and loud as she unleashed the energy inside her.

John looked down and saw a golden glow emit from Izzy's body. "No!" he exclaimed, seeing what the demon hunter was about to do.

Sigfried turned around, his face contorting in fear as he watched the blinding light emitting from Izzy's body in awe. His psychic power diminished, releasing Nikki from his grasp.

Nikki gasped for air, looking in horror at her sister as her body glowed with white light. "Izzy!" Nikki exclaimed over the deafening roar of the power being emitted.

Izzy screamed one last time before releasing the energy inside her. Sigfried screamed in pain as his snake tail exploded, sending pieces of flesh and green blood everywhere.

Nikki fell to the ground after the blast, feeling something snap inside her being and heart—a dark feeling in the pit inside her stomach. The familiar connection she had with Izzy faded away until it was no more. The red-headed girl shook her head, trying to clear it, when she saw one of the dropped short swords on the floor. She hurried toward the blade, grabbing it. She turned toward Sigfried, who was on his knees. The girl jumped from where she was and brought the blade down across Sigfried's extended arms. Sigfried bellowed in agony as a severed limb fell uselessly across the holy-water-covered floor. Nikki looked behind the vampire and saw Izzy's lifeless body lying on the tiled floor in a pool of green blood and flesh mixed with holy water.

Nikki's heart stopped, seeing Izzy's lifeless body lying awkwardly on the tiled floor. The red-headed demon hunter rushed toward her fallen sister, her heart searching for their telepathic bond. There was no response.

Anna kicked up from where she was and jumped onto Sigfried's chest, grabbing hold of the vampire. The petite demon hunter scrambled behind him and pulled at his bat wings, hearing the bone pop. Sigfried screamed as he twirled violently, trying to shake the demon hunter from his back. Anna held on tight and cried out, straining with all of her demon hunter power, putting her tennis shoes on the vampire's back and pulling on the wings until flesh and bone ripped from Sigfried's back.

Sigfried fell on the holy-water-covered tiles, screaming in pain as his body twitched, rolled over, and burned in the consecrated liquid. Anna jumped and landed hard with her tennis shoes on the vampire's chest, cracking his chest cavity. The vampire tried to grab Anna's throat, but the girl grabbed his remaining arm and struck right above the elbow. The extremity cracked, causing Sigfried to scream in agony as his broken limb fell uselessly on the tiled floor. Anna pulled hard on Sigfried's black chain with the blue orb, ripping it from his neck. Sigfried screamed, feeling his power diminish considerably with nowhere else to go.

Anna turned toward Nikki, tears streaming down her eyes as she cradled Izzy's pale, lifeless body in her arms, trying in vain to wake her sister up. Anna ran toward her sisters just as John reached both girls. "Izzy!" Nikki screamed. "Stay with me!"

"No! No! No!" John exclaimed as he grabbed Izzy's body from Nikki's arms. The Guardian put his ear on her chest, not hearing a heartbeat, and seeing the girl was not breathing. John's mind was on fire as he positioned his hands over Isabella's chest, locked his fingers, and started the CPR process engrained in his mind. His palms pushed firmly against her resisting chest as the Guardian counted in his mind. After a few seconds, he clamped Izzy's nose and breathed air into her mouth.

Victoria and Luis reached them, forgetting about the defeated vampire as they saw John frantically compress Izzy's chest. His face looked full of anguish.

"Come on, Isabella!" John screamed at the young girl. John looked around and saw Nikki sobbing and feeling powerless, full of sorrow. Anna had tears in their eyes, witnessing another demon hunter perish under her watch.

An idea flashed into John's mind. "Nikki! Anna! Grab each of Izzy's hands! Hurry!"

Nikki and Anna obeyed the order without asking questions while the Guardian continued his CPR. John looked at both demon hunters pleadingly. "You have to give part of your life force to Izzy!"

"How do we do that?" Nikki asked, visibly scared, seeing her sister's inert form.

"Use your demon hunter power!" John ordered. "Close your eyes and will your demon hunter energy into Izzy!"

Anna and Nikki looked at each other, unsure of how to proceed. Anna did the sign of the cross and held Izzy's right hand tight. Nikki took a deep breath and closed her eyes. Seeing her sister like this reminded her of her mom. She held Izzy's left hand and closed her eyes tight, trying to send her energy to her sister. The guilt flooded her mind and heart as the memories flashed before her eyes. For a brief moment, she neither felt nor heard anything but John's grunts as he continued to press onto Izzy's chest. There was an emptiness in her heart. Something had faded. A familiar and ever-present link was broken. The red-headed demon hunter then felt the demon hunter energy within her. Nikki could feel it move through her body as electricity. The seventeen-year-old girl felt the energy flow and could see Izzy's energy fading in her mind. Without hesitation, she lent out her energy into her sister. In her mind, she could see Anna doing the same.

John continued pressing on Izzy's chest. *Not again,* the Guardian thought to himself. *I won't let this happen.*

Time seemed to stretch for eternity when suddenly, Isabella's body jerked up. Her chest rose as if inhaling its first breath. The seventeen-year-old girl opened her eyes and saw her Guardian looking at her.

The room seemed to exhale as John felt relief wash over him, seeing the demon hunter he watched over regain her heartbeat and begin to breathe again.

Nikki grabbed hold of Izzy and hugged her tight, "I thought I lost you," Nikki whispered in her ear as tears continued to stream down her eyes. The red-headed demon hunter then turned her attention toward Anna, mouthing the word *thank you* before embracing her sister again, who was trying to sit up.

Isabella felt like her head was about to be split in two. "What happened?" she asked John while grimacing in pain.

"You won," John said softly. "I'll explain later. Try to rest."

Izzy attempted to get up, but the dizziness got the better of her, and she laid down for a few seconds in the puddle of holy water, trying to recollect her thoughts.

Nikki and Anna, seeing their sister alive and well, turned their attention to the crippled vampire trying to crawl away. Nicole took Izzy's golden crucifix from around her sister's neck as she stood up. Both she and Anna looked at Sigfried with rage in their eyes as they approached him. Nikki saw the bane that almost cost Izzy's life. Anna saw the being that had tormented her for weeks. Victoria softly put her hand on Anna's shoulder, signaling her to release the chains with the orb in her hand. Anna nodded at her older sister, handing her the medallion before continuing toward the defeated vampire.

"Do you feel like talking, Sigfried?" Nikki asked the vampire as he tried to crawl away, burning slowly in the holy water. "I'm really going to enjoy tearing you apart more than you already are."

"To hell with you!" Sigifried spat out as he grimaced in agony. "I have nothing for you!"

Nikki approached Sigfried, sat on his chest, and stuck Izzy's golden crucifix down his throat. Smoke started to emit from his lips as the vampire gazed back at the red-headed demon hunter with panic in his eyes. "Who did this to you?" Nikki asked as she removed the crucifix from his mouth. "These enhancements are not natural."

Sigfried laughed at the demon hunter and the Guardians, his voice coarse. "You will live in the dark," the vampire said. "Demon hunters rise and fall, whether by me or another demon. I'm an instrument of Chaos. Darkness will fall upon you no matter how much you..."

Sigfried did not have time to finish as Nikki stuck the crucifix back inside his mouth.

John frowned at Nikki's conversation with Sigfried as he helped Izzy sit up. "Take it easy," John said to his demon hunter. "Don't push yourself."

The Guardian looked at the vampire as he struggled under the pressure of the red-headed demon hunter. "Nikki!" John called out. The blue-eyed demon hunter turned her attention toward her Guardian. "This beast caused Anna grief and despair. Have her kill him."

Nikki looked at John, removing the crucifix from Sigfried's mouth as she stood up. The seventeen-year-old girl looked at Anna. "This is the vampire responsible for the death of our sisters. Do what you must."

Anna nodded as she pulled her trusty stake from the back pocket of her pants.

Luis and Victoria turned away as they only heard Sigfried scream in agony, accompanied by the sound of tearing flesh. They knew what Anna was doing. A few minutes later, the sound of the vampire exploding into dark ash echoed around the room.

John looked at Izzy, who now had Nikki at her side, helping her stand up. The Guardian then proceeded to inspect the black robe that the vampire used, which lay on the tile floor. His body felt a wave of relief as he breathed in.

Victoria and Luis hugged Anna, who remained kneeling with tears streaming down her eyes. The horror that had plagued their city had come to an end.

Luis stood up and looked at John, who flipped the robe from side to side as if he had searched for something. Luis approached his counterpart, who was visibly distraught by the entire ordeal. "Sigfried did not kill Angie, did he?"

John turned the robe inside out, and a white business card fell into the water. The young Guardian picked up the card and read it. *Anna, Balish, and Raymond LLC D. Anderson.* The card had a phone number and a Los Angeles address. "Sigfried was an instrument," John said, putting the card away in his shirt pocket. "Just as the demon that killed Angie."

"Angie killed that demon when she unleashed her demon hunter power," Luis concluded.

"Angie was alone when it happened," John said, looking at Izzy, who needed Nikki to support her as they started walking up the stairs. "She did what was needed. And now we must do what is asked of us as Guardians."

"Are we going after the hand that wields the instrument?" Luis asked, understanding what John meant.

John looked up at his counterpart, nodding. John stood up and looked at his demon hunters. "Let's head back to the hotel and get some rest. We need to discuss next steps."

CHAPTER VII

Lake Tahoe, Nevada, USA: Feb 8, 4:45 a.m.

GRACE STRUCK THE WU chu wooden dummy hard, spinning it from side to side. She hit, dodged, and blocked easily as she practiced her technique at half-speed. She could feel the rogue demon hunters watching her every move, studying them. The Hawaiian demon hunter was no stranger in always having eyes on her. She remembered the times back in Hawaii when she would attend exclusive high-society events with her parents. At a young age, she had learned to behave and conceal when needed. That was the reason she was moving and striking at half speed. She could feel her superior powers, even at that speed, compared to the older demon hunters surrounding her.

Then there was Leah. Grace turned her attention to the blonde seventeen-year-old girl who watched her from the far wall with an icy stare. Grace could feel the energy brewing inside of her. Izzy and Leah both had similar essences. But Grace could feel a slight deviation in the blonde's power. It was raw, fueled by anger and hate, unlike Izzy's, whose essence was driven by sheer will, compassion, and love. *They're like yin and yang,* Grace thought to herself.

All of a sudden, Grace felt an oppression in her heart. She stopped her maneuvers around the dummy as she held on to it for support. She felt as if something was torn away from her heart. Grace looked up, searching for Leah, who had disappeared from the room. Grace closed her eyes and tried to reach out with her senses to the missing essence in her heart. She stood still in the gym for what seemed to be an eternity with her hand on her chest. After what seemed like hours, she felt something move back into place. Grace could feel her heart whole again. The Hawaiian demon hunter opened her eyes and saw the other demon hunters stare back at her with puzzled looks.

Grace continued her training routine, trying to process what had just happened. *Izzy's fine,* she thought while sensing Roxanne and Sylvie watching her from the computer stations. Grace composed herself, hiding her feelings, pushing away the disturbing thoughts, and focusing on the demon hunters watching her. She faked a smile the best way that she could. *Got to keep it together,* Grace thought, focusing back on the wooden dummy. *They're evaluating me.*

Roxanne turned her attention toward Sylvie. "Grace is all that you said she was," the dark-eyed demon hunter said.

Sylvie frowned as she walked away and signaled for Roxanne to follow her. "Grace is holding back. She's stronger than this."

As both demon hunters walked up the stairs, Roxanne spoke up. "You can't trust her. Her parents were both Guardians. The Guardian's way is too ingrained in her."

Sylvie nodded as they reached the second level of the mansion. "I'm aware," the purple-pinkish-haired demon hunter said. "It's worth a shot if we can turn her. With her great fortune backing her up, she would be a great asset."

"She won't share that with us," Roxanne said. "She doesn't share it with the Guardians, let alone us."

"The Guardians don't need her money," Sylvie said as she entered her room. "We do."

"I think you're wasting your time," Roxanne said. "We should've killed her and Elizabeth as the contract required us to do."

"You don't see the big picture," Sylvie said. "With Elizabeth and Grace alive, others will pay three times as much. If I can channel Grace's power for a few days, we can profit from her in the Abyssborne."

Roxanne nodded. "At least it's not one of our girls."

There was a knock on the door, causing both rogue demon hunters to turn, seeing the dark-haired woman in the lab coat in the doorway. "What is it, Veronica?" Sylvie asked.

"Just informing you that we lost Yazmine and Nancy," Veronica said with zero emotion in her voice. "Their bodies could not take the punishment and never recovered.

Roxanne sighed and looked at Sylvie, who turned her back to Veronica. "They knew the risks," Sylvie said. "Cremate the bodies and do what you need to do."

Veronica nodded and walked away while Roxanne looked at Sylvie. "Yazmine and Nancy were good. We lost two good assets."

"But we have an Arzkang demon at our disposal," Sylvie said with a smile. "And we're over three dozen strong. We'll manage without them."

Sylvie's phone started to ring. The woman answered the video call, and a man in his early thirties appeared on the screen. "Mr. Daniel Anderson," Sylvie greeted. "How may I help you?"

"I am just asking for an update on the contract placed on Elizabeth Somiere and Grace Wu." the man asked.

"Going great," Sylvie said. "They're my prisoners now."

Daniel Anderson frowned at the response. "That was not what I specified in the contract."

"Don't worry," Sylvie said. "We'll have them participate in the Abyssborne. You received the invitation, didn't you? You can see the contract fulfilled with your own eyes."

Daniel Anderson nodded with a knowing smile. "You do put up quite a show," the man said. "I'll stop by your complex."

"Excellent," Sylvie said. "Ensure your fingers are ready to carry out that wire transfer."

"You have been very reliable for the last few years, Sylvie," Daniel said. "Hela Corp has been more reliable than other life forms out there. Undead forms included."

Sylvie noted the change of tone in Daniel's voice as he said that. "Did Sigfried fail?" Sylvie asked.

"Unfortunately for him, he has," Daniel said. "Fortunately for you, my firm will double the contract if you can take care of Nikki and Izzy."

"The risk is greater," Sylvie stated. "You know my crew and the results we produce. With the Abyssborne coming up, doubling what the original contract specified will not do. We're talking about the former leader of the Demon Hunter Division and the top three demon hunters in the region."

Daniel Anderson nodded. "Name your price."

"Ten times the original contract. Plus exclusive incursions with your firm after the job is done."

Daniel Anderson smiled. "Done."

"Prepare the paperwork," Sylvie said. "Bring it to the complex and enjoy the show."

Sylvie hung up the phone and looked at Roxanne, who had a look of awe on her face. "Told you the Arzkang demon would come in handy. Get the women ready. We must prepare for our guests."

"Are you ready?" Roxanne asked as Sylvie headed toward the end of the room where a solitary painting hung. Sylvie opened the portrait, revealing a small secret door with a metal safe embedded into the wall.

"I'm always ready," Sylvie said, opening the safe and pulling out golden chains with a dark blue orb hanging at the end.

Lake Tahoe, Nevada, USA: Feb 8, 4:45 a.m

ELIZABETH HAD HER LEGS crossed and her eyes closed while concentrating on her breathing. The growls and thumping from the lower level made it harder for her to focus and center her mind. The presence of the Arzkang demon on the premises tugged hard at her heart. She knew her husband, daughter, and Nikki would come to rescue her and Grace. Exposing them to this demon was just too dangerous. She needed to find a way to warn them.

Suddenly, Elizabeth had an uneasy feeling in the bottom of her stomach. Elizabeth grimaced, sensing the connection to her daughter lost. The blonde demon hunter opened her green eyes. She could feel her heart and soul being torn as if the most precious thing in the world was being taken from her. The woman stood up, grasping and pulling the chains hard. Her calm and serene demeanor disappeared from her face as she strained, trying to yank the chains from the wall. Elizabeth grunted in vain, missing her demon hunter strength. Her heart started to beat faster and faster, letting her anxiety reach fever-pitch levels as she tried to escape.

The sensation stretched out to what seemed an eternity when it ceased. Elizabeth felt the connection back, with her heart and soul restored. Elizabeth tried to reach out to her daughter with her mind, but the telepathic barrier was still there. The blonde demon hunter's heart skipped as a familiar essence entered the room where she was chained up. Elizabeth took a deep breath and tried to compose herself as she looked behind her. The silhouette of Leah peeking behind a stone column came to The Guardian's view. Her blue eyes were beautiful and intense.

"Hello, Mommy," Leah whispered as she stepped from behind the column. "Did you feel it? Izzy gone? Did you feel the sensation tear at your soul? Did it hurt?"

"What did you do?" Elizabeth asked.

Leah smiled at Elizabeth. "I wish I could take the

credit." The blonde demon hunter got closer to the Guardian and studied her features. Leah seemed to want to caress Elizabeth's face but did not touch her. "It feels like looking in the mirror," Leah said, admiring every inch of Elizabeth's face, eyes, and hair. "But it's not. This is real."

Elizabeth took a deep breath. Something happened to Izzy. She was sure of it. But she could feel that she was now okay. Now, she had Leah to contend with. Elizabeth gave in to the sensation, feeling Leah's demon hunter aura. It was identical to Izzy's, but it seemed to vibrate with a slight difference in frequency. "Seeing you standing there all grown up... it does feel like a dream," Elizabeth said, trying to focus her thoughts on seeing her lost daughter face-to-face for the first time.

"You've only seen me in your dreams," Leah said. Her deep Slavic accent pierced Elizabeth's heart. Her daughter had grown up far from her reach. "Did you ever think I was real?"

"Your father and I always had you in our hearts," Elizabeth responded.

"Lies! Lies! Lies!" Leah exclaimed, waving her arms as she stepped away from Elizabeth. "You can't help yourself, can you?"

"If you could peer into my mind, you'd know I wouldn't lie about that."

"I've peered into Izzy's mind," Leah said, touching her temple as if she were pointing a gun to her head. She made the motion of shooting her brains out, bending her neck to the side.

Elizabeth shivered, seeing the pantomime dramatization. It was like seeing an insane version of her daughter act in ways that a mother could never imagine. "Why her?" Elizabeth asked. "It's me you're angry at. It's me and Sean."

"Was it fate that separated us?" Leah asked. "Destiny or providence? All of that is a big joke."

"If we knew where you were, we would have searched for you until the ends of the earth," Elizabeth said. "We did search for you."

Leah laughed. "Did you?"

"We had nothing to go on but nightmares," Elizabeth said. "I had nightmares. Sean always painted about you. We both somehow knew. We didn't understand how, when, or why?"

"Twin daughters separated at conception," Leah pondered. "I know it's not your fault, Mommy. Izzy fell from the heavens when you defeated Daristos—an exchange for the unbalanced power in the world."

"And where were you?" Elizabeth asked. "Izzy was alone in that plane of existence."

"I was on the other side of the mirror," Leah said as memories flooded her mind.

The blonde demon hunter turned her back to Elizabeth as the room turned white in her mind. She saw four-year-old brown-haired and green-eyed Izzy sitting on the white plane with a book of ancient Latin in her hands. Leah tried to reach out, but an invisible barrier stopped her from reaching her sister. She turned around, and there was nothing on her side of the invisible wall.

Suddenly, the white room started to change color. The white slowly turned to yellow, then orange, and finally red. As the room changed color, so did the temperature. It increased at an alarming rate.

122

Leah looked at her body. She was no longer a seventeen-year-old teenager but a four-year-old girl. The room started to be engulfed by large red flames. Leah screamed as the fire burned her tiny body but did not consume it. Seconds became minutes. Minutes became hours. Hours became days. Days became weeks. Weeks became months. Time lost its meaning in the hellish torment.

Then, the pain, torment, and suffering stopped. The four-year-old girl looked up, and it was dark and cold. The white plane was gone. In its place, Gray, broken-down stone structures towered and surrounded the little girl.

The little girl heard a growling sound behind her. She turned, seeing a four-legged animal, bigger than her, growl and bark at her. The animal attacked the blonde child, only for her to scream and grab it with her bare hands, smashing it against the ground. Leah yelled as the creature yelped in pain while the girl ripped the animal open, tearing its limbs from its body. Blood spurted across her face as she brought an end to the four-legged creature.

Leah heard a scream from behind her. She turned around and saw a burly man with dirty garments around his body. A filthy, bushy beard adorned his face while he screamed at her. "Моя собака! Ти вбив мою собаку!" The taller man tried to grab her, but Leah pushed him away, flinging him against the concrete wall behind him.

A woman with dirty blonde-gray hair and ripped dirty clothes screamed behind her. The girl turned toward her while the woman rushed to the man's aid. "СТІЙ!" the woman shouted. "Він справедливий і старий!"

The woman helped the older man stand up as they looked at Leah, unsure what to do. The older man smiled, revealing a toothless grin. "Ти сильна маленька дівчинка," he said. "Думаю, ти заміниш нам собаку."

"Do you remember what they said?" Elizabeth asked, bringing Leah back to the present.

Leah turned toward her mother. "They were upset I killed their dog," Leah responded. "And they were upset I pushed the old man against the wall."

"Then they took you in?" Elizabeth asked, making the calculations in her head. "Where did you appear?"

"North of Ukraine. Near the Belarus border."

"They named you Leah?" Elizabeth asked, feeling a sting in her heart, not being the one who had named her daughter. "It's a beautiful name."

Leah looked at Elizabeth mockingly. "Are you trying to bond with me, Mommy? That time has long passed."

"I know it has," Elizabeth said. "There's nothing I can do about that. I do know you are part of me, just like Izzy. And you can't sever that connection, no matter how hard you try."

Leah screamed and threw a knife at Elizabeth's head. The blonde Guardian felt a slight sting on her cheek as the blade passed beside her face and stuck itself firmly on the concrete wall behind her. Elizabeth froze in disbelief, processing that her daughter had just thrown a knife at her face.

"I could kill you," Leah said coldly. "I feel that would cut the connection for good, wouldn't you agree?"

Elizabeth took a deep breath as she cleaned the blood from her right cheek and turned toward the knife sticking out of the wall. "Nice throw," she commented. She shifted her attention back to Leah's eyes and examined them. They were cold blue eyes. The demon hunter shielded her emotions, making it hard for Elizabeth to read. But for a split second, the Guardian saw a flinch in Leah. A sense of need and wanting. "I believe you could kill me," Elizabeth said. "But something stops you. Is it Sylvie? What is she planning?"

Leah smiled, almost relieved to change the subject. "She has great plans for you,"

"I am sure she does," Elizabeth said. "Would you mind sharing them with me?"

"I am not that easy, Mommy," Leah said. "Let's just say that her ideas align with mine and what I have in store for Isabella."

"I can't wait to see you together," Elizabeth challenged. "Maybe she can knock some sense into you."

"You have high hopes, Mommy," Leah replied, resenting the preference. Leah turned toward the octagon next to Elizabeth and tested the chains surrounding it. The blonde demon hunter smiled and turned her attention back to her mother. "I, for one, can't wait to see you in action."

After saying that, Leah made her way back up the stairs.

Elizabeth smiled and turned her attention back toward the blade impaled in the wall. Elizabeth looked at her chains and smiled. "You will see me, Leah."

Interstate 80, California, USA; Feb 8, 7:45 a.m

"BUT YOU'VE MADE SURE she's alright?" Sean asked with a slight panic as Aidan looked up at the Guardian's face. "Okay. Have her rest a bit while you tie up those loose ends. Ask Nikki to book the flight back to the States." Sean looked at Sabine, who had a refill on her glass of wine while he spoke. "No!" Sean continued. "Don't come to Lake Tahoe. Not with her condition like that." Sabine smiled, knowing what would happen, as she sipped her wine. "Okay," Sean relented. "But I have the lead on this. They do nothing without my say. I need to get a hold of what we're dealing with here. "

Sabine put down her glass as she received a notification on her cell phone. She read the message and started typing. She then turned her attention back to Sean.

"Take care of it, John," Sean said, feeling powerless. "I trust you." The Guardian hung up and looked at the vampire before him.

"All is well, I hope," Sabine said.

Sean nodded as he turned toward the limousine window and watched the sky. "They defeated the monster causing havoc in Mexico," Sean said. "They will be flying up this afternoon."

"I see," Sabine said as she continued looking at the Guardian.

"You can read my mind," Sean said, turning his attention back to the vampire. "Why bother asking?"

"It's a sign of trust, Sean," Sabine replied plainly. "I am more valuable to you as an ally than an enemy. And it would be best if you didn't worry about Isabella. She will recover soon."

Sean looked at Sabine inquisitively. The vampire returned a bored look. "I don't need to read your mind to know something happened to your daughter. The important thing is that she is now safe and recovering her strength. She will need it if she's coming to help us save her mom and sister."

"John is prepping her an antidote to recover," Sean said.

Sabine nodded her head. "Even though you have a strong and capable daughter, your concern is palpable. Imagine what the parents of other demon hunters go through every day—the pain of their daughters being thrust into an unknown peril."

Sean sighed as he sat back in his chair. "How does it feel to hear everyone's thoughts?" the Guardian asked, changing the subject. "Are the thoughts just out there, or do you get inside the head?"

"Good question, Sean," Sabine said. "Everyone projects their thoughts one way or the other. They lie within the surface of the mind. If I need something more tangible, I can force myself inside the mind and take whatever I want."

"Being a vampire and a demon hunter, do you share a connection with the rest of our girls?"

"I'm in the demon hunter phone book," Sabine replied. "But establishing a formal and stable connection that extends miles takes attuning. The amount of time your girls spend with each other and with Elizabeth helps establish that connection as second nature. But as with all things, there are advantages and disadvantages."

"Such as?" Sean asked.

"Lack of privacy, for one," Sabine said. "I would assume Elizabeth would have shared this information with you."

"She has," Sean said. "I just wanted to see to what extent you are connected to our girls."

"As I said," Sabine said, sipping her wine. "I'm in

the phone book."

The window that separated the driver from them lowered. Sean looked and saw Samantha take a right. "We'll be at our destination in fifteen minutes."

"Thank you, Sam," Sabine said. "Please take us to a hotel nearby. One that has a shop where we can purchase some fancy attire. Curse these demon hunters for doing this in the middle of winter."

"Would you like to involve me in your plans?" Sean asked.

"All you have to do is ask, Sean," Sabine said. "We're allies, you and I, after all. I just got the dossier of Hela Corp. Our rogue demon hunters are hosting an event called The Abyssborne. It's a small gala for select clientele to view what they offer."

"The Abyssborne?" Sean asked. "Cute name."

"Now you're reading my mind," Sabine said. "This Abyssborne seems to be a showcase for Hela Corp. They present their talent with small demonstrations of their abilities. They also have an auction for dead or alive creatures from the underworld. This year, they have a small treat for the audience."

"I am afraid to ask," Sean said.

"It seems that they are showcasing Elizabeth as their main attraction," Sabine said. "They have prepared small jousts with other demons and monsters. The attendants gamble on the outcome, and they purchase the flesh at the end—dead or alive."

Sean gritted his teeth in rage. He was aware of underground events like this. He was familiar with certain groups kidnapping demon hunters so they could participate against their will. The Guardians had specific protocols in place to protect the demon hunters. But sometimes, they fell through the cracks. And today, his wife and one of his girls were embroiled in a dangerous game.

"I've purchased our entrance for the event," Sabine said. "Hela Corp charges a hefty fee just to view the services."

"I'm afraid to ask how much I owe you for the granted access," Sean said.

"Nothing, Sean," Sabine said. "This one is on me. These demon hunters are only interested in money, which is not a problem for me. I bet that if you pay their asking price, I'm sure you can buy Elizabeth's and Grace's freedom."

"I won't do that," Sean said, looking out the window.

"Then what are you going to do?" Sabine asked inquisitively. "I'm genuinely curious. You teach your demon hunters fundamental rules: Protect the innocent. No human casualties. But this time, you have humans hurting you. I am curious about how you're going to deal with this."

Sean continued looking out the window while he formed a plan. "Our girls are heroines called to a higher purpose. They're pure, and they will remain as such." Sean stopped looking at the window and looked at Sabine. The vampire saw a dark rage in his eyes, which she had seen before. "The dirty work is left to their Guardians. That is where I come in."

Sabine nodded, not needing to read Sean's mind. She finished her glass of wine and looked at the Guardian before her. "Glad we agree, then," the vampire said. "I left that heroic path long ago."

CHAPTER VIII

Mexico City, CDMX, Mexico; Feb 8, 11:30 a.m.

IZZY COUGHED, SEEING DARK *green fumes surround her. The night sky was pitch black, and the ground below was a mystery, shrouded by the dense green fog. Izzy tried to make her way toward an unknown force that called out to her mind and heart.*

As if the fog had parted just for her, Izzy gasped in horror, seeing her twin sister before her, twirling a jackal knife with a five-inch blade and dragon-body handle. Behind her hung the beaten and unconscious bodies of Grace, Nikki, and Elizabeth.

"I missed you, little sister," Leah said. "You are going to wish you stayed dead."

"Stop it, Leah!" Izzy said as she took a step closer toward her sister.

Leah stepped right behind Elizabeth and pulled on her blonde hair, exposing her throat and placing her knife on it.

"Don't!" Izzy warned.

"Is that a threat, little sister?" Leah asked. "If I kill Mom,

will you break the unspoken rule of not killing humans?"

"Is that what you want?" Izzy asked, standing straight.
"Create blind hatred in me so that I become like you?"

"Why don't we give it a try?" Leah said, swiping the
knife hard across Elizabeth's throat.

Izzy tried to move, but her body froze on the spot,
seeing Elizabeth twitch, gag, and choke as her chest became
drenched in blood. Soon, her body stopped twitching.

Izzy's eyes filled with tears as she watched, powerless,
as Leah stepped toward Grace with her blood-stained knife.
Nikki struggled to release herself from the chains but was
unable to. Izzy could sense powerful magics cursing the
black chains that had her red-headed sister trapped.

Leah caressed the knife against Grace's cheek. Grace's
cold, dark stare penetrated Izzy to her core. In one swift
motion, Leah released Grace from her chains and handed
the dark-haired demon hunter the blood-stained knife.

"How can I hurt you?" Leah asked Izzy as she stood
behind Grace. "How about I destroy everything you hold
dear, and what little is left, I corrupt."

Grace twirled the knife in her hand and flung it at
Nikki's unprotected chest.

Izzy's eyes widened, seeing the blade sink into Nikki's heart.

"NO!" Izzy screamed, sweat streaming down the
side of her face.

Nikki woke up with a jolt from the couch across
from Izzy's bed. She looked at her sister, sweating due
to being covered with three thick serape bed covers.
Nikki quickly got to her feet and scrambled toward
Izzy. "Izzy!" Nikki called out. "I'm here! I'm okay!"

Izzy looked into Nikki's blue eyes and hugged her
sister. "You saw it, right?"

"I did. She's just playing with you. It's not real."

"We have to help Grace," Izzy said. She suddenly felt lightheaded.

Realizing this, Nikki helped her sister lie down again. "You need to regain your strength," the red-headed demon hunter said. "You're in no condition to execute a rescue right now."

"Grace is running out of time," Izzy said with a weak voice. "I shouldn't have betrayed her the way I did."

The room door opened, and John stepped in with a black medical bag in his hand. "Are you okay?" the Guardian asked. "I heard a scream."

"She had a bad dream," Nikki said, standing up and turning toward her Guardian. "She's still weak."

John walked toward the brown-haired demon hunter, pulled a wrist-style blood pressure monitor from his bag, and slid it into place on Izzy's hand. While the small white machine did its job, the Guardian pulled out a small pen light from his breast pocket and looked into Izzy's green eyes. He then took Izzy's pulse while she had a glazed look. "Your blood pressure is low, but it's slowly stabilizing," John said. "Your body is trying to recover, but it's taking time."

"I can feel it," Izzy said as she looked around her bedroom. She closed her eyes, hoping for the room to stop spinning. She opened them again, and slowly, she focused on her Guardian looking at her.

John stared directly into Izzy's eyes. "Promise me you'll never do that again," John said with a pleading stare. "There's no gain in dying like that."

Izzy could see the hurt in John's eyes as she silently nodded.

John stood up and looked at Nikki. "At what time will your uncle land to take us home?"

"Two and a half hours," Nikki said.

"I'll have Anna bring you both something to eat," John said. "After that, pack your gear because we're leaving." Saying that, the Guardian walked out of the room, shutting the door behind him and leaving both demon hunters alone.

"You cut that too close to the heart, O'Brien," Nikki said as she started packing her bag.

Izzy took a deep breath as she looked at her sister's back. "I couldn't come up with another option. We were running out of time."

Nikki stopped packing for a second as she relived the battle. She turned toward her sister. That was when Izzy noticed Nikki's blue eyes were red from excessive crying. "I know," Nikki said. "Anna was good, but we needed Grace with us this time."

"I know," Izzy said, sensing a little bit of strength return to her as she sat up while Nikki continued packing. "I messed things up with Grace. I thought I was doing the best for her."

"I believe you," Nikki responded as she zipped up her bag and turned her attention toward Izzy's gear. "Grace was right, you know."

"About what?"

"The reason she helped you fight Dante was because she didn't want you to go through the pain she went through in losing her parents," Nikki said. "She didn't hesitate in bringing down that bastard and his minions."

Izzy remained silent as Nikki turned around from packing. "You have your mom and dad, Izzy," the red-headed demon hunter continued. "I have my dad and my brother. Grace only has you and me. No one else. Neil is Grace's Dante, and she needed our help."

"I understand that now," Izzy said.

Nikki nodded as she finished packing Izzy's gear and turned toward her. "Then let's go and rescue your mom and our sister. Are you up for it?"

Izzy was about to answer when there was a knock on the door. Nikki opened it, revealing Anna carrying a tray with what seemed to be two red bowls of soup. "My mom prepped this for you two. My brother and sister added a little kick to accelerate your anabolic state."

Izzy and Nikki looked at each other as they each grabbed a bowl. The smell was delicious, but already, Izzy's eyes had begun to water in response to the spice level.

Anna looked at both her older sisters with a big smile on her face. "It's chicken pozole," the girl said. "The best and spiciest in the city."

Nikki nodded and took a big spoonful. Her eyes widened as soon as the spice reached her tongue. Slowly, her face started to turn red. She turned toward Izzy, who was trying to swallow the mouthful as tears began streaming from her eyes.

"Drink it all," Anna said. "You will regain your strength in no time with that."

"Do you have a glass of water?" Izzy wheezed out.

"Nope," Anna said as she sat on the couch across from Izzy's bed. "It has a better effect without water. Try eating it fast. It will alleviate the spice."

Both Izzy and Nikki gulped down the food as fast as they could. Izzy could feel the heat stream down her throat and into her stomach. She felt her insides on fire, but she kept the food down.

Nikki's eyes and nose watered as she ate the dish. She felt like a volcano was erupting in her mouth, and lava was streaming down her esophagus.

When both girls cleared their bowls, they looked at Anna, expecting some mercy. There was none as the Mexican demon hunter stared back at her older sisters. "I'm coming with you to the States. I'll help you rescue Elizabeth and Grace from whatever prison holds them."

Izzy started coughing, feeling intense heat in her throat. "My dad has eyes on the ground. I'm sure he'll brief us once we get there."

Nikki looked at the ceiling, looking for relief as she wiped the tears from her blue eyes. "Fighting alongside your dad this time. This is going to be great."

Izzy tried to smile at her sister but was unable to, feeling she was running out of breath. The heat level inside her mouth was excruciating.

Anna looked at both girls before standing up and pulling out two water bottles from her pants pockets. She threw the bottles at each of her sisters. "I'll pack my gear, then," she said.

The petite, dark-haired girl walked out of the room with a smile as Izzy and Nikki gulped down the contents of their water bottles. Anna knew that water would only spread the heat. She smiled more when she heard her sisters gasp behind the wooden door.

*

VICTORIA RODRIGUEZ LOOKED AT the large-screen setup in front of her—six twenty-nine-inch monitors lined up in a two-by-three formation. The young Guardian took a sip of her coffee as she peered at the security perimeter of the hotel on the left side of the displays, while seeing software algorithms doing their thing on the right side. The software was chewing on the keywords "Hela Corp," and "Anna, Balish, and Raymond LLC." The top center screen had the website splash screen of Anna, Balish, and Raymond LLC, while the bottom had a picture of a handsome gentleman in his early thirties named Daniel Anderson in a designer suit.

Luis Rodriguez entered the office and looked at all the screens, focusing on the algorithm running on the right side. "Working like clockwork," Luis said, turning toward his twin sister. "Saves you hours in research, doesn't it?"

"It does," Victoria said, memorizing the contents of Daniel's biography. She then turned toward her taller brother and smiled. "You're not as *menso* as you look."

The algorithm flashed a few seconds, and then a single document appeared with green text and a black screen. "Wanna race, *mensa*?" Luis asked.

"You're on," Victoria said, accepting the challenge. "John will declare the winner."

"Done," Luis said.

As if the twins could read their thoughts, both started reading the green text as quickly as possible. The words flowed before their eyes as their gifted memory absorbed the information. After a few minutes, both brother and sister finished reading the lengthy compiled document just as John entered the room.

"How is Izzy?" Victoria asked.

"She's recovering," John replied. "Her demon power is severely depleted, but she's alive. And that is all that matters."

"How are you holding up?" Luis asked. "What happened hit a little too close to home."

John tried to smile at the twins but was unable to. "My last words to Angie were for her to give me time. Her death opened the door and gave Isabella a chance today. It gave an additional option. I think that is a win on that front."

Victoria and Luis looked at each other and then at the image of the dark-haired man on the lower center screen. "We have another win," Luis said.

"Daniel Anderson," Victoria said. "A senior consultant for a large firm based in Los Angeles. The firm provides several services for high-end clientele, specializing in science, technology, public relations, and legal services. They offer out-of-the-box solutions for those who can afford their services."

"Why would Sigfried have a human's business card?" John asked.

The twins looked at John as if he were stupid. "For a genius, you're kind of slow," Luis teased.

"I have other specialties, you dorks," John retorted back.

"Anna, Balish, and Raymond LLC is a front," Victoria said. "A very successful front dealing with normal human beings who are wealthy enough to pay for what they offer."

"I wrote an algorithm that uses AI to cross-reference anything we want in the dark web," Luis said.

"And the firm has exclusive clientele in the underworld," John concluded.

"See," Victoria started teasing. "You got the answer."

"The firm has been providing services for demons, vampires, warwolves, and other types of hellspawn," Luis said. "They've been operating for over two centuries, based on the information my algorithm dug up."

John looked at Luis and smiled a bit. "You're proud of your little program, aren't you?"

"Hey," Luis said. "You remember how long it took us to review our books. With this thing, we can do it in minutes."

"These guys have been behind some serious stuff," Victoria said. "Their most recent exploits were dealing with the vampire clans in Europe and North America to unleash Apocalyps. They were behind the scenes on the assault on the St. Helena Hellspot."

"They are responsible for the deaths of Anna and Theresa," Luis said.

"That piece of information is something The Guardians in Ireland will find interesting, " John said.

"There's a link of several Guardians disappearing, along with some demon hunters from Colorado, Nevada, Utah, Nebraska, and the Dakotas," Victoria said.

John's mind flashed for a moment. "Pull up a map of North America," the Guardian ordered.

Victoria looked perplexed but pulled up the map on the top screen. "The girls found the Tome last year," John said.

"What?" Victoria exclaimed.

"And you haven't shared it with us?" Luis asked.

"The Guardians are still processing it in Ireland," John said. "But based on the estimates, North America will have a cataclysmic supernatural event."

"Do you know where?" Victoria asked.

John shook his head as he looked at the states where demon hunters and Guardians were reported missing. "I calculate a large city up North."

Luis looked at the map, and his eyes widened. "They're clearing the path. They're weakening the defenses, so the event has little to no resistance from the demon hunters."

"When will this happen?" Victoria asked

"Two more years," John said. "Send the information to Ireland so that they can process it. All this information needs a long-term plan."

"There's more," Luis said as he looked at Victoria.

John looked at both twins, waiting for a response.

"The same firm is responsible for all the things that have been happening in Mexico in the past five years," Victoria said.

John took a deep breath as he processed the new information. He looked at the picture of Daniel Anderson and then at the twins. "These are humans that are running the firm?" John asked. "Not demons? You said the firm has been operating for over two centuries."

"Daniel Anderson is a thirty-three-year-old man from California," Luis said. "He may be working for someone more supernatural."

"And this guy is backing everything in the past five years?" John asked. "A human man?"

"Not only that," Victoria said. "He is backing Hela Corp."

John had to sit down as he looked at both twins. "WHAT?"

Luis nodded as he typed something on the keyboard. "Hela Corp has been freelancing their services for Anna, Balish, and Raymond LLC. They've carried out half a dozen assignments in the past year alone."

"They are financing an event tomorrow night for Hela Corp called The Abyssborne," Victoria said. "A special gala where they show off the demon hunters who fight for their side, as well as other pet projects."

"From the documents I've read," Luis said. "Daniel Anderson himself put the bounty on Elizabeth for Hela Corp to perform the deed."

John rubbed his head as he tried to process the information. The demon hunters could take on any undead creature from the underworld. But now their enemy was their flesh and blood. "Exclusive event?" John asked.

"Very high-end," Victoria said. "Fully booked, but maybe I can figure out how to smuggle our team in."

"Sean is not going to like this," John said.

"It's in our hands now," Luis said as he looked at Victoria. "For Andrea, Maria, Blanca, Mercedes, and all the demon hunters we've lost these past years."

"Luis is right, John," Victoria said. "The demon hunters have enough burden to carry. It's up to us to carry this load."

John took a moment to reflect on what Nikki and Izzy would say if they knew what he knew. "I agree," the dark-haired Guardian noted.

"One more thing about Hela Corp," Luis stated.

"What is it?" John asked.

"Besides Elizabeth, The Abyssborne is promoting a fully controllable Arzkang demon," Luis said.

"An Arzkang demon?" John said, looking at the twins. "How the hell did they pull that off?"

"Based on the invitation, Hela Corp will showcase a way for the Arzkang to receive orders without question," Victoria said.

John nodded and looked at Luis. "They want to play hardball. We can play hardball. Pack me The Judge."

"It's just a prototype," Victoria said.

"I'm not sending our demon hunters with nothing to face off against an Arzkang demon," John said.

"I hope the ammo works," Luis said.

"It has to," John stated. "For our demon hunters, it has to work. Double the dose when you pack it."

"Who's that?" a voice interrupted the Guardians.

John, Victoria, and Luis turned to see Anna at the office door. The demon hunter approached the monitor and saw a human's face on the bottom screen. "Who is this?" she asked again, looking at her brother and sister.

"Do you recognize him?" Victoria asked.

"He was inside a parked limo at the club two nights ago," Anna said. "I remember him smiling at the bouncer at the door before driving off."

"Are you sure it was him in that limo?" Luis asked his younger sister.

"I'm positive," Anna said, looking at the twins. "Who is he?"

"We're still figuring it out," John said. "The important thing is that you took care of Sigfried today."

Anna looked at the three Guardians and nodded. "Izzy and Nikki are almost ready," the young demon hunter said. "I promised I would accompany and help them out with Grace and Elizabeth."

John nodded and looked at Victoria and Luis. "I need one of you to fly north with us," John said. "The one who stays continues investigating this firm and all their deeds."

Victoria and Luis looked at each other as they extended their fists simultaneously and shook them three times. Victoria pulled out a rock while Luis pulled out scissors. "Okay," Luis said. "One of us will go with you and help out."

"Let's do this," John said, standing up.

CHAPTER IX

Lake Tahoe, Nevada, USA: Feb 8, 2:00 p.m.

GRACE STEPPED OUT OF the bathroom, wearing a black long-sleeved crop top and matching black leggings. A white towel covered her black hair as she dried it in front of the mirror. Her dark eyes peered into her reflection, pondering her next steps. With Sylvie's proposal bouncing around in her mind, she had trained for a while and gotten a few hours of sleep. She knew Elizabeth was still in the bowels of the mansion, but the possibility of getting her hands on Neil was too close for her to ignore.

Suddenly, a tug on her insides caused her demon-hunter senses to perk up. She could feel a disturbance in the air. A knock on the door of her room interrupted her thoughts. "Come in," Grace said as she turned around.

The door opened, and Sylvie and Roxanne walked in. "Did you get some rest?" Sylvie asked, her voice dripping with too much concern for Grace's comfort.

"A bit," Grace said as she sat on the bed and put on

her white sneakers. The raven-haired demon hunter extended her hand toward an almost-empty fruit bowl and grabbed two green grapes from the small cluster left on the plate.

"Have you had time to contemplate Sylvie's offer?" Roxanne asked.

"I guess I won't decide until I see you have Neil," Grace said, standing up and tying her hair into a neat ponytail. The unease in her stomach was too strong to ignore now. She knew that Neil was near.

"Then you're in luck," Sylvie said with a sly smile drawn across her face. "He's waiting for you downstairs."

Grace's heart started beating faster upon hearing the news. She tried to hide her emotions, but her eyes betrayed her.

"You can accept my proposal after seeing him," Sylvie said. "Unlike Elizabeth, I care for the needs of my demon hunters."

"Let's go," Roxanne said, motioning Grace to exit the room.

Grace felt very lightheaded, unable to control her heart rate. She could feel Neil's unmistakable essence nearby as she walked through the hall and down the stairs. The other demon hunters watched as the trio made their way down to the cellar.

As Grace entered the bowels of the mansion, the first person she saw was Elizabeth, sitting on the floor with her legs crossed and eyes closed. A plate of untouched bread and water sat on the floor next to her. Grace, Sylvie, and Roxanne were making their way to the octagon when Elizabeth opened her eyes and peered into Grace's. Elizabeth smiled and gave Grace a reassuring look. She then closed her eyes again and continued to sit quietly.

Grace was confused by what Elizabeth had said to her with that look. Despite their predicament, the senior demon hunter was in a bizarre state of peace.

Roxanne guided Sylvie and Grace to the back of the cellar, where a large metal door stood. The growls behind it grew louder as they approached. Roxanne opened the door that led to a black staircase leading to a lower level. The growls grew louder as the trio descended the stairs, bringing a shiver down Grace's spine.

When they reached the bottom of the stairs, Grace was not surprised to see a long white hall with thick glass that separated individual rooms. Each room contained several living demons, vampires, hellhounds, or hellspawns chained to the wall, just as she had seen in the security feed. At the end of the hall, four demon hunters dressed in black waited.

Grace was walking the hall with Roxanne and Sylvie when she saw the Arzkang demon smash his giant fist against the reinforced glass. Grace looked at the behemoth seven-foot fury beast for the first time. His humanoid frame was massive and muscular, covered in white fur. His sizeable white snout revealed long, sharp fangs that could tear into human flesh like butter. Grace noted the blood-stained claws as the monster smashed the reinforced glass over and over again. The big ruby-red eyes pierced Grace's soul. The demon hunter felt tense seeing a monster five times stronger and faster than a Hillion. She and her sisters had never faced a demon of that caliber.

Sylvie smiled at Grace, knowing the Arzkang demon had caught the demon hunter's attention. "You have no idea the price tag on this bad boy," Sylvie said.

"I can't imagine," Grace responded as the beast cried a war growl and continued pounding the reinforced glass.

"Now imagine how much people will pay to see this beast in action before I sell him," Sylvie said.

"Anything that faces this monster will get torn to shreds," Grace said.

"I know," Sylvie said as she looked at Roxanne. "And people will love it."

Roxanne motioned for them to continue at the end of the hall where the demon hunters stood. As Grace approached, she finally saw Neil, who stood in the middle of the white cell, looking straight into her dark eyes. The six-foot-one vampire stood still, with a sly smile on his face. His three-piece gray suit looked a bit dirty with a small tear, but other than that, he looked impeccable.

"As promised," Sylvie said, presenting her prize and gift to Grace. "The ancient one, Neil."

"I've walked this world for over two thousand years," Neil said. "I can't remember being surprised by someone in such a long time."

"I am full of surprises," Grace said as she gritted her teeth.

Neil stepped toward the glass and looked down at the five-foot-three demon hunter. "I guess that is what you're worth," Neil said. "Everyone has their price, Grace. And I guess yours was pretty low."

"Pay no attention to the undead," Sylvie whispered

into Grace's ear. "The vampire is trying to throw you off your game like he has done all your demon hunter life, but he doesn't control you anymore. No one does. You are free."

"The surprises keep on coming," Neil said with a smile, stepping back while his eyes stared into Grace's soul. "You're so desperate for the truth that eludes you. I guess your father was right. Your impatience and anger are the source of your weakness."

Something snapped inside Grace as she smashed her fist against the glass. "Shut up!"

"Always proving my point," Neil said. "But you and I will dance soon enough." He turned toward Sylvie and stared directly into the rogue demon hunter's eyes. "I am going to enjoy tearing you apart."

Sylvie was surprised at the vampire's comment. "For an ancient vampire, you're not that bright," Sylvie stated. "We captured you."

Neil turned around and leaned against the back wall, crossing his arms with a confident smile. "Indeed, you did."

Sylvie was about to respond when the white lights inside the dungeon turned off, and a red light flooded the room. A blazing alarm boomed through the speakers integrated into the ceiling. Roxanne touched the communicator in her ear, trying to hear what was happening. "Talk to me! What's happening?" Roxanne's eyes widened, hearing the response as she looked at Sylvie.

"What is it?" Sylvie asked.

"Elizabeth escaped?" Roxanne said. "She has broken off her chains, took out two of our girls, and she's escaped the property."

"Things do get interesting around here," Neil said with a sly smile.

Roxanne and Sylvie glared at the vampire while conflicting feelings and emotions bombarded Grace's mind. There was a sense of peace, knowing Elizabeth had escaped her predicament. But her Guardian left her alone to fend off the rogue demon hunters. Or did Elizabeth think that she'd betrayed her, leaving her behind? *Did she think so little of me?* Grace thought to herself.

"I have a great idea," Neil piped in from his cell, capturing the attention of the demon hunters. "Why not send Grace with a few demon hunters to capture Elizabeth again? It would be a great test of her loyalty."

Grace grimaced at the thought and looked at Sylvie. "That's not part of the deal," Grace protested.

"The deal is that I give you Neil if you join us," Roxanne said after thinking for a few seconds. "What better way to test your demon hunter skills than to capture the great Elizabeth Somiere?"

"Demon hunter of legend," Neil said, adding more fuel to the fire of emotions Grace was going through. "Wasn't that what you always wanted, little girl? To be the best of the best?"

Grace glared at the ancient vampire, who extended his arms with a knowing smile. "Don't worry, sweetheart," Neil said. "I'm not going anywhere. Once you bring Elizabeth back, you can have a one-on-one with me."

Grace turned toward Sylvie with rage in her eyes. "Give me these four demon hunters," the raven-haired girl stated, motioning at the girls who had brought Neil in. "And keep that psycho blonde demon hunter out of my way."

"You got it," Sylvie said, beaming with satisfaction. "Roxanne will accompany you. She will be my eyes on the field for this excursion."

Grace glared at Neil, who waved goodbye to his demon hunter as she stormed off.

*

ELIZABETH MADE HER WAY through the snow-covered woods as she zipped the black parka she had borrowed over her torso. Sylvie's mansion was a hundred yards behind her as she made her way in the twenty-seven-degree weather. The day was cloudy, but there was enough light for her to see a way through the woods. Her mind tried desperately to break the magic that blocked her mental connection to her daughter. She needed to warn her before they approached the mansion with a rescue party.

The blonde demon hunter jogged in the snow for fifteen to twenty minutes before reaching a clearing. She could feel the magic from the mansion weakening as she reached the end of the clearing. She leaned against a ponderosa pine tree and sat behind it, putting her back against the mansion's direction. Elizabeth crossed her legs and closed her eyes, expanding her demon hunter energy that had returned to her when she picked the lock from the cursed chains. She pulled out Leah's knife from the back of her pants and twirled it. *Thank you, daughter*, Elizabeth thought to herself as she tried to reach out to Izzy.

Soon, Elizabeth's mind brought her to a projection of the green prairies of Ireland next to Izzy's oak tree.

Elizabeth opened her green eyes and calmed her heart, waiting for her daughter. Soon enough, Izzy appeared, running toward her. Both mother and daughter's minds embraced for what seemed forever. An overwhelming sense of relief washed over Elizabeth, seeing her daughter alive and well.

"Are you okay?" the blonde demon hunter asked. "I felt our connection snap for a few seconds."

"I'm fine, Mom," Izzy said. "I will tell you everything when we find you and Grace. Where are you?"

"I don't have time," Elizabeth stated. "Grace and I are somewhere near Lake Tahoe. A rogue demon hunter named Sylvie captured us and is preparing something involving me. I'm not sure what it is. They're trying to recruit Grace to join them."

"Grace won't betray us. She won't betray you."

Elizabeth grabbed Izzy by the shoulders as both peered into each other's eyes. "Look into my mind," the blonde demon hunter said. "Leah is here."

"I know," *Izzy replied as her mind fed off Elizabeth's thoughts and emotions of what had transpired in the past hours—the sense of sorrow Elizabeth felt on both coming face-to-face with her flesh and blood daughter, and Grace's desperate need for answers. Neil was in the compound, ready to wreak havoc.*

Izzy then turned pale as she heard a roar from Elizabeth's mind. "They captured an Arzkang demon?" *Izzy asked her mom.*

"You have to be careful," Elizabeth said. "Warn your father."

"Why can't we talk freely with our thoughts?" Izzy asked. "Nikki and I can't reach Grace."

"*Sylvie has created a magical barrier that blocks our efforts,*" Elizabeth replied. "*We can't communicate inside the compound. But you, Nikki, Grace, and I are attuned to each other. The spell can't hold us if we're together inside the mansion.*"

"*These are demon hunters,*" Izzy said, shedding light on her doubts. "*They're not demons or vampires we're dealing with.*"

"*You and Nikki will figure something out,*" Elizabeth said to her daughter, kissing her head as tears streamed down her eyes. "*I will take care of Grace. You find a way to get us out of here.*"

Izzy looked behind her oak tree and saw Grace walking up to them. Izzy stepped to the side and yelled at Grace. "Please take care of my mom!" the green-eyed demon hunter said.

Grace stopped briefly as Izzy's single thought pierced her entire being. The image of both Elizabeth and Izzy talking flooded her mind. The demon hunter motioned the women who followed her to stop. She turned to see Roxanne wearing the Hela Corp black parka, and the other demon hunters behind her. "Stay here," Grace ordered. "I got her."

Roxanne nodded to the four rogue demon hunters as they watched Grace walk up to the pine tree before her. As she turned around, she crouched next to Elizabeth, who sat cross-legged, looking into Grace's black eyes. "I'm sorry," Elizabeth said. "I'm truly sorry I couldn't provide the answers you seek."

Grace felt Elizabeth invite her to peer into her mind for the first time. Elizabeth and the Guardians' numerous attempts to link the connection between

Neil and her parents were palpable. There was also great remorse for Elizabeth's failure to gain her trust that she was looking into the matter.

Grace looked back at Roxanne, trying to hide the conflict in her eyes as the rogue demon hunter pulled metal chains from her backpack. Grace turned back to Elizabeth. "Get up," the seventeen-year-old demon hunter ordered.

Elizabeth nodded as she handed Grace Leah's knife. Roxanne and the other demon hunters approached and wrapped the metal chains around Elizabeth's body, immediately taking Elizabeth's strength.

Roxanne raised her fist and tried to punch Elizabeth in the face, but Grace blocked it. "We got her," Grace said." We can't damage the goods before The Abyssborne."

Roxanne looked surprised at Grace's bravado but slowly nodded, giving the Hawaiian demon hunter full reign and authority.

Grace pushed Elizabeth's chained body and forced her to march back to Sylvie's compound, trying to hide the emotions that engulfed her. Elizabeth had indeed attempted, but had failed to bring closure to her needs. Yet it was Sylvie who put all her resources at her disposal. And now Neil was within her reach.

Grace could feel Roxanne try to peer into her mind right before they entered the compound's boundary. Grace turned toward Roxanne and glared at her. "Do you need something from me?"

"You have cold blood in your veins, Grace Wu," Roxanne said with a hint of admiration. "But I want to know if you have any doubts lingering in your mind."

"We have a deal," Grace said. "You give me Neil, and I join your little team."

Elizabeth stopped in her tracks, causing the small squad to stop. "Keep on walking," Roxanne barked at the blonde Guardian.

Elizabeth turned toward Roxanne and then toward Grace. "What will happen if you obtain everything your heart desires from Neil, and it still doesn't bring the closure you seek?"

Grace thought for a second and scowled at Elizabeth, letting her rage and hatred be her drive. "I will beat the closure from his undead body."

Elizabeth nodded as she continued walking toward the compound.

Grace tried to push away the uneasiness about what she was doing. She relived the memory of Neil over her dead parents over and over again in her mind, fueling her resolve. She needed to do this. No matter what it took.

CHAPTER X

Lake Tahoe, Nevada, USA; Feb 8, 5:30 p.m.

SEAN PACED BACK AND forth in his hotel room while he listened to his daughter over the FaceTime phone call. "What else did you see?" Sean asked.

"Hela Corp has these chains that zap mom's demon hunter powers," Izzy replied. "That is how they're keeping her prisoner."

Sean nodded. "It will take more than that to keep your mom out of action. Still, we need to help her."

Izzy turned her face away from the camera. She then faced her father again. "Lieutenant Wells says we will be landing in two hours," Izzy reported.

"Okay," Sean said. "How are you holding up?"

Izzy paused for a few seconds before responding. "My strength is coming back. John says it will take a few hours before I'm fully powered up. Nikki and Anna fueled me up with their energy, making my recoup time faster."

"Glad to hear that," Sean said.

"Dad?" Izzy asked. "I asked Mom about us taking these rogue demon hunters out. She said we would think of something. So far, Nikki, Anna, and I are drawing a blank."

Sean stayed silent momentarily, thinking carefully about what he was about to say. "Stay to the rules, Izzy. We go in. We rescue Grace and your mom, and then we get out. Neutralize all human opposition. Do not terminate."

Izzy smiled a bit, despite the tension. "You make it sound so easy."

"I try," Sean said, smiling a bit, knowing his daughter and her team were strong enough to handle the task.

A knock on the hotel room door caught the older Guardian's attention. Sean opened it, and Samantha walked in with a dry cleaning bag in her arms. Sean motioned Sabine's driver to come in while he continued speaking to Izzy. "Trust in John and Victoria," Sean said. "They will guide you on this."

"Okay," Izzy said. "Do you want to speak to John?"

"Yes, please," Sean said, motioning to Sam to place the dry cleaning bag on the chair while he continued the call.

"Hello," John said over the phone.

"I'm near the Hela Corp Location with Sabine," Sean said. "She's gotten me an entrance. Not sure how they will react when a vampire enters the premises through the front door."

"According to our readings, their loyalty depends exclusively on how deep your pockets are," John said with a shrug. "I guess the Guardians' payroll is not enough for them."

"We don't play that game," Sean said. "Meet us at the location I sent you. Any thoughts on getting our demon hunters in position?"

"Victoria is working on it," John said. "But we're sure not paying for a seat at the table as you are."

"I'm not paying the tab," Sean said. "Sabine is putting up the cash, upfront. Her motives do not clash with ours as far as getting in."

"Deep pockets," John said. "It pays to be immortal."

"I agree," Sean said, looking at Sam, who waited patiently. "John. About the rogue demon hunters."

"I'm aware," John said, interrupting Sean. "Luis and Victoria are on board. We've informed Ireland, and we have their support on this."

"And the other humans involved in this?" Sean asked. "Are you on board?"

"We will follow Guardian protocol," John said without missing a beat. Sean studied John's eyes, seeing a fierce determination in them.

"It's part of the job," Sean said. "Contact me when you land."

"Will do," John said. "See you at the hotel."

"And John," Sean said before hanging up.

"What?"

"We have a pending conversation on what happened with Siegfried," Sean said. "That was too close."

"I understand," John said.

"Thank you," Sean said. "For being there for Izzy."

"It's my job," John replied.

"Okay," Sean said. "Talk to you later."

Hanging up, Sean turned toward Samantha, who was still in the room. The stunning young Black woman stood at five feet six inches. She carried herself with confidence and grace, wearing a tailored black pantsuit that hugged her form in all the right places, with matching polished black booties. A crown of shoulder-length dark curls framed her round face, celebrating her natural beauty.

"I'm sorry to interrupt," Sam said. "Lady Sabine had me pick up your suit for tomorrow's event."

"Thank you," Sean replied, opening the dry cleaning bag and pulling out a black suit with a white silk shirt and black bow tie. "Will you be joining us?"

"Lady Sabine needs my expertise inside," the woman replied. "So yes. I will be at your side temporarily during the incursion. I promise not to get in the way. I'm good at not being seen in dangerous situations."

"Elizabeth mentioned an older man accompanying Sabine," Sean said. "Your father, I assume."

"Yes," Sam replied. "He's retired now, and now I take his place."

Sean examined Sabine's driver, looking into her eyes. "How does that work? I mean. How do you put in your resume that you work for a two-thousand-year-old vampire?"

"I assume the same way that your Guardians apply for a job," Sam replied without missing a beat. She then mimicked reading a headline in the air. "Looking for a candidate willing to care for young girls risking their lives fighting demons, vampires, and other monsters that go bump in the night."

"I concede," Sean said, smiling at Sam's wit. "But working for a vampire? How does it work without her feeding on you?"

"You couldn't help yourself in asking, could you?" Sam said with a sly smile drawn on her face. "Just as demon hunters and Guardians, Sabine abides by a code. That code impedes her from feeding off my family and me."

"I see," Sean said. "How did your family come into Sabine's services?"

"Around the late eighteenth century," Sam replied, "my family was subject to a blood curse that wreaked havoc among my clan. Death and pestilence followed wherever we roamed. Lady Sabine broke the curse, but in doing so, a new blood link was created between my family and her."

"Hence, your family is tied to her," Sean concluded.

"She brings prosperity to my family," Sam stated. "In return, we provide a human face to her bidding. We walk in the daylight while she works in the shadows."

Sean nodded as he gained insight into who Sabine really was. "Are you happy serving at her side?"

"A similar question could be asked of anyone called to serve," Sam responded as she looked out the window. "Some rogue demon hunters are unhappy with the arrangement the Guardians created. Maybe some Guardians are not pleased with that as well. Isn't that how it works with any organization of human beings? Dealing with that pesky free will?"

"None of our demon hunters or Guardians are forced to serve," Sean said. "Families are called. Some have said no."

"And how many have said yes because they feel forced?" Sam asked. "And how many said yes because they have a true calling to do what they believe is right?"

"Are you doing what's right?" Sean asked.

Sam turned away from the window and looked into Sean's dark eyes with fierce determination. "I know I am. Just as you're convinced that you are."

"Noted," Sean said.

"Is there anything else I can help with?" Sam asked.

"That will be all, thank you," Sean replied.

Sam started walking out of Sean's room when she turned and faced the Guardian. "Lady Sabine said that you should rest. There's nothing to do until tomorrow night. Regroup. You will need your wits and strength."

Sean frowned as Sam closed the door behind her. The sensation in the pit of his stomach felt as if he had walked straight into the mouth of a dark and bottomless abyss. The Guardian walked toward the window and saw Aidan outside by the trees, camouflaged by the snow and the trees. One thing was for certain. If someone did hurt his wife and daughter, there was no hell on earth that would stop him from destroying the culprits.

Lake Tahoe, Nevada, USA; Feb 8, 5:30 p.m.

"WE'RE BEGINNING OUR DESCENT," Lieutenant Wells declared over the loudspeaker of the private aircraft.

Izzy buckled up as she felt the aircraft start doing its maneuvers. The young demon hunter tried to focus her mind on something else while they landed. With all the commotion in Mexico, her mother and Grace being held by the rogue demon hunters, and the fact that these were new conditions she was required to operate in, she needed time to distract herself. It was challenging.

The seventeen-year-old girl admired the interior of this particular aircraft. It was a bit bigger than the one they flew from California, and definitely more luxurious. Nikki's uncle had called in a considerable favor to fly them using this jet. The seats were spacious, with plenty of legroom and space to walk around.

Izzy turned her attention to Anna, who sat beside her by the window. She had been silent the entire flight. In front of them, Victoria worked arduously on the black fingerless gauntlets they had tested against Siegfried. A pair of magnifying glasses were perched on her head as she adjusted the weapons with her set of tools.

Behind Victoria, John is working on a portable chemistry set. During the flight, he barely spoke except when on the call with Sean. The young Guardian adjusted his reading glasses as he mixed a powdered solution in a glass beaker. He then proceeded to add two different sets of fluids to the powder.

"What are you two working on?" Izzy asked.

Victoria looked up at Isabella and then back down to the gauntlets. "Adjusting your weapons for battle," the mechanical engineer said. "The projectiles are calibrated to penetrate flesh. I'm reducing the tension in the firing mechanism so that they only perforate the skin."

"That won't help against demons," Anna said.

"You won't be fighting demons," John stated. He looked at both demon hunters and thought a moment before he spoke. "Well. You will fight demons and vampires, but won't use the gauntlets against them."

"They will be for the demon hunters," Izzy said softly to Anna.

"Firing the projectiles at them will only scar them," Victoria said.

"Enough for this solution to kick in," John said as he grabbed a roll of wooden projectiles and added them to the blue liquid he had just mixed.

"What's that?" Anna asked.

John was about to answer when the cockpit opened, and Nikki stepped out. "Uncle Tony has the aircraft," the red-headed girl stated. "He didn't want me flying after all we've been through."

"You feeling okay?" John asked.

"I'm fine," Nikki replied. "I'm worried if O'Brien will be one hundred percent for this."

"I'll be fine," Izzy said. "I'm not getting benched on this one."

"It's okay," John said. "There's still time. Izzy will be ready for the incursion tomorrow."

Nikki walked toward Izzy and playfully punched her arm before sitting beside her. Her heart felt complete as the vivid connection linking the demon hunters was re-established.

"As I was saying," John continued. "The gauntlet's projectiles are heavily dosed with a powerful sedative exclusive for demon hunters."

"The same formula used on Elizabeth and Joy back at The Gathering?" Anna asked. "I thought the Guardians were done using that poison."

John and Victoria exchanged looks before John continued speaking. John put the beaker down on the table and looked at the three demon hunters. "How would you deal with demon hunters who are trying to kill you?" John asked. The demon hunters remained silent. "You three have shed blood, sweat, and tears in battle. You have a common bond. How would you deal with it if one of you betrayed the other two?"

"Loaded question," Izzy mumbled, looking at Nikki. They both thought the same thing, with their sister Grace in mind.

"It sounds archaic," Victoria said. "The exception proves the rule. There is a chance demon hunters use their powers irresponsibly, hurting innocents in the process."

"I've made modifications to the formula," John explained. "The poison used on the demon hunter line had the objective of putting the demon hunters down."

"And this one?" Nikki asked.

"We don't hurt our own," Victoria replied.

"This formula is different," John replied as he grabbed the beaker with a blue liquid solution. He dropped a few more wooden projectiles inside and sealed it. "Clara helped me test it out. Once the arrow hits the demon hunters, a powerful muscle sedative will nullify their strength. I've also added a sleeping agent that will remove the women from the playing field for forty-eight hours."

"What happens after that?" Izzy asked, looking at Anna and Nikki. "Other creatures will be in that compound, based on what you've told us. That will leave them helpless to defend themselves against these beasts."

"That is where you have to intervene," Victoria said. "You have to neutralize the demon hunters from the playing field, and then take care of the real threats. Otherwise, you expose yourself to fighting on two fronts."

"So will they," Nikki said.

"They operate on a different code," John said. "They'll not hesitate in killing you or letting you be killed if you stand in their way."

"What if we have to make that choice?" Anna asked

John took a deep breath. "It's self-defense, girls," John said. "Victoria and I are working so that doesn't happen. But if it does, there is no talking them down. There is no negotiating. It's either you or them."

"This is not cold-blooded murder," Victoria reassured the girls. "All three of you are true heroines. You're above that. And we'll help you so your hands are not stained with innocent blood. That's our job."

"Suppose we manage to achieve all this," Izzy said. "What happens to the rogue demon hunters once they wake up?"

"Clara and other demon hunters are flying in for clean-up duties," John said. "The rogue demon hunters will be transferred safely to Ireland, where The Guardians will take the proper measures."

"And those measures are?" Nikki asked.

"Rehabilitation," Victoria said. "We do everything in our power to set them in the correct ways. Or at least make sure they use their powers by our code."

"And if they refuse?" Anna asked.

Both John and Victoria looked at each other; John was the one to respond. "The Guardians will cross that bridge when they get to it. Right now, our main focus is to rescue Elizabeth and Grace."

"How do you expect us to deal with the Arzkang demon?" Izzy asked. "From what I read, that monster is unkillable."

"That will be the main focus after taking out the demon hunters," Victoria said. "We're not sure what state Hela Corp has captured this animal in. But we have a possible solution if it's at full strength."

John pulled out a small metal canister that looked like a fat bullet. It was ten centimeters in height and four cm in diameter. The round tip had a silver coating, while the main body had a red stripe around it. "The Arzkang at full strength can't be pierced with any forged weapon. The white fur hides heavy-duty skin that's impenetrable with our conventional blades."

"You want us to use a grenade launcher?" Nikki asked. "I'm an Air Force girl. I don't use those types of weapons."

"And we're not asking you to," Victoria said.

"We're not sure if modern weapons can pierce its skin, either," John said.

"That's why Luis developed this," Victoria said. "A projectile that we will fire at the monster. Once it strikes him, the canister will release a special gas that will weaken the demon."

"For how long?" Anna asked.

"Based on Luis's calculations, one to two minutes," John said.

"Cutting it a little close," Izzy said, looking at her sisters.

"But it opens the window," Victoria said. "A perfect opportunity to take it out."

"We're not letting you face this type of demon empty-handed," John stated. "You'll be prepared; we'll have your back the entire time."

Isabella looked at John, and there was a fire in his eyes that had not been there before, a hidden rage within his determination to keep them safe. All the girls nodded in agreement, dropping the conversation. Izzy turned toward Nikki, who was now buckling up as the plane started its final descent. She opened her mind to her sister, who acknowledged the connection. *How are we supposed to pull this off?* Izzy asked Nikki in her mind.

Nikki pointed at Izzy's chest, signaling the golden crucifix that hung from her neck. *Your praying hasn't let us down so far.*

Izzy smiled as she grabbed the crucifix and started whispering to herself in Latin.

CHAPTER XI

Lake Tahoe, Nevada, USA: Feb 8, 9:30 p.m.

ELIZABETH STOOD STILL WHILE the three rogue demon hunters had her tied with obsidian-infused black chains. Around the octagon rings, she saw a large black cage take shape. The cage, made of deep black metal bars with a black metal mesh, was imposing, with its walls reaching the ceiling of Sylvie's cellar.

Elizabeth saw a dozen demon hunters in the cellar with them, including Grace and Leah, who stood beside Sylvie. With her arms crossed, Sylvie stared at her demon hunters, who were working on putting the large cage into place, silently evaluating the progress. She turned toward Elizabeth with disdain in her eyes.

"It's looking nice," Elizabeth said, admiring the cage. "Although, I've never been a fan of black."

"Joke all you want, Liz," Sylvie said. "This cage will seal your fate."

"Unless my daughter helps me escape again," Elizabeth said with a smile, looking at Leah. "Thank you, Leah. You were a big help."

Sylvie sneered at Leah, who only stared at Elizabeth with rage in her eyes. Sylvie pulled out Leah's knife and handed it to the blonde demon hunter. "You're an idiot. Don't let her get to you."

Leah scowled at Sylvie's insult as she grabbed her knife, storing it behind her back.

"It's not her fault, Sylvie," Elizabeth said. "It's natural for a daughter to aid her real mother, even if it's at a subconscious level."

Sylvie fumed at Leah, who was about to rush at Elizabeth but was stopped by one of the demon hunters at the last moment. "Get out of here," Sylvie ordered Leah.

Leah scowled at Sylvie as she walked away from the group of demon hunters and headed toward the lower level.

"It will take more than your phony bachelor's degree in psychology to get out of this one," Sylvie said, turning back toward the blonde Guardian and demon hunter.

"Don't forget my Masters," Elizabeth said, taunting Sylvie. "It's not easy being a mom and a demon hunter and still having time to study."

"It doesn't matter," Sylvie said, stepping toward Elizabeth as she motioned the cage. "Admire where you'll spend your last days. No world-ending scenario where the hell spots open. No heroic death-saving friends and family. You will die fighting for your life inside that cage. Alone. As you have always been. And I will make a profit from your death."

Grace tensed up, hearing Sylvie express Elizabeth's

fate. "Cage is set," one of the demon hunters reported.

"Excellent," Sylvie said, turning toward the women holding Elizabeth's chains. "Ladies, please guide Mrs. O'Brien Somiere inside the cage and remove those heavy shackles."

As Grace looked on, trying to hide her emotions, the demon hunters followed orders without question. "The cage is infused with obsidian," Sylvie said. "There is no other way out except the door you walk through."

"Interesting," Elizabeth said as the demon hunters removed her iron bonds. All three demon hunters walked out of the cage so Roxanne could close the entrance, sealing it with a heavy metal padlock. "I'm glad that my death will be the only source of joy in your life."

"Oh, it will," Sylvie responded, stepping up to Elizabeth's face. "I can't wait for my Arzkang demon to tear you apart."

Grace felt a shiver down her spine. Deep down, she knew this had been Sylvie's plan all along. But hearing her say it out loud just brought a sense of doom in the pit of her heart. Her parents' words echoed in the back of her mind. *A warrior's true strength is the person fighting alongside you. So give honor and respect to them, and it will be returned to you.*

Grace looked directly into Elizabeth's green eyes and fired a single thought at her with her mind, hoping to break through Sylvie's blocking shield. *Trust me!*

For a brief second, Grace noticed Elizabeth's look of understanding, which relieved the seventeen-year-old girl. "That's a bad idea, Sylvie," Grace said out loud.

All the demon hunters turned toward Grace. Sylvie

and Elizabeth had a look of surprise written all over their faces.

"What did you just say?" Sylvie asked.

"It's a bad idea to have the Arzkang demon kill Elizabeth," Grace reiterated.

Roxanne stepped up toward the black-haired demon hunter. "That's the contract we're getting paid for. Her head on a silver platter."

Grace sneered at Roxanne as she stepped to her side and looked toward Sylvie and Elizabeth. "Do you know how many people want a piece of the great Elizabeth Somiere?" Grace asked. "The contract you have to kill her doesn't specify how or when. Why not make money off her before killing her?"

Sylvie contemplated Grace's idea briefly while Grace took a step forward. "The Abyssborne is a chance to showcase our power," Grace continued. "Why not showcase Elizabeth's power against a few lower-class demons and vampires? Have our guests make wagers on her life while she fights them off. We don't sacrifice our demon hunters for that."

"And when Elizabeth is at her weakest," Sylvie pondered for a second.

"You can handle the wagers with staggering odds with her against the Arzkang demon," Grace concluded, turning toward Elizabeth. "It's the smartest play to capitalize on one of the greatest demon hunters on the planet and make a hefty profit."

Roxanne looked impressed as she looked at Grace. "Now I understand why your sisters call you the Ice Princess."

"You need to leave emotion at the door, doing what

you need to do in this line of work," Grace said as she looked at Elizabeth.

"I guess you win, Sylvie," Elizabeth said, not lowering her green eyes from Grace. "You've turned one of the best demon hunters on the planet against me."

"It's easy when you fail to give them what they need," Sylvie said. "I have Leah, and now I have Grace."

"Go claim your prize," Elizabeth said to Grace. "He's waiting for you downstairs."

Grace looked at Sylvie, who nodded her approval. Grace turned toward the metal staircase that led to the lower level, only sensing Elizabeth's thoughts directed at her before leaving. *Be careful.*

The steps down to the lower level felt eternal. The fact that she bought Elizabeth a few minutes before she faced the Arzkang monster did little to comfort her aching heart. The price was too high to pay with the answers so close within her grasp. As she walked in front of the white-furred monster, the emptiness in her stomach intensified. The beast growled at her as those red-orbed eyes stared directly into her soul. She had only read about that particular demon but had never faced it before. Its tight muscles wrapped up in hard skin cover, all hidden by a soft fur coating. No blade was sharp or tough enough to penetrate it. The sharpness of the fangs and claws was beyond anything the demon world had to offer. They could tear human flesh as if it were butter. The power behind the monster was the last bestial characteristic. No guardian or demon hunter had been able to measure it accurately. The closest comparison was that it was stronger than ten vampires.

"It's impressive, isn't it?" Neil said, bringing Grace back to reality.

Grace continued walking down the white hall, seeing Neil sitting at the back of the wall of his cell, one leg extended, while the other was bent with his knee pointing to the ceiling. "How many demon hunters did Sylvie sacrifice to capture that demon alive?"

Grace remained silent as she stared into straight into her nemesis' black eyes. "You can answer, child. You're one of them now."

"Several," Grace relented.

"I see," Neil replied. "I guess Sylvie took to heart the famous demon hunter and Guardian motto. Death is a necessary evil. As long as someone else is dying."

"Why did you kill my parents?" Grace asked. "What did they do to you that they deserved to be killed by a former Guardian?"

Neil's confident smile disappeared as he stared into the seventeen-year-old's eyes. "Are you scared?" he asked.

"No," Grace responded.

Neil stood up and slowly walked toward the glass. He looked down at the five-foot-three demon hunter. "Liar," he whispered. "You reek of fear. Just like that little girl who had her dead parents at her feet."

"Shut up!" Grace hissed.

"I thought you wanted to talk," Neil said. "This is us talking."

"Why?!" Grace screamed at him as she banged on the glass with both her fists. Her scream echoed through the hall, her rage at its peak.

"No," Neil replied stoically. "Do you honestly think

throwing a temper tantrum will make me talk? Are you really that naïve?"

"Tell me!" Grace ordered.

"Calm down," Neil said. "Learn to control your emotions. Isn't that what your parents tried to teach you? If you don't control that rage, rage controls you."

Grace blinked for a second, remembering the lessons her mom and dad had given her.

"Are you seriously considering his opinion?" Leah asked from the entrance of the white hall.

Grace turned toward the rogue demon hunter as she slowly walked toward her. If Izzy looked like Elizabeth with brown hair, then Leah was her exact twin. Leah's blonde hair had a lighter tone than Elizabeth's, and her icy blue eyes could pierce anyone's soul.

"You're truly pathetic," Leah continued as she stared into Grace's eyes. "You begging the vampire who killed your parents is the saddest thing I've seen in my life."

"You know nothing about our history," Grace said.

"I know enough that he has control over you," Leah said. "I've read about you: Brave Grace Wu, the strongest of the three of St. Helena. Dominated by a single bloodsucker."

"That's not nice, Leah," Neil said, admiring the blonde demon hunter. "We all have a purpose in this world. Don't interfere with Grace's destiny."

Leah pulled out a stake and tapped the glass barrier. She looked at Neil and then at Grace. "What would happen if I killed him for you?" Leah asked. "Would you be thankful that I vanquished the demon that killed your parents? Or would you resent me for taking the answers from you, knowing they die with him?"

"Knowing what I know about you," Neil pondered for a second. "You would do what would hurt her the most, just to hurt Isabella."

Grace looked in fear at both Neil and Leah. "Open the door," Neil offered as he took a step back and exposed his chest. "Take your best shot."

Leah reached out toward the button that guaranteed Neil's freedom right before Grace grabbed her wrist and flung the blonde demon hunter toward the opposite side of the hall. Leah rolled in the air and landed in a crouched position as Grace squared off.

"Stay away from Neil," Grace ordered. "He's mine."

"Why should I?" Leah asked with a grin on her face. "I'm a demon hunter, and he's a demon. It's my duty to kill him."

"I kicked your sister's ass," Grace said. "I don't mind kicking yours, too."

"I guess I hit your head too hard with my knee," Leah retorted. "If my memory serves me, you were the one who was lying unconscious in that graveyard."

"How exciting," Neil said, genuinely amused. "Two demon hunters fighting over me. It's been a while since something like this has happened to me."

Leah lunged forward, firing heavy haymakers aimed at Grace's face. The raven-haired demon hunter blocked Leah's powerful blows with difficulty. The blonde demon hunter changed tactics and did a foot sweep, which Grace jumped over, firing a haymaker of her own. Leah blocked the attack and fired a knee strike aiming at Grace's midsection, which Grace blocked, pushing Leah away.

Both demon hunters squared off again. Grace had

studied Leah's moves when she was training, and when she fought her in the cemetery. With no element of surprise from the Slavic demon hunter, this would be an evenly contested battle.

Grace adjusted her stance and took the initiative to attack high. Leah blocked Grace's haymakers just as the dark-haired demon hunter shifted her move set again and tried to connect with a knee strike to the abdomen. Leah blocked, but left her head exposed as Grace struck her face twice, snapping her head to the left and right.

Leah took the strikes in stride as she fired a kick of her own, connecting with Grace's chest and pushing the girl back.

Grace took a step back but did not relent. Her rage flaring, she pushed forward, striking with left and right punches aimed at the face, which Leah blocked. The demon hunters' arms clashed as each tried to dominate the other with sheer strength alone. Hatred and rage fueled their power and their desire to win.

Leah pushed Grace's arms upward, leaving her exposed as she struck with a straight punch to the face. Grace was staggered due to the blow, as Leah proceeded to kick her opponent with a right kick to the temple. Grace felt her ears ringing after the kick as she blocked Leah's onslaught. The sheer power was formidable. Grace felt a kick to her left leg, leaving her off balance. Leah took the initiative as the fight shifted in her favor, striking true with three direct jabs to Grace's unprotected chest.

Grace grunted in pain, but she was not done yet. As Leah tried to strike a fourth time, Grace grabbed her arm and pressed three sensitive areas. Leah screamed in pain as the pressure built into her arm, rendering it powerless.

Taking advantage of the situation and with Leah's arms under her control, she flung the blonde demon hunter toward the glass barrier that protected Neil. Leah screamed in pain as her body crashed against the glass and then the floor.

Grace let her rage drive her as she hammer-fisted Leah's face several times while the rogue demon hunter was on the floor. She only saw a white flash, no longer in control for a moment, her rage doing all the pummeling. Grace's mind flashed at the sight of her mom and dad looking on. Then, the image of Izzy and Elizabeth flooded her mind. She was no longer beating Leah, but her sister and their mother. But that image did not deter her from hammering away at Leah. It wasn't until she felt several hands grab her arms and pull her away.

Leah looked up and saw several demon hunters restraining Grace. The blonde girl lunged at her opponent, only for three demon hunters to restrain her, too.

"That's enough!" Sylvie ordered.

"I told you to keep that bitch away from me!" Grace screamed at Sylvie.

"We're not done yet, Ice Princess!" Leah screamed back, wiping the blood from her face. She then tried to approach Grace, but several demon hunters restrained her.

"You're right, Sylvie," Neil said, amused at the action as he admired the cracked glass wall that imprisoned him. "The Abyssborne hasn't even started, and I'm already entertained. I'll give you half a million if you put Grace and Leah together in your underground tournament."

Sylvie turned toward Roxanne and pointed at Grace. "Take her to her room until she cools off," the rogue demon hunter leader ordered.

"I'm not done with Neil!" Grace protested.

"You're done for the day," Sylvie said. "I will let you talk with him after you cool off."

"No!" Grace screamed as the demon hunters dragged her away. "You can't do this! We had a deal!"

"Cool off, Grace," Sylvie said, focusing on Leah now.

"Nice talking to you, Gracie," Neil said, coyly waving his hand goodbye to his demon hunter. "See you soon."

Sylvie turned toward Neil while Grace's protests echoed in the castle's bowels. "You're on thin ice," she said to the vampire. She then turned toward Leah, who was cleaning the blood from her face. "What happened?"

"She got her ass kicked," Neil said with a hint of pride in his voice. "That's what happens when you mess with my demon hunter."

Leah screamed as she lunged at the glass barrier, striking it with her fist. The glass cracked further as a result of the blow. An evil smile was drawn on Neil's face as he looked at the group of demon hunters gathered in front of him. "Careful, ladies," the vampire said. "You don't want to set me loose."

Sylvie looked at Leah's battered face and frowned. "Clean yourself up," Sylvie ordered. "And stay away from Grace."

Leah shrugged off the demon hunters restraining her as she looked at Neil, who smiled. "Good luck on the next fight," Neil called out to Leah as she stormed out. He then looked at Sylvie while admiring the cracked glass wall. "You sure know how to pick them."

"Leave us," Sylvie ordered her demon hunters, not losing eye contact with Neil. The women silently obeyed, exiting the cellar and leaving the ancient vampire with their leader.

"Half a million," Neil repeated. "That number has your interest?"

"Petty change for a vampire who has walked the world for two millennia," Sylvie responded.

"But that's your focus, right?" Neil asked. "Wealth? It's not honor, pleasure, or power. You desire riches."

"Riches can buy you anything," Sylvie responded.

"And the Guardians did not share their wealth with you," Neil concluded. "So you focused your power on obtaining what you couldn't have."

"The Guardians limit our power," Sylvie said. "We are free now to choose our own destiny, and obtain what we're worth."

"I respect that," Neil said. "Still interested in my offer?"

"Perhaps," Sylvie said. "I am a businesswoman, after all. If Grace doesn't pan out, I'm willing to explore another path to wealth."

"I'm not going anywhere," Neil said as he stepped back from the glass and leaned against the back wall.

Sylvie nodded and exited her dungeon with a sly smile on her face.

CHAPTER XII

Outside Lake Tahoe, Nevada, USA: Feb 8, 10:30 p.m.

ISABELLA BLINKED HER EYES hard, hugging herself to keep warm, with only her leather jacket as an extra layer for the weather. She looked at the dashboard thermostat from the SUV, reading thirty-two degrees outside. The demon hunter shivered from the back seat, looking at her right side. Nikki looked comfortable with her bomber jacket, which provided all her needed warmth. On her left side, Anna's body language told a different story. She had a jean jacket and a thick sweater, which was still not enough to battle the cold, as she hugged herself as well.

"The airplane cockpits always have a cool ambiance," Nikki said to her sisters. "You should have been with me when I was with my dad in Alaska. That was a blast."

Anna glared at Nikki, shivering. "I should have given you an even hotter version of that pozole."

"I grew up in Ireland most of my life," Izzy told Anna. "I never got used to the cold."

The sixteen-year-old demon hunter looked at her sister, her teeth chattering. "Is the heating on in the car?" she asked.

"It is," Victoria said from the passenger's seat. She was also covered in several layers as she looked up the snow-covered road. She turned to the driver's side, seeing John was comfortable in his white dress shirt as he maneuvered the vehicle. "I hate you, Canadian boy."

John smiled at her Guardian counterpart. "T-shirt weather," he replied as he admired the pine trees on each side of the road. "Almost like back home." He turned his attention to the rearview mirror, seeing the demon hunters ride in silence. "No communication yet?" he asked.

Nikki and Izzy shook their heads. John nodded. "We're almost there," he said. "Keep your instincts up."

The Guardians and demon hunters drove to a lodge where Sean waited outside with a young woman. Both were dressed in signature black Canada Goose parkas. Coming to a stop, the girls got out and rushed inside the lodge, where they would be warm. John stood outside and shook Sean's hand.

"Samantha," Sean said, addressing his companion. "My associate, John Simmons."

"A pleasure," Sam said, extending her hand, which John shook.

"Likewise," John replied dryly as all three entered the lodge.

The lodge's main lobby was neatly furnished with cushioned armchairs and sofas. Soft fur carpets covered the wooden floors. Izzy, Anna, and Victoria crowded around the raging stone fireplace. Next to it, a wooden staircase led to the upper levels. Nikki was at a wooden table where a feast with all types of food had been served and was ready to be consumed. The red-headed demon hunter wasted no time, cramming as much food as she could on her small plate.

"Ladies," Sam called out to the demon hunters and Victoria. "Lady Sabine welcomes you. She has reserved this lodge for us all for the next few days. The only personnel who will be working is the waiting staff. I've arranged warm jackets and winter clothing in your sizes, in your rooms on the second level. The food is warm. Help yourself to hot tea and cocoa."

"Where's Sabine?" Izzy asked.

"I'm up here, Isabella," the ancient vampire responded. The demon hunters turned their attention toward the top of the stairs where the raven-haired vampire stood. Her stiletto knee-high black boots clicked on the wooden staircase as she made her way down confidently. The elegant class she displayed matched the aura of grace the vampire carried. Black dress pants with a white turtleneck blouse contrasted nicely with her pale skin and light green eyes. "Do you want to rest? Or are you ready to work?"

"Did you check out Sylvie's compound?" John asked Sean.

The older Guardian nodded as he motioned the demon hunters to join him at the far table opposite the fireplace, where drawings of the compound were placed. "Samantha managed to get these for us," he started. "A visual inspection has six women covering the inner perimeter. We couldn't check the back or sides, but I would put at least twelve demon hunters guarding the compound."

"Do we know the total?" Nikki asked as she took a bite of a Nutella-covered croissant.

"Thirty-six demon hunters in total," Sabine said. "All capable warriors, aged between twenty-five and thirty-five years old."

"I'm curious how you got that number," Izzy pondered.

"I pay good money to be informed," Sabine said, pulling out a bottle of pills from her pants pocket. She dropped a few in her hand and popped them inside her mouth. "Hela Corp deals with several acquaintances from the underworld."

"That leaves more than half the force inside," Anna said. "We're only three."

"Don't sell yourself short," Victoria scolded her sister softly. "These demon hunters are not as strong as you. And we have Grace and Elizabeth on the inside."

"Correct," Sean said. "Our plan is for Sabine, Sam, and I to enter The Abyssborne as guests tomorrow night. With Samantha's help, we will disable the outer perimeter security feed located here." Sean pointed to the spot on the drawing. "We'll signal you to start taking out the demon hunters on the outside perimeter."

"What about demons and vampires trapped inside?" Izzy asked Sabine. "Do you have a number on those?"

"The main threat is the Arzkang demon," Sabine said. "Other than that, I am sure of two dozen vampires and soldier demons."

"We've dealt with numbers like that before," Nikki told Izzy. "With Anna and Grace there, those won't be a problem."

"It's the demon hunters that I'm worried about," Izzy voiced her concern.

"You girls talk with such confidence that Grace is on your side," Sabine said. "What makes you so sure?"

"She won't betray us!" Izzy and Nikki exclaimed simultaneously. Both girls looked surprised at their response.

"I hope you're right," Sabine said.

"Any ideas on how Sylvie is controlling the Arzkang demon?" Sean asked.

John looked at Victoria, who pulled a black chain with a dark blue orb from her backpack.

"What the hell is that?" Sean asked.

"We were hoping you had an idea," Victoria said, putting the orb on the table. "The master vampire from Mexico had it on him when the girls defeated him."

"It's a glenix orb," Sabine said, taking a step forward and looking at the large jewel. "It's been a while since I've seen one."

"Do you know what it does?" Nikki asked.

"It's a magical item," Sabine said. "Witches and warlocks attune to it to control the undead. It takes a lot of psychic energy to control a vast number of demons and vampires with one of those things."

"Or plenty of demon hunter horsepower to control a single demon," Izzy concluded.

"Do you know the origin of this?" Sabine asked. "These are hard to come by. I've heard only a dozen exist on the planet."

Victoria and John looked at each other and then at Sean. "We have a theory," John said. "A third player has been coordinating efforts against us."

"It all points to a consulting firm in Los Angeles that has been undermining our efforts," Victoria said. "We're still researching them."

John looked at Sean and Sabine. "This firm seems to be bankrolling Hela Corp, and Elizabeth's demise. Not to mention the deaths of several of our demon hunters and Guardians."

"If that's true," Sean stated as he looked at the group, "They may be present tomorrow at The Abyssborne."

"Wouldn't be surprised," Sabine said.

"Wait," Izzy interrupted. "If we manage to break Sylvie's connection to the Arzkang, that will leave a dangerous wild demon on the field without regard for what it destroys."

"I don't see another choice," Sean said.

Nikki and Izzy looked at each other and then at Anna. The odds were severely stacked against them.

"Our main goal is to free Grace and Elizabeth," Sean said, reaffirming their primary objective. "Crippling Hela Corp is a distant second in our priorities."

"We'll have a lot of enemies inside," Anna noted. All turned toward the youngest demon hunter. "Not only the rogue women wanting to kill us and the demons inside, but the attendants of The Abyssborne, I'm sure, are not fighting the same battle that we are."

"What can we expect from them?" Izzy asked Sabine.

"I'm at a loss on that one," the ancient vampire said. "Previous events like this gathered fifty to sixty high rollers paying millions for Hela Corp's services."

"Human?" Nikki asked.

"All kinds," Sabine answered.

"We may not be enough," Izzy admitted.

"You're forgetting one thing," Sabine said. "I'll be inside."

"Will you be on our side this time?" Sean asked.

"The question hurts, Sean," Sabine said. "We have an accord. I don't break agreements. You'll have to trust me."

"Okay," Sean said as he turned his attention toward his demon hunters. "Once the outer perimeter is secure, break through the front door."

"Frontal attack?" Izzy asked.

"They won't see you coming," Sean responded. "By that time, I'll be next to your mom."

"And Grace?" Nikki asked.

Sean looked at John and then at the girls. "You girls have to break Sylvie's barrier tonight and reach out to her," Sean responded. "You've got to get through to her."

Nikki looked at Izzy. "Let's take turns tonight," the red-headed demon hunter said. "Get some rest to recover. I'll wake you up so that you can take a shot at it."

Isabella nodded at her sister.

"Get some rest," Sean ordered the team. "All of you. We'll have a wild night tomorrow."

Samantha stepped up to the group. "Follow me," she said. "I'll guide you to your rooms."

Izzy, Nikki, and Anna started to walk up the stairs, leaving the Guardians alone with the ancient vampire. "You didn't mention your twin," Anna said to Izzy.

"I have nothing on that," Izzy said. "I guess I will figure that out tomorrow. Right now, it's all about my mom and Grace."

"If Leah is an obstacle?" Nikki asked.

"You both will know what to do," Izzy said. "But knowing her, she will focus on me when she sees me."

Nikki stopped for a moment and looked at her sister. "I got your back on this," she said. "It doesn't matter what Leah injects in your dreams; she doesn't control you."

"I know," Izzy said, rubbing her sister's arms. "Thanks for not giving up on me."

"What are sisters for?" Nikki asked as she looked at Izzy and Anna.

Lake Tahoe, Nevada, USA; Feb 9, 2:30 a.m.

GRACE TOSSED AND TURNED in her bed. Sweat dripped from her upper body, soaking her black top. The nightmare was intense.

She was fighting against the blonde demon hunter who refused to go down. The black obsidian-infused metal cage trapped both of them inside, in a battle to the death. Every punch and kick Grace connected brought the blue-eyed demon hunter down, but she stood right back up as if the blows she'd taken had meant nothing. Her blonde hair covered her battered face, but her blue eyes were still visible. They were full of hate.

Grace moved around the octagon like a skilled dancer, entirely in control of the fight. Leah struck high, but Grace quickly blocked and spun, connecting with a solid kick to the chest, sending the seventeen-year-old girl flying against the metal cage.

Grace admired the defeated opponent as dark myst surrounded her. She moved toward Leah, only to see the beaten and bloodied form of Elizabeth staring back at her. Grace looked in horror as she stepped back. She almost toppled over, seeing Izzy's battered and broken body at her feet. Grace tried to open the door, but her demon hunter strength was taken away from her when she touched the cage.

"Hatred only brings suffering," Neil said behind the cage. Grace felt a wave of fear wash over her. She turned around and saw her sister and adoptive mother's bloody corpses hanging from the cage walls. "Your hatred did this," the vampire whispered in her ear.

"No!" Grace exclaimed. "This is not real!"

"You're a killer," Neil said, stepping right in front of her. "A killer who has not purged her fear."

The vampire grasped Grace's shoulders and pushed her against the cage. "Purge your fear!" the vampire ordered.

But the fear had grasped the pit of Grace's soul. Her demon hunter strength was gone. She looked at herself as if she were in an out-of-body experience. She saw a scared thirteen-year-old girl seeing her dead parents at her feet. "Why am I so scared?" Grace asked herself.

"What are you afraid of?" Grace heard her father whisper to her. She turned around, seeing her parents look at her adoringly. "What are you afraid of?" her father asked again.

"I'm afraid this is a mistake," Grace admitted to herself. "I'm afraid I'm not really chosen. The skill and strength are all a lie."

"Is it a lie?" her mother asked. "Would we lie to you?"

"Never," Grace responded.

"You're not alone, Gracie," her father said. "And you are chosen to do this. You have to live that truth."

"You're not alone anymore," her mother said as she pointed behind her. Grace turned and saw Izzy, Nikki, Elizabeth, Sean, John, and the rest of the Guardians.

"We will never lie to you," her father said. *"Just remember. We did it because we love you."*

Grace woke up with her father's words resounding in her mind. Sitting alone in her bed, she contemplated everything that had happened the past few days. She stood up and entered the bathroom, pouring water over her face. She tied her hair in a ponytail, looking outside her window at the snow-covered landscape. She slipped on her shoes and the Hela Corp parka and exited her room.

The emergency lighting provided by Sylvie's compound was the only light source in the hallway. The raven-haired demon hunter jogged through the carpeted hall and down the stairs, only to see several demon hunters watching over the security monitors.

A blonde demon hunter in her early thirties looked up from her workstation and noticed Grace. "Sylvie ordered for you not to see Neil," she said.

"I'm not going to," Grace responded. "I feel the need to kill some undead. Is anyone available for an early morning hunt in the woods?"

"You can't leave the compound," the blonde demon hunter said.

"Watch me," Grace replied. "I can't stay cooped up any longer. I need to dust some undead. Have you lost that urge?"

The blonde demon hunter sighed and pressed on her earpiece. "Tina and Helena," the blonde demon hunter spoke. "Meet Grace Wu at the front entrance and accompany her on a night hunt. Yes. Sylvie will authorize this."

"Thank you," Grace said as she approached the

front door. She tried to feel Leah's essence, but it wasn't palpable to her senses. As she opened the door, Grace saw two demon hunters in their Hela Corp parkas. Both women looked in their late twenties. One had light brown hair, brown eyes, and light skin. The second one had curly, short red hair, one side shaved, light brown skin, and dark eyes. "Helena and Tina, I presume?"

"Come on, Ice Princess," the girl with the light brown hair said. "Let's see you in action in your own habitat."

"Try to keep up," Grace said. "Let's see if those old bodies still have what it takes."

The raven-haired demon hunter started running north of the compound, with Tina and Helena at her heels. The snow height put a damper on their speed, but all three demon hunters powered through. Slowly but with purpose, the distance between them and the compound grew. "Do you feel it?" Grace asked Tina and Helena. "The call of darkness. We're hunters. The creatures of the night are terrified by us. Maybe we can capture a demon and bring it for The Abyssborne."

"There are no demons or vampires in these parts," Tina said. "We cleared it."

Grace turned toward both women with a surprised look on her face. "Are you sure you're demon hunters?" she asked with an incredulous tone in her voice. "The dark energy is like a magnet. You feel it in the pit of your stomach."

Grace continued walking until she reached the clearing where she captured Elizabeth. The raven-haired crouched as she looked at the opposite side of the snowed-down glade. "Across from here," Grace whispered to Tina and Helena.

Helena looked across the field and saw nothing. "What is it?"

"Three vampires," Grace said as she inspected the pine trees. "They seem lost. Probably fresh out of their graves."

"How do you know this?" Tina asked, apparently not feeling anything.

"I'm seriously going to report you to Sylvie," Grace sounded desperate. "Let's surround the clearing. No noise. Follow my lead."

Slowly, Grace led Tina and Helena to the side of the clearing. Almost reaching the end, Grace motioned them to stop. "There're four of them," Grace whispered.

Tina and Helena were on high alert now. Grace motioned them to move forward to the left and the right of her. All three demon hunters crouched down, waiting for the vampires to attack.

"Behind us!" Grace exclaimed.

Tina and Helena turned around just as Grace touched a nerve point on each of the other two demon hunters, right where their necks and shoulders met. Immediately, both demon hunters went limp and fell unconscious in the snow.

Grace took a sigh of relief as she crouched on the snow between both demon hunters and crossed her legs. She closed her eyes and took a moment to think about her sisters and Elizabeth. She shook her head, knowing this had to be done. Slowly, she opened her mind, reaching out to Izzy and Nikki, hoping one would answer.

The Hawaiian demon hunter stood by a large oak tree in the middle of a green prairie. The night sky was replaced by beautiful blue. This was the spot where they'd first experienced their minds uniting. This was their mind sanctuary when they needed to regroup and share privately. Today, it was empty.

Grace felt a tug in her heart; she turned around and saw Izzy looking back at her. Both girls stared at each other for a few seconds as if they searched for the words to speak before their minds embraced, sharing a mutual sign of relief.

"Are you okay?" Izzy asked. "We've been trying to reach you for so long. I've been trying to reach you."

"I'm sorry," Grace managed to say, tears accumulating.

"No," Izzy said. "I'm sorry. I should have realized the pain Neil has caused you. I should have seen it. I should have supported you to the fullest. I failed you."

"I'm sorry," Grace said. "You were worried about me. You were protecting me from going too far. I understand that now."

"Are you okay?" Izzy asked. "Is my mom okay?"

Grace shook her head. "Sylvie is planning for Elizabeth to fight the Arzkang inside an obsidian-infused cage. That is the main attraction for The Abyssborne. I bought her some time to fight a few vampires before the main event, but it's not much."

"How many demon hunters does Sylvie have in her ranks?" Izzy asked.

"Three dozen," Grace responded based on her gathered data. "The security perimeter is guarded by eight demon hunters, with rotations every ten hours. Not sure how it's going to be tomorrow."

"How many demons has she captured?"

"With the Arzkang demon, I counted six Anharran, three Kulaks, two Yamanh, and five vampires," Grace reported.

"Did they capture Neil for you?" Izzy asked, already knowing the answer.

"How did you know that?" Grace asked her sister. She peered partially into Izzy's mind, capturing superficial thoughts. "Sabine is with you?"

Izzy silently nodded. "Dad made a deal with her. She would secure a way into the compound if he helped her get Neil out."

Grace's rage started to boil and Izzy sensed the loss of connection. "She was the only lead dad had," Izzy said, trying to calm her sister down. "We wouldn't be this close to you if it weren't for Sabine."

"Does he plan on rescuing him to hand it to her?" Grace asked.

"Not if I can help it," Izzy said to her. "I won't let him until you get the answers you seek."

Izzy's determination brought ease to her heart. But it was putting them all at significant risk. Both demon hunters were fully transparent about each other's intentions. "What's your dad's plan?"

"He goes in tomorrow as a potential client for Hela Corp, along with Sabine," Izzy said. "An hour later, we take out the outer perimeter defenses, and then Nikki, Anna, and I storm the front door."

"To get me and your mom out," Grace concluded.

"That's the main objective."

"Sylvie is not going to stop," Grace said. "Her hatred for The Guardians is too much."

"We can't kill her," Izzy said. "Mom and Dad trust that

Nikki and I will figure it out. So far, both of us are drawing a blank."

Grace shook her head. There was no way either side would walk away from this battle without casualties, and she still needed to contend with Neil.

"Did Leah hurt you?" Izzy asked.

Grace turned toward her sister. "She does hate you," Grace said. "Her sole purpose in life is to make you suffer. And if taking me, Nikki, or your mom out will cause you pain, she will do it without hesitation."

Izzy contemplated the variables laid before her. It felt as if she was going to war where the enemy wanted nothing but her death, but she couldn't come to grips with the fact that she could end a human life.

"Let's rescue my mom," Izzy said. "We get another demon hunter in the playing field. Then we take out the Arzkang to finally contend with the demon hunters and Neil."

"I hope you have a better plan than beating them to a pulp to do this," Grace said.

"John has us covered," Izzy replied. "Just follow our lead once we're inside with you. John says that Sylvie's spell will be nullified once the three of us are in close proximity to each other. That gives us a tactical advantage."

Grace couldn't help but smile. "We spent months trying to block our thoughts from each other. Now, we must open the floodgates of feelings and emotions to stand a chance with these odds."

"We've gotten out of scarier situations than this," Izzy said, trying her best to sound brave. "Right?"

"Right!" Grace echoed her sister.

Both sisters stared at each other for a moment. "I have

to get back," Grace said. "I'll be waiting."

"We'll get you out," Izzy said. "And we'll get you the answers you need."

Grace opened her eyes, still sitting on the snow. She looked at the sky, seeing that it was clearing up and stars were beginning to appear. She crouched and glanced at the unconscious demon hunters at her feet, still out cold.

The raven-haired demon hunter stood up and started moving around them using different variations of katas and marital arts forms. Her father and mother had ensured she was proficient in at least three of them. She moved from side to side and around the women's bodies at her feet. Her form was perfect. After a couple of minutes, she had drawn sweat. She looked at the snow, and the sequence of moves was plastered around her and the bodies of Sylvie's demon hunters.

Grace crouched down and started shaking the girls. "Hey, wake up!"

Both demon hunters stirred in the snow. As their eyes focused, they both looked at Grace staring down at them. "They got the jump on us," Grace said as she helped them stand up.

"Where are they?" Tina asked.

"Fought them off," Grace said. "Let's report this to the team. We can't have undead on the property while The Abyssborne takes place."

CHAPTER XIII

Outside Lake Tahoe, Nevada, USA; Feb 9, 3:30 a.m.

IZZY SAT ON THE bed with her legs crossed. She had reached out to her sister, Grace, and explored her thoughts. She had a clear idea of the odds they faced, but it did not bring ease to her anxious heart. Grace was exposed in the center of Sylvie's compound all alone, trying to play both sides with over three dozen rogue demon hunters ready to kill her at a moment's notice. By examining Grace's thoughts, Izzy could sense her sister's naive belief that she could rescue Elizabeth and get the information she wanted from Neil. Grace was stubborn in her conviction; it could be her end. *I would be if I were in the same position,* Izzy thought to herself. *I was in the same position once.*

The green-eyed demon hunter stood up and exited her room. The dark hallway of the inn was empty, but there was no place where Sabine could hide. The shadows could not conceal her dark energy from Izzy's hunting instincts. The vampire was pacing alone on the lower level. Her essence was almost palpable to Isabella.

Share...

The misty thought floated into Izzy's mind. It vibrated differently, but it had the signature of a former demon hunter. Isabella ignored it and walked toward Anna's room. She knocked softly, hoping her younger demon-hunter sister was awake. She waited a couple of seconds before the Mexican demon hunter opened the door. The girl looked rested compared to how she had been the past couple of days. "You got through?" she asked.

Izzy nodded and motioned for her to follow. Anna nodded and walked behind her older counterpart. Not bothering to knock, Izzy silently entered Nikki's room, seeing her sister resting in bed.

"Nikki," Izzy whispered.

The red-headed demon hunter stirred, hearing her name. She had just gotten to sleep, but the instruction both girls had shared earlier was explicit. Wake the other one up if you made contact. "Did Grace reach out to you?" Nikki asked as she slipped on her red-framed glasses and looked at her sisters at her door.

Nikki nodded as she sat on Nikki's bed while Anna sat on the armchair beside the nightstand. Izzy looked at both demon hunters and started sharing everything Grace had told her, and the thoughts and emotions that bled through their conversation.

"Neil's got her number," Nikki said. "She's terrified of him. Part of me wants to pull her away, but he's the only one who can provide the closure she needs."

"I still don't know how we're supposed to pull this

off," Anna said. "These are not simple vampires were facing. These are former sisters of our order."

"If these were a horde of demons, I would be more confident," Izzy said. "Right now, I feel like we're fighting with both hands tied behind our backs."

"Would you do it?" Nikki asked the dreaded question.

Izzy thought for a moment. "My mom and dad have talked to me about it," Izzy said, looking at Nikki and Anna. "When push comes to shove, we have to defend ourselves. But it's a last resort. I never imagined I would have to do this."

"Luis and Victoria never brought the subject up," Anna confided. "Our Latin American team is very tight. I guess they've never been in a situation like this."

"And yet here we are," Nikki said. "My dad says that when facing this type of situation, he would return to basic training. He measures the success of an encounter on two things. Was it a successful encounter? And zero innocent casualties."

"Sylvie measures success by how much money she makes, no matter who gets hurt," Izzy replied.

"And from what we've heard, these demon hunters are not innocent," Anna said. "They've made a choice."

"But is the price of that choice their lives?" Izzy asked. Her mind was torn. And she could feel her sister's doubt as well. Second-guessing themselves could cost them their own lives.

"Gone are the days when a young virgin for a human sacrifice was all the bad guys needed to achieve their goals," Nikki said. "Why does this have to be about money?"

"Simpler times," Izzy said with a sad smile.

"Have you ever killed a human?" Nikki asked both of her sisters.

Izzy turned toward her sister and stared deep into her blue eyes. "Never," Izzy replied. "Have you two?"

Nikki shook her head. "Not even by accident. And accidents do happen in our line of work."

Anna shook her head, being in the same boat.

"So here we are," Izzy said.

Nikki was about to say something when all three demon hunters felt the essence of the master vampire behind the closed door, causing all of them to look up. "Come in," Nikki said as Izzy stared at her, surprised. Nikki shrugged. "It's her place. It's not like she can't go anywhere she pleases."

The door opened, and the pale, raven-haired vampire entered. "You made contact," Sabine said. "Is your sister still on your side?"

Nikki glared at the vampire, while Izzy showed a more secure demeanor, having sensed Grace's thoughts and emotions firsthand. "She's on our side," the brown-haired demon hunter replied.

"I'm glad you truly believe that," Sabine said. "You underestimate the power Neil has over Grace. Not easy to shake off. And she still has not learned the lesson she's meant to learn."

"What lesson is that!?" Nikki exclaimed, standing up. "And why is HE teaching it? Do you know why he tortures her so?"

"We're teachers, Nicole," Sabine said. "This has been our purpose for over two millennia. Some lessons are just harder than others. Remember the lesson that I taught you?"

Nikki glared, remembering her skull smashing against a concrete pillar at the hand of the master vampire.

"Pain makes us stronger," Izzy replied.

"Indeed it does," Sabine said, turning toward Anna. "You are no stranger to pain, am I correct, young Anna?"

Anna looked surprised that the master vampire knew her name. The elegant demon before her gave her a strong sense of familiarity—a profound connection, unlike the one she felt with her sister demon hunters, but nonetheless ever-present.

"You've experienced death," Sabine said to Anna. "You've held your sisters' heads on your lap and watched them gasp their last breath. Even though they didn't say it, they spoke to you with their eyes. Their last words were defiant, but their eyes begged you for help."

Anna looked down as her eyes watered. All the bottled emotions inside started to boil over—all the unprocessed grief.

"Don't look down," Izzy instructed her younger sister. "Look into her eyes and acknowledge the truth."

Nikki looked surprised at her sister's response, while Sabine nodded in agreement. Anna looked at Sabine, her dark eyes filled with pain. "Embrace the pain," Sabine instructed. "We're demon hunters. We strive through pain. We learn from it."

Nikki looked at Izzy, Anna, and finally at Sabine, realizing what she was doing. The vampire curtsied. "You're welcome," she said.

"Pushing us physically and mentally makes us stronger," Nikki said, understanding the lesson the vampire was teaching them. "Those are some twisted lessons you ancient ones have."

"You've felt it," Izzy said to her sister. "Your body is stronger and faster after our first encounter with her. You've noticed it."

Nikki thought momentarily, realizing it took her less effort to deal with the undead when it was her turn to patrol. She'd dismissed the idea, considering the demons and vampires she had recently faced were too weak.

"You've felt it, too," Sabine said to Izzy. "Haven't you? You tapped into something no demon hunter should. It almost cost you your life. It sure cost Angie."

It was Izzy's turn to look surprised. "How do you know about that?"

"I read the reports on the deaths of each demon hunter," Sabine said. She then looked at Nikki. "I have nothing but time." She then turned toward Izzy. "In your case, I overheard your father's conversation with your Guardian. The technique is forbidden for a reason."

"It was the only way to get out of there alive," Izzy said.

"You have to find another way," Sabine said. "The demon hunter power is volatile. Our bodies can wield it, but if we lose control, we explode. You must find a way to channel that energy properly. You must help your sisters reach their full potential."

Izzy thought for a moment about the staggering odds they faced. "You walk into battle tomorrow," Sabine continued. "You've got a secret weapon, all three of you. You have to find a way to wield it appropriately."

The nature of their demon hunter power flooded into her mind. Izzy stood up and looked at Nikki and Anna, sharing her thoughts—the memories of her encounter with Apocalypse in the nightmarish dimension. The truth being exposed to her was as clear as daylight.

Nikki finally grasped the idea: "We embody the full power of a being of light."

"Works in theory," Sabine said as she pulled out a bottle of painkillers from her pants pocket. The vampire opened it and dropped a few pills in her hand, then swallowed them whole. "The solution to your problem is my ultimate demise. As the power of the demon hunters increases, tapping into their true nature inside their bodies, the demon inside me slowly dies."

All the demon hunters turned toward the vampire, who shrugged. "Death is a necessary evil," the ancient one said. "But my time has not come yet."

"It would be easier if you shared everything you know," Izzy said. "Our Guardians could prepare better instead of us scrambling at the last minute."

"You're all not ready for what is to come," Sabine said. "And until you do, the truth will be hidden from you. I need you alive." The vampire then focused on young Anna. "All of you. Your body and mind must be ready."

"How can we prepare if we have no idea what's coming?" Anna asked.

"Everything is in the Tome," Sabine said. "All you need to know is in the Tome. Even the reason why Neil killed Grace's parents is there."

Izzy and Nikki looked at each other, bewildered. "What?" Nikki exclaimed.

"It's not your place to figure it out," Sabine said. "The correct time will come when the truth will be revealed to her. The only obstacle her parents did not foresee was this cursed organization of Hela Corp. But that will end tonight."

The demon hunters looked at each other, unsure what to think of that last comment. Sabine had a stone-cold, emotionless look on her face. "Be ready," she instructed the three demon hunters. "Rest now and focus on your secret weapon. All of you will use it tonight." Saying that, the vampire strolled out of the room like a dark, foreboding shadow.

Lake Tahoe, Nevada, USA; Feb 9, 6:30 a.m.

GRACE'S EYES FLUTTERED AS she woke up. She sat on her bed and tried to regain her bearings, taking in the strange settings of the room that Sylvie had prepared for her. She missed her bed and her bedroom back in St. Helena. She missed her sisters. The solitude of her personal quest felt overbearing. The demon hunter pushed the negative sensations down to the depths of her heart. *I'm not alone,* she thought to herself. *They will come and help.*

The demon hunter tied her raven hair in a neat ponytail and stepped out of bed, heading toward the shower. She turned it on, letting the ice droplets start to flow from the silver showerhead above. Taking a deep breath, she stepped in, feeling the frigid water pierce her skin like tiny needles. The ice-cold shower had been part of her training since she was eight. It honed her muscles and helped her mind focus. She then let the freezing water wash over her body while her thoughts replayed her conversation with her sister.

It wasn't what her mind told her directly that caught her attention. It was the raw emotion that surrounder her aura. Guilt, plain and simple. She felt she had let her down in her time of need and failed. She was trying to make amends—not out of self-pity, but compassion.

Izzy's emotions mirrored what she felt, in a way: shame and selfishness. Her obsession with Neil had led her to a path that, if it weren't for her sister, would have been one of no return. She wasn't willing to take that step, neither for herself nor for the closure she needed. The memory of her parents and how they viewed her was too important.

As she exited the shower and dried herself, Grace's mind wandered toward what her former Guardian and Elizabeth had said. They'd known her parents well. If indeed they had given out the order to be killed by a vampire, the question would be why. Grace knew her parents loved her. Their death could not have been in vain. It had to be so important that they needed to leave her.

Grace closed her eyes. The final words of her parents rang in her mind. *Don't be afraid,* her father said. She stepped out of the bathroom and went into her bedroom as her mind tried to figure out the riddle her parents left her. *What does Neil have to do with all of this?* She thought to herself. *A two-thousand-year-old Guardian turned into a vampire received a request from my parents. Why would they do that?*

Grace quickly dressed in her black Adidas gear when a knock on the door interrupted her thoughts. "Come in," Grace instructed, preparing to continue with the charade.

Sylvie and Roxanne stepped into the room. "Good morning," the rogue demon hunter greeted. "Did you sleep well?"

"A little," Grace said. "I needed to get a hunt out of my system. We pulled two of your demon hunters to go out, but the demons got the jump on us."

"I heard," Sylvie said. "I had to coax the information from both Tina and Helena. I can't believe they were surprised by a pack of vampires. Maybe you can help them hone in on their instinct. Their skill should be evolving, not regressing."

"It's this place," Grace said. "Something is messing up our sensibilities to the darkness. I barely felt it, but they were present."

"That's good," Roxanne said. "We can't have rogue vampires during The Abyssborne feasting on our clientele."

"Well, not before they pay up," Sylvie noted, half joking.

"So, what's the plan for today?" Grace asked as she tied her black trainers.

"We put the finishing touches on today's events," Sylvie said, motioning Grace to leave the room.

Grace followed Sylvie's lead as she stepped out of the room. "High-end clientele will start arriving at seven p.m.," Sylvie said as she walked with Grace at her side and Roxanne close behind. "I set up these events by serving some champagne and hors d'oeuvres. I give the guests a chance to mingle with our best demon hunters. I want them to see Elizabeth inside the cage on this event and admire her."

"Showcasing the main course this early?" Grace

asked as they reached the top of the stairs, and all three women started descending. "In the event my mom and dad offered pitch sales, we saved the best for last."

"I came up with the idea so the clientele could see that this was not a myth," Sylvie said. "We have indeed captured her."

"Lock her downstairs," Grace recommended as she looked at the monitors with the security feed of the compound. Five demon hunters watched over the screen while a group trained on the side. Grace could see that both Tina and Helena were surrounded by six demon hunters, who took turns attacking them while they defended themselves. Leah was nowhere to be seen. "Set up one of the monitors so the clientele can see a live feed of her wrapped in chains. Then, she tests her skills against the demons, leaving the Arzkang for last. In the meantime, showcase sparring sessions on the mats while the main event starts."

Sylvie smiled as all three demon hunters stepped in front of the monitors. "I like how you think, Grace Wu," Sylvie said. "I want to show you something."

Sylvie motioned one of the demon hunters to flip on the security feed. As the cameras circled the compound, Grace could see the exterior, with demon hunters standing guard around the building. The cameras flipped toward the lower levels where the large octagon cage stood, while Elizabeth sat in the middle of the ring with her legs crossed. Finally, the image flickered on the cells where the vampires and demons were kept. Neil stood with his back against the wall, looking at the cracked reinforced glass blankly.

"Our security feed works on a closed circuit," Sylvie

explained. "We store video surveillance content for about a week before purging it."

Sylvie signaled an olive-skinned demon hunter to flip a switch. One of the monitors displayed a recording of Grace's fight with Leah. The raven-haired seventeen-year-old demon hunter crossed her arms and stared at the monitors, admiring Leah's fighting style and her own. Grace shivered, seeing the rage on her own face as she struck with all her might at the blonde demon hunter in the recording. Her hatred was ablaze, and it was similar to what Leah projected. In that fight, she and Leah had the same fuel pushing them forward. Grace felt a little sick inside, seeing what she was becoming. Grace frowned, watching herself throw Leah against the glass wall that protected Neil. The teenager now focused her attention on Neil, who was admiring the fight he was witnessing. Grace noticed that proud look on the vampire's face as he witnessed her unleashing her rage upon Leah, especially in the moment where she started hammer-punching Leah on the head.

"I thought you were more graceful than that," Roxanne quipped, admiring Grace's rage in the recording.

"I was angry," Grace muttered under her breath, not taking her eyes from Neil. That look of pride in him because of her actions shook her to the core. *Why do you torment me?* Grace thought to herself as the vampire smiled at her in the recording.

"This is my favorite part," Sylvie said as she ordered another monitor change.

Grace's heart sank, seeing the screen cameras

pointing to the clearing where she had led Tina and Helena. Cold sweat started dripping from her forehead as she saw a recording of what she had done to the rogue demon hunters a few hours ago.

"I wanted to see for myself how you dispatched four vampires," Sylvie said coldly.

Grace was about to run when heavy chains were wrapped around her body. *How could I be so stupid?* Grace thought to herself, finally sensing Leah's essence behind her. As the obsidian-infused chains wrapped around her body, she felt her power abandon her.

"I'm so disappointed in you," Sylvie said, turning toward the raven-haired girl as Leah kicked the back of her legs, forcing the girl to her knees.

"Told you," Roxanne said to Sylvie.

"Can I kill her now?" Leah asked as Grace tried to find the strength to set herself free.

"No!" Sylvie said as she grabbed Grace's chin and forced the girl to look at her. "This Ice Princess is too valuable. Millions of dollars valuable."

"Billions," Grace gasped as Leah pulled hard on the chains.

Sylvie turned her attention toward the monitor, observing Grace sitting peacefully on the snow with her legs crossed. "Your sisters don't have a chance against me," Sylvie spat. "No matter what you told them."

"You don't know my sisters," Grace spat out.

"Stubborn little girl," Sylvie said. "Stop being foolish! You're grounded! Look at my girls, my hardware. I've got Elizabeth and an Arzkang demon under my control. You think two girls can stop me?"

"I can't wait for them to try," Leah said as she pulled

harder on the chains, causing Grace to scream in pain. She tried to hold it in, but without her demon hunter power, she couldn't help it.

"I'll make you a deal," Sylvie said, pondering for a second. "I will make a trade with you. Why don't you attempt to buy me off? You have access to your family's fortune. Make me an offer for your life, the life of Elizabeth, and your sisters. Ballpark number."

Grace shook her head. "I've looked into your mind," Grace said.

"Bullshit!" Sylvie retorted. "My compound makes it impossible for you to do so."

"I don't need my demon hunter powers to know what you desire," Grace said. "You have no honor. No code. You're a basic mercenary. Yes, money drives you. But you've tasted capturing two of the best demon hunters on the planet. You won't release us. Not for all the money in the world."

Sylvie gritted her teeth as Grace spoke. Grace smiled defiantly. "You're nothing but an ordinary whore for high-end lowlifes."

Sylvie screamed at the demon hunter, striking Grace with a backhand slap across her right cheek. The raven-haired girl's head snapped to the side. The familiar metallic taste in Grace's mouth accompanied her aching cheek. She moved her head from side to side, trying to stretch her neck and shake the cobwebs off as she stared defiantly at her tormentor. "Say goodbye to your operations," Grace warned. "My sisters will burn it to the ground."

"I know now how I'm going to start my event tonight," Sylvie said. "You will join Elizabeth in the cage. You will fight with all your might. And when the demons tear you apart in my octagon, the great Elizabeth Somiere will face the same fate as you against my Arzkang demon, with your lifeless body and blood as a canvas."

"Bring it!" Grace exclaimed.

Sylvie ordered Roxanne and two demon hunters to grab Grace's chained body. "Stick her in the cage with her Guardian. Don't let them out of your sight." Roxanne nodded as the other two demon hunters dragged the girl away toward the dungeons below, leaving Leah empty-handed.

"You cheated me again," Leah said, her rage boiling. "No demon or vampire on this earth should end her life. She's mine. Her, Nikki, and finally, Izzy."

"I haven't cheated you," Sylvie said. "I'm creating the perfect setting for you to kill her. Once she fights our demons below and she's at her weakest, then you have my permission to end her life."

Leah growled at Sylvie and walked away. The rogue leader looked at the demon hunters who stood by, awaiting orders. "Prepare yourselves, ladies," Sylvie said. "We'll have a wild night."

*

ROXANNE LED HER DEMON hunters toward the cage where Elizabeth waited. The blonde demon hunter and Guardian stared silently as the women smashed Grace against the metal cage face first. Grunting in pain, she was dazed as they removed the chains, while Roxanne opened the padlock that kept the cage shut. The women threw Grace's stunned form inside as she sprawled unceremoniously inside the octagon while

Roxanne locked the cage door again.

Elizabeth knelt in front of Grace, trying to help her up. "Are you okay?" the Guardian asked, her voice filled with genuine concern.

"I couldn't do it," Grace said, looking at the floor as her fists smashed against it in frustration. She felt the same way she had felt when she first met Elizabeth. "I wanted to do it so bad. I wanted to betray you. I wanted to betray Nikki and Izzy. But I couldn't."

"I know you wanted to," Elizabeth said. "What stopped you?"

"My mom and dad," Grace said. "I dreamt of them alive and well. They looked so real."

"What have I taught you about your dreams?"

"They represent my fears and desires," Grace said, looking at her Guardian with teary eyes.

"Your parents live here with you," Elizabeth said, pointing at Grace's heart. "I'm sorry I couldn't help you get the necessary closure."

Grace nodded, hugging Elizabeth. As she did, she felt a weight lift off her shoulders. She didn't understand how or why; she just felt relieved. Right in the middle of that cage, she felt honest acceptance of her pain—no false empathy.

"Did you manage to speak with Neil?"

Grace nodded as she wiped the tears from her eyes. "He said nothing that he hasn't said before."

"That you're a scared little girl?" Elizabeth asked.

"He says it all the time," Grace whispered as the anguish started filling her heart.

"And are you afraid?" Elizabeth asked.

Grace looked at Elizabeth with a puzzled look.

Elizabeth sat on the floor next to Grace. "I've seen you battle monsters I would never have dreamed of fighting," Elizabeth started. "I've seen you fly into the air with a Hell Gargoyle and take down demon trolls and countless vampires. I've never seen you afraid of anything since I've met you."

"And right now, I'm afraid," Grace concluded, feeling the anguish in her heart. Closing her eyes, she could see her dead parents at her feet.

"The way Neil repeats this in your nightmares, and when he sees you," Elizabeth said, "I don't think he's trying to torture you."

"How do you know?" Grace asked.

"A master demon from hell has tortured me," Elizabeth said. "Neil is simply pointing out something that may not have been obvious to you until now."

"That I'm afraid?" Grace asked.

"But of what?" Elizabeth nodded. "Did your parents ever tell you how to figure that out?"

Grace thought for a moment. "Once. I think."

"Love and truth," Elizabeth said. "Those extinguish our fears. The problem is figuring out what we're afraid of."

Grace thought for a moment as the memories flooded her mind. Her parents' words had lingered for years.

"What do you fear?" her father asked.

"I'm afraid this is a mistake. I'm no demon hunter."

"Love and truth push out fear," her mother said. "That is the source of your strength."

Grace turned toward Elizabeth, who had a soft smile on her face. "You are chosen for great things,

Grace Wu. Don't let rage blind you from seeing what you can achieve."

Grace Wu nodded as she looked around and saw the two demon hunters standing guard. "You've been locked in for a while. Any ideas on how to get out?"

"Sure," Elizabeth said. "I was just waiting for you to join me so I could execute a well-laid plan to get us out of a cage that, if we touch it, takes our powers away."

"Seriously," Grace said. "You have a plan, right?

"Sean has never let me down," Elizabeth said as she lay down on the floor, looking at the ceiling. "I'm sure he's grilling John and your sisters to get us out of here. When they get us out, we have to be ready."

"So you plan to wait?" Grace asked.

"I plan to trust in our team," Elizabeth said. "Are they still going to let us fight the lower-tier demons before we deal with the Arzkang demon?"

Grace nodded. "Sylvie controls it somehow."

"That information will be vital if we could reach out to your sisters," Elizabeth said.

Grace pondered on something that she had felt in Izzy's thoughts. *Can you hear me?* She thought out to Elizabeth.

Elizabeth looked surprised as she looked at Grace. *I can now,* she thought back. *How?*

Grace thought out to her Guardian, *we can do it since we've been attuned to each other for so long. Our powers can break Sylvie's spell when Izzy and Nikki are nearby.*

Elizabeth nodded. "Good to know," she said to her demon hunter. "We're going to teach these women and all of Sylvie's clientele what two demon hunters attuned to each other can do. Are you ready?"

Grace nodded. "Let's do it."

Outside Lake Tahoe, Nevada, USA; Feb 9, 12:30 p.m.

John Simmons examined the two plain black metallic rings in the palm of his hand. Putting one down on the wooden table, he inspected the remaining one, slipping it on one of his fingers. He twisted the ring, and a small quarter-inch needle popped out from the palm side. Carefully removing the ring, he dipped it inside one of the blue glass beakers on the table. He then repeated the same exercise with the second ring.

"Are you sure Sean knows what he's doing?" Victoria asked from the opposite side of the table. Her mind focused on the open black gauntlet bracelet on the table. Her hands held fine tools, adjusting the firing mechanisms of her creations.

"He's handled worse situations," John said as he mixed the solution inside the blue beaker with a metal spoon.

The dark-haired Guardian looked up at her counterpart, who was focused on the rings being drenched in the liquid. "Do you have two of those in my size?" she asked.

John smiled at the question, pushing a small wooden box across the table. Victoria put down her tools and opened the box, revealing two silver rings. "You shouldn't have," the woman said, slipping on the jewelry pieces.

"Rotate the rings counterclockwise for the needle to pop up," John explained.

"How many doses?" Victoria asked.

"You get five on each," John said. "Just remember

that is one dose per demon hunter. Over one, and you put them out in a coma they may never wake up from."

"I don't see anything wrong with that idea," Sam said as she walked up to the Guardians with three large cups of hot coffee on a silver tray.

"We don't kill our own," Victoria explained as she grabbed a cup from Sam's tray.

"Even if they are threatening your sister?" Sam asked, handing a cup to John and keeping one for herself.

Victoria smiled at the nuanced question. "I guess the circumstance will dictate my proper response."

"I see in your eyes that you've already made up your mind," Sam said. She then turned toward John. "I see it in you, too."

"We're here to help our demon hunters," John replied. "The burden of their calling is heavy enough. We ensure they don't pile on any more than what they already carry."

"Do they know?" Sam asked both Guardians.

"They don't need to know," Victoria said.

"Interesting," Sam wondered as she sipped her coffee.

"What is?" John asked.

"What I've read about the new Guardians and the relationship with their demon hunters is that you give them freedom of choice," Sam said. "They're free to choose their path. One of the main reasons we're all in this mess right now."

"Is there a problem with that?" Victoria asked, getting a bit defensive. *It's hard enough for our girls and us to do our job—and have someone question the nature in which we do it.*

"Not at all," Sam said. "I find it quite noble. From

what Lady Sabine has shared with me, this was not always the case."

"But you're still not convinced," John said as he removed the last two rings from the solution they were being drenched in.

"No system is perfect, John," Sam said. "Trust me, you try to do the best for your demon hunters. No one questions that."

"I sense there's a 'but' coming," Victoria said.

"But if you give them freedom," Sam started, "and you hide what you do behind the scenes, you rob them of that freedom to think for themselves whether your actions are morally correct or not. What would the three demon hunters upstairs say if they knew what you guys do in the shadows?"

"Betrayed," John said, thinking about Izzy, Nikki, and Grace. "That's why they don't need to know."

"It's what you do," Sam said. "There will be a lot of 'innocent' bystanders in tonight's event. And not necessarily the demon hunters, which, in my opinion, are not innocent."

"You know Sylvie's clientele?" John asked.

"I went through their profiles," Sam nodded. "Half of them are human. Rotten to the core, but human nonetheless."

"Did you read up on Daniel Anderson from Anna, Balish, and Raymond LLC?" Victoria asked.

"The consultant," Sam replied. "He's an interesting fellow. It seems he's bankrolling these women. I guess he's invited to verify the product of his firm's investment."

Both Victoria and John nodded at each other with a

knowing glance. "What's your role in all of this?" John asked, changing the subject.

"My role?" Sam asked. "My role is to provide support for Lady Sabine on the ground. In this case, create an opportunity for your girls to act." The dark-haired woman pulled out from her pocket two little black devices, each no bigger than a remote car starter.

"What are those?" Victoria asked.

"Data disruptors," Sam replied, showing one device to both Guardians. "It scrambles IP addresses, impacting video over IP and other communications protocols."

"That's what will disable the security feed," John told Victoria.

"Correct," Sam said, walking toward the bar and picking up her silver tablet. She did a few swipes and pulled out the wire diagram of the compound. "Thanks to Lady Sabine's connections, we managed to obtain this."

Victoria put down her fine tools and walked over to Sam and John, looking at the tiny screen. "The security diagram?" the female Guardian asked.

Sam nodded. "Sixty minutes after we're inside, I disrupt the signal, and Hela Corp goes blind to the outside world." Sam then held up the second device in her hands and handed it to John. "This will light up the moment the security feed is down. Your signal to strike."

John motioned to see if he could grab hold of the tablet. He expanded the map and selected to show all the cameras. The cameras surrounded the perimeter and covered an extensive section of the property, from the pathway to the entrance to the pine forest behind the installations.

John zoomed in closer to the farthest regions, seeing several cameras installed near a clearing at the edge of the property. He recollected what Izzy had shared with them early in the morning. "Damn," John muttered under his breath.

"What is it?" Victoria asked.

"I think Grace got discovered," the Guardian said.

"How can you possibly know that from this image?" Sam asked, somewhat bewildered yet impressed at the young Guardian.

John stood up and started pacing the carpeted lobby, his brain on fire as he processed the information his demon hunters and Sean had provided. "Sylvie has a spell blocking all communications from the Demon hunters to the outside world using their power," John stated. "Elizabeth managed to escape and found a clearing where she could communicate."

Victoria looked at Sam and then at John, putting the pieces together. "Grace did the same today, so they got her on camera stepping outside the boundaries of the spell."

"What makes you think that she's in captivity?" Sam asked both Guardians. "For all we know, Sylvie let her communicate with her sisters to draw them out."

Victoria looked at John, waiting for his answer. "I've seen these girls in action," he said. "They're bound by something beyond sweat and blood. Grace would never turn on her sisters."

"You know her that well?" Sam asked. "Even if they had to choose between the answers that eluded her and her friends?"

"Do you know?" Victoria asked Sam. "Why did Neil kill Grace's parents?"

Sam shook her head. "My father told me that I should trust in the wisdom of the Ancient Ones. They've walked the earth for millennia and thrived."

"They're never wrong?" John challenged. "Made an incorrect call?"

"If they did, then I'm not aware of it."

Both Victoria and John looked at each other. They started packing their gear as if they had read each other's thoughts. "Did you finish?" John asked.

"Gauntlets are ready," Victoria replied. "How about your rings?"

John nodded as he put the black rings inside a wooden box. He grabbed another pair of silver rings that he slipped on his left and right hands. "Let's find Sean and go over this crazy plan of his."

CHAPTER XIV

Lake Tahoe, Nevada, USA: Feb 9, 6:30 p.m.

SEAN STRUGGLED TO STRAIGHTEN his bow tie and was failing miserably at the task as he looked in the full-length mirror.

"It's still crooked," Izzy said, sitting on her father's bed with her legs crossed.

"Thank you, Captain Obvious," Sean said. He turned around and signaled her to approach him.

Izzy stood up and started adjusting her father's tie diligently. "Are you sure this is how you want to do this?" she asked.

"It's going to work," Sean replied, looking at the ceiling while his daughter fixed the accessory around his neck.

"You're putting your life in the hands of a stranger," Izzy said. "Not only yours but Mom's and Grace's."

Sean looked down at her daughter. "I'm trusting her because you trust her," he said.

Izzy looked surprised as Sean looked into her green

eyes. "I know you talk to her with your telepathic connection," her father continued. "You seek to understand the source of your power, and you think she can provide the answers you seek because of her long life."

"She told you?" Izzy asked.

Sean smiled. "No," he said. "But you just did."

Izzy scoffed at her father, letting go of the tie as she sat back on his bed, looking at the floor. "Isabella," Sean called. "Look at me."

Izzy looked at her father, searching for the words to say. "Why are you doing this? You have your mother and me. Why do you need someone else's opinion on your powers?"

"Because I know what you guys know," Izzy replied. "I've read every book in the Guardian's library. I've read every word in Mom's journal. I've listened to all your stories, and the answers are not there. All of us are on a different level now after we unleashed Apocalyps. I want to understand why there is a sudden change. What can Nikki, Grace, and all the other demon hunters do with this hidden power?"

"Why?"

"I need to understand our limits," Izzy said.

Sean sat next to his daughter. "We almost lost you yesterday, Izzy."

"I know," Izzy answered.

"No, you don't," Sean said quietly. "You are so important in this world. Your purpose is not to go out like that."

"Like Mom did?" Izzy asked. "I read her journal, remember? You also risked your life countless times. I thought you knew I can't be spared of that."

Sean stood up and crouched before his daughter, looking deep into her eyes. "You are not your mother. You are not me. You are more than us. Your purpose is far greater than you can possibly imagine."

"But I need to know," Izzy replied.

"Not risking your life, you're not," Sean said, trying not to lose his patience. It was like speaking to a wall. He had taught his daughter well, and now he was asking her not to take the risks he and her mother had taken. She was stubborn, just like him and Elizabeth.

"It's part of the job, Dad," Izzy said. "If I hadn't done it, you would have three dead demon hunters. Thanks to John, we're all still here."

Sean stood up and turned toward the mirror, grabbing his black jacket and putting it on. "I know it's part of the job," he said. "The Guardian in me understands. The dad in me is just like every other dad."

"Like every other mother and father who has a demon hunter for a daughter," Izzy replied. "No matter how hard you try, you can't avoid this."

"Are you ready for the nightmares?" Sean asked, looking at her.

Izzy took a deep breath before she spoke. "I know they're coming," she replied. "It's part of the job."

"Your mom had no one to turn to when this happened to her," Sean said. "Because of that, she almost got her best friends killed."

"It's different with me," Izzy said, standing up. "I have Mom, you, and my sisters to help me out."

Sean hugged his daughter tightly. He hated that she took that gigantic risk. But he would have taken it in a heartbeat for the women he loved. So would Elizabeth. Why would their daughter be any different? He kissed her forehead. He then took one last look in the mirror.

"You look great," Izzy said.

"I know," Sean replied with a confident smile. "You think I shouldn't trust Sabine?"

"We're in this far," Izzy shrugged. "No turning back now."

"Did she say something new about your powers?" Sean asked. "Something we didn't know before?"

"We definitely changed the polarity," Izzy said. "From negative to positive. That has many benefits for us, but it's slowly killing her."

"Easy solution to that," Sean said, turning around. "You've got to find a way to turn her human."

Izzy smiled. "Like you did?" she asked. "Isn't that one thing in every millennium? I thought you won the lottery on that."

"There's more than one way to skin a cat," Sean replied. "The question is, is she willing?"

"I think she's hiding something," Izzy said. "She needs the power of a vampire for a reason. Something related to the Tome. For what will come, she must be a vampire and a demon hunter."

"Be careful exploring her mind," Sean warned, noticing what his daughter was doing. "Remember that is a two-way street."

"I'm aware," Izzy said. "Want to talk about Leah?"

"I was waiting for you to bring her up," Sean replied. "She falls into the same category as the others, Izzy."

"She's uncooperative, Dad," Izzy said. "She will stop at nothing to kill Mom, you, and me. Well, torture us first, then kill us."

"Your mom is still alive," Sean replied. "I don't think she can will herself to do it. There is rage in her, but she's conflicted. She's not completely lost."

"High hopes for your lost offspring," Izzy said with a sly smile. "What makes you so sure?"

Sean turned again toward his seventeen-year-old daughter. "It's in our blood," Sean said. "No matter how misguided she is or how frustrated she feels, she won't do it. Our ties are too strong. Your mother and I have felt it. You must have felt it."

Izzy thought about that for a moment, nodding her head. "That doesn't mean she won't hurt us."

Sean sighed. The memories of the countless times he and Elizabeth hurt each other flooded his mind. "That runs in our family, too," Sean said. "Come on. We're running late."

Both father and daughter exited the room and headed back to the inn's lobby, where Nikki, Anna, Victoria, John, Samantha, and Sabine waited.

"Wow," Sabine said, admiring the older man in his black tuxedo. "You clean up well, Sean. I see now why Elizabeth keeps you around."

"You're not a fan of long-term relationships, are you?" Sean fired back, looking at the Ancient vampire. She wore a sleek black dress and a slit for her legs, showing off her four-inch black Christian Louboutins. The raven-haired vampire would turn the heads of anyone at the gathering.

"I'm over two thousand years old," Sabine said. "Relationships come and go. Are you ready?"

"Let's do this," Sean replied, grabbing his long

black trench jacket while Sam helped Sabine put on her red coat.

The Guardian looked at the demon hunters who would help with this endeavor. They all wore puffy black Canada Goose jackets, ready to embrace the cold. Sean turned toward John. "Synchronize your watch," he said. "You guide the girls and wait for the signal that the security is off. Take out all the rogue demon hunters in the perimeter. By then, the front door will be clear for you to walk through."

"Understood," John said as he pulled out a wooden box with the rings inside and gave it to Sean.

Sean opened the box and slipped the rings onto his fingers. "They're ready?" Sean asked.

"You won't have any problems with them," John replied.

"What about our girls?" Sean asked the Guardians. "What firepower besides the gauntlets?"

"Izzy and Nikki will be carrying dual battle axes. Wooden stakes are attached to the pommels for all four weapons," Victoria replied. "As soon as Elizabeth and Grace are in play, they will have a weapon in their hands. Anna will be on crossbow duty, taking out the undead."

Sean looked toward Anna. The youngest demon hunter had a determined look on her face. "You look ready, Anna," Sean commented.

"The least I can do is to be here for my sisters and Elizabeth. We'll get them out," Anna said, turning toward Nikki and Izzy.

"Your team is set," Sabine said. "Should we go?"

"Let's get our girls out of there," Sean ordered.

As soon as the team exited the inn, the dark-furred wolf jumped out of the snow-covered woods and sprinted toward Izzy. "Aidan!" Izzy exclaimed, kneeling and hugging her pet. She then turned toward her father. "How did you get him here?"

Sean shrugged. "He just tagged along. Can't seem to get rid of him."

"I guess you have your little bodyguard with you now," Sabine quipped.

Izzy smelled her wolf and inspected his fangs. "You've been hunting," she said. "You're in your domain."

"Can you ask him not to tear the rogue demon hunters apart?" Nikki asked. She had grown accustomed to the animal being around them. She still had her reservations, though.

"He'll behave," Izzy said as Anna petted the wolf, who licked her hand.

Nikki turned toward Sean. "I'm surprised you survived that trip with him."

The wolf growled at the comment as Nikki growled back at him.

"Okay," Sean stated. "Board up. Aidan is on your team now."

Izzy motioned her wolf toward the black SUV, followed by Anna and Nikki.

"Izzy has a pet wolf?" Victoria asked John as they headed toward the front of the vehicle.

"Great pet to have," John said, jumping into the driver's seat. "Second line of defense."

Sean watched the SUV come to life as John drove off with their team to the assigned location of the property's compound. He then walked toward the limousine and joined Sabine as Sam pulled out of the inn's driveway.

"You have a great team, Sean," Sabine noted as they approached Sylvie's compound. "Probably one of finest I've seen in my lifespan."

"That says a lot," Sean said. "Do you remember them all?"

"It's more about the events surrounding their service," Sabine said. "But you guys are memorable just because you've broken many ancient rules. And that has worked for you."

"Do you remember your parents?" Sean asked.

Sabine was perplexed by the question. "I've lived over three hundred years," Sean continued. "The only true happiness I've ever felt is with my wife and daughter. Despite all the perils this dark world offers, I see my daughter truly happy and complete. That's a parent's satisfaction."

"I guess that's what makes your generation of demon hunters so unique," Sabine said. "Before you broke the rules, demon hunters fought alone. Now, they fight alongside of and for their loved ones. Gives them a reason to continue the battle and not fall into despair."

"Do you remember your parents?" Sean asked again.

"They died before I died," Sabine said, shaking her head. "No one left but my Guardian."

"Is Neil your Guardian?" Sean asked.

Sabine smiled and shook her head. "Neil is an old friend."

Sean nodded as they slowly approached Sylvie's compound. Already, a line of high-end vehicles was forming to get in.

"These demon hunters won't recognize you, right?" Sabine asked.

"They shouldn't," Sean replied. "I'm a senior Guardian, and I deal with things from the outside. I never got involved with the demon hunter business at the ground level until just recently. The files on the Guardians are all pictureless. On the other hand, Elizabeth has always been the face of the Demon Hunter division. Most demon hunters who do know me are invited to The Gathering. I doubt any of that batch of girls jumped ship."

"What about your daughter?" Sabine asked. "She's in there too, and you can't hide your face from her."

Sean sighed. "Leah's original focus has always been Elizabeth and me to hurt Izzy. When Izzy found comfort in her sisters, they became a target. Her current nightmares passionately involve them one way or the other. If I were her, I would be near Elizabeth's side. On the lower levels of the mansion."

"You are confident of your deductions," Sabine admired.

"I was a private eye for five years," Sean said. "How did you know about Leah? Izzy mentioned that you met her before."

"I travel the world a lot," Sabine said. "I was in Romania when I bumped into Leah. At first, I confused her with Elizabeth. But that is when I peered into her thoughts. The fear. The pain. The suffering."

"Why does she hate Izzy?" Sean asked.

"You know why, Sean," Sabine replied. "While your daughter was nurtured in a loving and safe environment while she grappled with her demon hunter powers, Leah was tortured physically and mentally in a hellish dimension before being thrown into a world that was not prepared for her. The cold world molded her character into this killing machine until Hela Corp got their hands on her."

"If she's such a wild card, I doubt Hela Corp can control her," Sean said.

"They don't need to control her," Sabine said. "She's an instrument in their warfare. They only need to wield her. And as of today, the girl fits perfectly with Hela Corp's agenda."

"I told Izzy she's not lost," Sean said. "That's what Elizabeth sees. Did you see that?"

Sabine shook her head. "I couldn't look beyond the hate without exposing myself," Sabine said. "She resents Izzy and her family with all her being."

Sean nodded. "Are you absolutely sure about this?" Sabine asked again. "Will you be recognized?"

"I'm pretty sure," Sean said. "If Leah, Sylvie, or one of her demon hunters recognize me, this will end before it gets started."

Sabine nodded. "If this goes south, don't try to stop me from what I will do to get Neil out."

Sean nodded, knowing perfectly what she meant. He then turned his attention back to the road.

"These rogue demon hunters really go out for their event," Sam quipped, seeing the high-end vehicles in the line to get in. They approached the mansion via a heated cobblestone driveway, greeted by an impressive façade of natural stone and rich, dark wood. The architecture was a harmonious blend of rustic alpine charm and modern design, with large windows. An elaborate wrought-iron gate ensured privacy and security, with two demon hunters guarding the entrance.

"I can't wait to see how your team works out this problem," Sabine said, looking at Sean.

"They'll manage," Sean said, looking at the demon hunters guarding the gate. "They will remain true to the oath they've taken, just as you've remained true to yours."

"I'm a demon hunter, after all," Sabine said. "Can't say the same for Neil, though."

"Meaning?" Sean asked, knowing the answer to his question already.

"He'll remain true to his Guardian protocol," Sabine replied. "It's his burden to carry, just like yours."

Sabine's limousine slowly made its way toward the entrance of the compound. One of the demon hunters at the gate had a portable scanner in her hand. Sean noted the young woman was in her late twenties. Dressed in her Hela Corp winter jacket, the dark-eyed demon hunter focused on their car. The negative vibration Sabine's essence emitted was a dead giveaway.

Sam rolled down the window and opened her cell phone so their bar-coded invitation could be scanned. "Lady Sabine plus two guests?" the demon hunter asked Sam.

Sam nodded. "Your invitation has been flagged," the demon hunter said. "Before you enter the premises, our security needs to conduct a secondary inspection."

Sam nodded again and drove the limousine inside. The young woman could see several humans lining up toward the large lake house mansion—a shorter line with a few humanoid demons formed to the side. Five demon hunters were inspecting that line, armed with short swords strapped to their backs and crossbows in their hands.

Sam parked the limousine and stepped out, opening the door for Sabine and Sean. The Ancient Vampire and Guardian immediately caught the attention of the five demon hunters. "Is it you or me?" Sean asked.

"It's me," Sabine said. "Can't hide my nature to our kind."

A dark-haired demon hunter with green eyes and olive-colored skin approached them. "Invitation?" she asked.

Sam stepped up and pulled out her cell phone. "Lady Sabine," Sam stated. "She and her guests are here to inquire about your services."

"You're a vampire," the demon hunter stated, looking at the raven-haired woman.

"Nothing gets by you, darling," Sabine said as she grabbed Sean's muscular arm. "I see your reputation precedes you."

A second demon hunter approached them and used a portable metal detector. The thirty-year-old woman scanned their bodies, finding nothing out of the ordinary.

"We hunt demons and vampires," the original demon hunter stated. "Why do you need us?"

"A million pounds a month for your services," Sabine stated. "Details, I will go over only with your boss."

The dark-haired demon hunter looked at all three before signaling them to follow her. They climbed the stone steps of the mansion only to be greeted by the red-carpeted lobby. The insides of the manor were equally luxurious as from the outside. Stone and wooden finishes gave the interior a rustic design.

A demon hunter handled their coats as they continued making their way inside. Men and women dressed in long gowns and black tuxedos exchanged silent conversations as they admired the extravagant interiors. The demon hunters were the only ones who seemed out of place in the gathering, wearing their signature Hela Corp apparel. Nonetheless, they were versed in intellectual conversations with their clientele. Each group had at least one demon hunter explaining their purpose, from the bits and pieces of what Sean could overhear from their hushed discussions.

Also in attendance were vampires and other humanoid demons. Sean saw a couple of soldier demons dressed in black tuxedos, their eyes lit up with soft blue flame. They were powerful, but not as strong as an average demon hunter. The women were on high alert around the demons, giving them a warm welcome but always remaining on their guard. The demon hunters were ready to strike at a moment's notice.

A dark-skinned demon hunter approached the group. "Greetings," she said. "Welcome to The Abyssborne. My name is Roxanne. Sylvie would like to meet you in person. May I ask who requests our service?"

"That would be me," Sabine said. "Lady Sabine at your service, along with my partner, Michael O'Shea, and my assistant Samantha."

"Glad to make your acquaintance," Roxanne said. "Please follow me."

Sam's eyes inspected her surroundings. Her attention was immediately drawn to the computer lab setup that only two demon hunters guarded. The terminals were all on. She looked at the ceiling and saw all the security cameras with green lights. *Closed circuit,* Sam thought to herself.

"Wait," Sabine said, turning toward Sam. "Samantha. Stay here. What Michael, Sylvie, and I are about to discuss does not concern you."

Sam nodded, staying near the lab and nodding at the demon hunters.

"Sorry about that, Roxanne," Sabine said. "Please let us continue."

Roxanne nodded and guided Sean and the ancient vampire toward a small living room to the side of the mansion. A purple-pinkish-haired woman talked to a tall, dark-haired man dressed in a black suit while both shared a drink. "Sylvie," Roxanne called out. "Lady Sabine and her partner, Michael O'Shea."

"Thank you, Roxy," Sylvie said, putting her glass on the coffee table near her and extending her hand. "I saw you made a last-minute purchase to join us, and I wanted to meet you in person."

Sabine extended her hand as Sean extended his to the dark-haired man. "Michael O'Shea," Sean stated.

"Daniel Anderson," the man replied, shaking Sean's hand.

"Anderson," Sean repeated. "From Anna, Balish, and Raymond?"

"You've heard of me?" Daniel asked, quite surprised.

"By reputation alone," Sean responded coolly. "Several acquaintances highly recommend your services."

"Interesting," Daniel said. "I always inform my customers not to mention my name or my company."

"Indeed," Sean said. "That is exactly what they said."

"If I may be so bold," Daniel said. "Who mentioned my name?"

"A vampire," Sean replied. "I was a liaison for certain clans in Eastern Europe."

"Ah, yes," Daniel said. "Nasty bit of business a few years back."

Both men stared into each other's eyes before Sean broke eye contact and turned toward Sylvie and Sabine. "A thousand apologies, ladies," he said. "It seems we men have monopolized the conversation."

"No need to apologize," Sabine said, turning toward Sylvie. "In this world, there is nothing better than finding people with common goals."

"And what is your goal, Lady Sabine?" Sylvie asked. "For your last-minute purchase, you certainly tickled my curiosity."

"Several," Sabine said. "I'm what the underworld calls an Ancient One."

Sylvie frowned at the title as she turned toward Daniel. Immediately, two demon hunters alongside Roxy approached on each side of both Sean and Sabine. Sabine only smiled. "It's okay, ladies," the vampire said, extending her hands. "I come in peace."

"You are here for Neil?" Sylvie asked.

"He's part of my clan," Sabine said. "Not sure how you tracked him down. We're very good at hiding our tracks. We've remained hidden for thousands of years."

"We're very good at what we do," Roxy said, measuring the vampire.

"We noticed," Sean stated. "I've worked hard to keep the Ancient ones hidden for some time now. Not even The Guardians and their demon hunters know of their existence."

"I wouldn't go that far," Sylvie said. "Some have exclusive knowledge."

"And yet no one found them until today," Sean said. He turned toward the demon hunters who were crowding them. "Is it possible for your women to give us some room and a drink?"

Sylvie momentarily thought and signaled for the demon hunters to back down. "Please," the rogue demon hunter said. "Let's take a seat."

Sylvie motioned for them to sit around the coffee table as the three demon hunters stood guard around them.

"Are you also interested in my business?" Sabine asked Daniel.

Sylvie interjected. "Daniel and his firm have an interest in Hela Corp. They sponsor a percentage of what you see here today. Consider his firm a silent partner."

"Interesting," Sabine said. "Does that mean that by doing business with you, I'm doing business with his firm?"

"No," Daniel said. "Hela Corp is a more hands-on contractor for my firm. If Hela Corp can't provide certain services needed for the human world, that's where I step in."

"Glad we have our cards on the table," Sean said as a demon hunter brought a crystal bottle of whisky with several crystal glasses. Sean looked for Sylvie for approval, which she granted by simply nodding. The senior Guardian poured himself a glass.

"The fact that you caught our scent and captured Neil fascinates me," Sabine said. "That is what piqued my interest. If you can track us down, what stops other interested parties from doing the same thing?"

"We had an incentive," Sylvie said. "A recruitment ploy for one of the best demon hunters on the planet."

"The demon hunter knew about Neil?" Sabine asked.

"More like he made his presence known to her," Sylvie responded, sipping her drink. "The vampire killed her parents. We offered the vampire in exchange for her services."

"That is your recruiting method?" Sean asked. "Fulfilling their deep desires guarantees loyalty?"

"It's worked so far," Sylvie said, motioning to the demon hunters surrounding them.

Sabine scoffed as she looked at Sean. "Neil needs to control his impulses with demon hunters," the vampire said. She then turned toward Sylvie and Daniel. "He makes a sport out of killing demon hunters. Tortures them before taking their life. I assume this demon hunter was his pet project."

"Pet project," Daniel repeated as he drank from his glass. "He got involved with a top-level demon hunter."

"You are familiar with this girl?" Sean asked.

"It's our job to know," Daniel replied. "The demon hunters and the Guardians are a tiresome nuisance to the objectives of interested parties. We have to keep tabs on the best of the best."

"It seems you failed to turn her to your side," Sabine said.

"Who says we failed?" Sylvie asked, almost challenging the vampire.

"I can still feel Neil," Sylvie said. "His essence is present in this compound. If you had succeeded, Neil would be dust now."

Sylvie nodded. "This demon hunter's ties to the Guardians are far too great. So you will see her in action instead."

"Excellent," Sabine said. "Can we talk business on me purchasing Neil back from you?"

Sylvie looked interested in the proposal. "You want to buy him from me?"

"Isn't this what you do?" Sabine sounded confused as she looked at Sean, then turned her attention back to Sylvie. "You sell your services. You sell demons and vampires. Is he not for sale? Or was his only purpose an offering to your demon hunter?"

"I guess we can discuss a price now," Sylvie said, looking at Roxy. "Neil had lost value to us and was to face annihilation. But since you seem interested in him, I think we can reach an agreement."

"Is he in good condition?" Sabine asked.

"Just a few tears in his suit, but he's fine."

Roxy approached Sabine with a calculator in her hand. "You can type your offer using this," the rogue demon hunter said.

"The moment of truth," Sean said with a smile as he adjusted the rings in his hands. "What is Neil worth to you?"

"More than you know," Sabine said, looking at Sean as she typed the amount on the calculator and handed it to Roxy.

Roxy handed the device to Sylvie. Sylvie was expressionless. "That seems like a low figure for an

Ancient One," the rogue demon hunter said.

"That's half of what I can offer," Sabine said.

"What else can you offer?" Sylvie asked.

Sabine smiled as she sat back and looked at Sean. "Since you have the great Elizabeth Somiere on display, how about I give you Sean O'Brien."

Sean's smile disappeared as he saw Sabine make her move. He was about to move before the demon hunters surrounding the group pointed their crossbows at him. Sean smiled at himself. "Well played," he muttered.

"I told you, Sean," Sabine said as she looked at Sylvie. "I will do anything for Neil."

"Welcome, Sean," Sylvie said. "Your wife and daughter are waiting for you downstairs."

CHAPTER XV

Lake Tahoe, Nevada, USA; Feb 9, 7:45 p.m.

GRACE SAT CROSS-LEGGED IN the middle of the octagon ring with her eyes closed, focusing on her breathing. She tried with all her might to block the noise from the outside world. She was not succeeding. She could hear the whispers of the men and women sitting around the black obsidian cage. She could feel the essence of the demon hunters who surrounded the area. She could feel Leah pacing right in front of her.

Breathe, Elizabeth, who sat beside Grace, instructed with her mind. *Breathe. Don't let anything distract you. We will get out of this together.*

Your daughter is impatient, Grace thought back.

There is no peace in her, Elizabeth replied. *She will be dealt with in due time. First, we must focus on getting out of here.*

Grace took a deep breath before feeling Sylvie make her way down. Both she and Elizabeth opened their eyes and saw her walking down with Sean, wrapped in chains. Right behind them were several demon hunters and Sabine.

Elizabeth stood up and walked up to the cage door, seeing for the first time the people who had surrounded the octagon. Grace followed close behind.

Leah was about to say something when she noticed her father being led toward the cage.

"I brought a little gift," Sylvie said to Elizabeth.

"Surprise," Sean said with a sly smile to his wife.

"Is this your attempt at rescuing us?" Elizabeth asked. "I've seen you execute better plans than this."

"Hey," Sean protested. "I'm here with you, aren't I?"

"It would be awesome if you were not chained up," Elizabeth muttered.

Sean turned toward Sylvie. "Do you mind if I kiss my wife?" Sean asked. "It's been a while."

Sylvie looked shocked at how lightly the Guardian was taking the situation. "No," she replied.

"It's okay, honey. We'll have time for that later." Elizabeth then turned toward Sabine. "I have you to thank for this reunion, don't I?"

"Elizabeth," Sabine said. "Death is a necessary evil. I did what I needed to do since your little demon hunter got Neil captured. And all for nothing."

Grace's temper flared. She wanted to lash out, but Elizabeth's thoughts pierced her mind. *Easy. Just play along.*

Grace took a deep breath and smiled at Sabine. "I'm sorry I allowed your hands to get dirty, Schoolmaster."

Sabine nodded as she looked at Leah. "We meet again, young Leah," Sabine said. "Still angry at your biological family."

Leah lashed out at the vampire, only to be

stopped again by Roxanne. "She's a client," Roxy said. "Behave yourself."

"Your sister is better at controlling her emotions," Sabine said. "That's why she has power over you."

Leah calmed herself down and looked at Sean again. Sean took a moment to admire his daughter's features. "We need to deal with your anger issues, young lady," Sean said.

Leah's rage boiled over as she pulled out her knife. "Easy!" Sylvie ordered. "Patience, Leah. Your prize is at our doorstep. It would be bad for you to ruin it." The purple-pinkish-haired demon hunter turned toward Elizabeth. "Your family is so complicated. Why couldn't you be normal?"

"We're demon hunters, Sylvie," Elizabeth replied. "Our lives are anything but normal."

"That ends tonight," Sylvie said. She turned toward two of her demon hunters. "Take Sean to the box office seats next to Daniel. I want him sitting right where his wife's blood will be splattered in his face."

The demon hunters obeyed as Sean looked at his wife and said, "Be seeing you, Beautiful. Good luck."

Sylvie looked at Sabine. "Once I finish my event here, I will release Neil into your hands," the rogue demon hunter said.

"I can wait," Sabine said as she looked at the demons and humans in attendance. "Can someone guide me to my seat?"

"Be a doll, Roxy," Sylvie ordered.

Roxanne nodded and guided Sabine to the side of the octagon, where the vampire sat next to a Galdamish demon. "Special seat for you," Roxy said.

"I'm sure it is," Sabine said, looking at the five-foot-five pink demon. The creature grinned, revealing jagged teeth as his red eyes examined Sabine from head to toe. He was dressed in a sharp and expensive black tuxedo that would make heads turn.

Sylvie then turned toward Grace. "Too bad you couldn't make it work out, Gracie. We could've done wonders with your powers and your money."

"Yeah," Grace said. "Too bad."

"Are you ready to showcase what you can do?" Sylvie asked. "Please put on a good show."

"Weapons would be nice," Grace said. "Just one short sword will suffice. I mean... you want to show off what demon hunters can do, right? It would be too bad if we died on the first encounter."

"Fine," Sabine said, motioning to the demon hunter who guarded the cell. "Hand them a single short sword to make it interesting. I know it will be useless when I unleash the Arzkang."

The demon hunter nodded as Sylvie took Leah's arms and guided her away from the cage. "Your sister is near," Sylvie said. "Go outside, patrol the grounds, and find her."

Leah smiled at the order and walked out of the cellar.

Sylvie turned around and faced her guests and the cage. "Friends," she announced. "Welcome to The Abyssborne. I have a marvelous treat for you this evening."

The rogue demon hunter walked toward the cage and pointed inside. "Tonight, I give you the privilege of seeing the demon hunter of legend, Elizabeth Somiere, in the flesh."

The crowd started murmuring, staring at the blonde demon hunter who had her eyes closed, taking in her situation.

"Alongside Elizabeth," Sylvie continued, "one of her protegees, Grace Wu. One of the best demon hunters on the planet."

Sabine admired Grace as she twirled the short sword in her hand. She then turned toward the ceiling and the walls, inspecting the security cameras. All the lights on them were green. Then, after a second, the green light turned a solid amber-red. Sabine smiled, looking at Sean, who sat next to Daniel Anderson. Two demon hunters guarded him. She saw the senior Guardian twirl the rings in his hands, focusing exclusively on what was happening inside the octagon. Sabine turned her attention back toward Sylvie.

"Tonight," Sylvie continued. "These brave demon hunters will display their strength and skill. That is the power you will have at your disposal."

Roxanne walked up to Sylvie with a large wooden box. Sylvie opened it and pulled out a large metal chain with a dark blue orb attached to it. She hung the chain around her neck and bowed toward Daniel Anderson. Daniel just lifted his glass and toasted it for Sylvie's event.

"I guess you're responsible for all this," Sean said out loud.

"I dabble a bit here and there," Daniel responded. "You're a smart man, Sean. Why not just ask directly."

"I don't bother to ask what I already know," Sean said. "But if I had a question you could answer, it would be... how many?"

Daniel smiled and turned toward The Guardian. "Indirectly? I'd say over one hundred."

Sean nodded at the number. "I figured as much."

"Let's watch the show," Daniel said. "Let's see if Sylvie can pump my numbers up. In my firm, we have a saying. There is nothing better than a dead demon hunter."

Sean took a deep breath as she saw the glow of the blue orb around Sylvie's neck. He turned toward Elizabeth, who had opened her eyes and stood beside Grace. *Hang in there,* Sean thought out to his wife.

Elizabeth and Grace looked at the end of the octagon, and a small trap door opened. *Whatever comes out,"* Elizbeth thought out to Grace, *take your time. Stall however you can. Give this audience a show and delay Sylvie in pulling the Arzkang out.*

A growl came from the lower level. Elizabeth and Grace focused on what would come out of the trap door. From the corner of her eye, Grace could see Roxy taking notes of the attendees while exchanging wagers on what would happen next. *Let's give them a show,* Grace thought out to Elizabeth.

The soft growls grew louder as a Kulak demon emerged from the trap door. The hound-like four-legged demon had gray-coloured skin and three fingers on each paw. Large, sharp, five-inch black claws extended from each toe as it lazily walked out. Its pointy gray snout revealed large fangs from the four-foot-long beast. The beast growled at the demon hunters as a second one emerged from the trap door.

"Get me a weapon," Elizabeth said as she separated from Grace by a couple of steps while the third demon appeared from the trap door.

Grace nodded as she twirled her short sword. One Kulak demon growled and launched itself toward Elizabeth. The demon hunter was ready and spin-kicked the monster right across its gray torso, sending the demon toward Grace, who swung the sword once. The sharp blade sliced through the neck like butter, separating the head from the body of the demon.

The other two demon hounds growled and lunged toward the demon hunters. Grace met with one demon's head and thrust her blade right inside the animal's mouth. The blade penetrated right through the soft skull, with dark black blood spurting out. The raven-haired demon hunter slid her sword to the side as the demon fell lifeless. Grace swung the blade a second time and severed both paws from the dead Kulak.

The last hellbeast launched toward Elizabeth, ready to tear her apart with its claws. The green-eyed woman grabbed the beast by the legs and twirled the demon three times before releasing it. The Kulak flew uncontrollably toward the cage entrance, its body crashing hard against the metal door and falling into a heap. As it recovered and stood on its four legs, Grace's blade came crashing down right through the middle of its skull, splitting it in two before the beast fell lifelessly on the floor.

We're near. The thought pierced Grace's mind. She turned toward her blonde Guardian, who nodded with a smile. She had felt it as well. *Hang in there.*

Elizabeth walked over to where Grace had severed the Kulak's paws and picked them up from the floor. She inspected the five-inch black claws and looked toward Sylvie. "These will do just fine," Elizabeth said.

Sylvie scowled as the blue orb glowed again. Six Anharran demons exited through the trap door and surrounded both demon hunters. The six humanoid demons were all five-foot-eight and wore black garments, all cinched with a black belt around their waist. Their skin was light brown and wrinkled as if it were a badly put-on suit over their bodies. The lower halves of their faces were exposed muscle tissue and pearly white fangs. Their fiery eyes stared at the demon hunters, ready to attack.

"Three for you and three for me?" Grace asked her Guardian.

"Sounds good to me," Elizabeth said.

Two Anharran demons attacked Grace with hard, precise blows. The dark-eyed demon hunter fended off with her sword, but by the nature of the attacks, she knew these demons were not pushovers. She sliced down and to the side, but the Anharran demons were just as spry as she was. As soon as she swung to one side, the demon cartwheeled out of the way and kicked toward Grace, who blocked with her blade.

A demon jumped over Grace and pinned her arms back while the other two took advantage of the situation. Grace jumped and kicked both demons in the face, pushing them back. She swung her head back and smashed the bridge of her captor's nose with the back of her skull. She then twirled her blade and decapitated the demon.

One of the Anharran demons kicked the sword from Grace's hand, causing her to wince in pain. One of the demons spun and tried to kick Grace in the face. The demon hunter dodged and did a handless cartwheel as the second demon attempted to do a foot sweep. The demons pushed Grace closer to the obsidian-infused cage as the fight progressed.

Realizing the danger she was in, the demon hunter changed tactics and allowed one demon to get close. As he swung a punch, the girl grabbed his arm and pressed hard on specific areas. The demon screeched in pain as it lost the feeling of its arm. Grace grabbed the entire extremity and swung him toward the metal door of the cage. The metal strained at the impact, but remained firmly attached to the cage.

Sylvie noticed the tactics both Grace and Elizabeth were attempting. She motioned for two of her demon hunters to move toward the cage entrance. Grace saw the demon hunter's movements as she rolled toward the side and picked up the sword she had dropped. The raven-haired demon hunter swung hard and to the right as the blade slit right through one of the demon's throats. Blood spurted out, staining the floor of the octagon.

The third beast growled at Grace and fired haymakers left and right, trying to connect with the girl, but she weaved and dodged with the finesse of a ballet dancer. The demon hunter plunged her blade directly into its chest, piercing the demon's body through. The beast spurted out blood from its mouth before Grace pulled out her sword, and the creature fell lifelessly to the floor.

Elizabeth had her trio of Anharran demons to deal with. She twirled the makeshift black blades from the Kulak demon and sliced them horizontally, pushing the demons back. One demon charged Elizabeth, but the blonde demon hunter ducked and thrust one of the claws right under the beast's jaw. The creature stopped in its tracks as the black five-inch talon pierced right through skin and bone. Elizabeth danced around him and connected with a spin-kick to the other two demons, pushing them away.

The blonde demon hunter pulled out the black claw from the first Anharran and threw the black blade toward the second one, who was standing up. The talon stabbed the beast right in the eye socket, causing the monster to screech in pain.

Elizabeth was already airborne as she fired a flying kick, connecting with the beast's face. Her boot made contact with the claw, sinking it deeper until it pierced the back of its skull. She then turned toward the last Anharran demon, who just extended his hands in a sign of peace. "Sorry," Elizabeth said as she connected with six successive blows to the chest. "It's either you or us." The demon fell to his knees just as the blonde woman grabbed his head and sharply turned it to the side, breaking its neck.

Both Elizabeth and Grace looked at each other and took a deep breath as the sound of the crowd erupted. The claps and cheers surprised both demon hunters, who turned their attention to the audience, captivated by their incredible display. They started yelling and screaming at Roxy and Sylvie with their respective bids.

Grace could feel Nikki and Izzy's essences nearby. *They're almost here,* she thought out to Elizabeth.

"We have to hang on," the blonde demon hunter said as five vampires emerged from the trap door. Both demon hunters steadied themselves before engaging again against the new threat.

CHAPTER XVI

Lake Tahoe, Nevada, USA: Feb 9, 8:05 p.m.

ANNA RODRIGUEZ EXHALED THROUGH her mouth, seeing vapor form before her eyes as she rubbed her hands, trying to keep them warm. It was the first time she had seen snow in her life. She knelt and scooped a handful, letting the cold seep into her hand. For a brief moment, she let her mind wander what it would be like if she were a normal sixteen-year-old experiencing the winter wonderland for the first time. She would be running and jumping in the white landscape, probably throwing a snowball at Luis and laughing about it.

The young girl wiped her hands on her pants as her older sister approached with a short sword in her hand and a small automatic crossbow in the other. Behind her, John handed a pair of black battle axes to Izzy and Grace while Aidan stood guard next to the black SUV, observing the surroundings.

"Are you okay?" Victoria asked her younger sister.

"Yeah," Anna said, grabbing the short sword and

strapping it to her back. She then grabbed the crossbow and inspected it.

"I made a slight adjustment," Victoria said. "A faster reload time gives you an extra two seconds."

Anna inspected her weapon. She treasured it wholeheartedly. She remembered when Elizabeth Somiere handed it to her. It made her feel unique and chosen. That feeling was long gone now.

"Will you retire with me?" Anna asked her older sister.

Victoria gave her sister a sad smile and shook her head. "We understand why you're giving up your post," she said. "And we fully support your decision. This choice does not invalidate the fact that you're still a demon hunter. Just because you are not the lead in Mexico doesn't remove your power or skill."

"Just the responsibility," Anna said, looking up at her sister. "I can't have more innocent girls die because of me."

"I know that you blame yourself, Anna," Victoria said. She turned around and looked at Izzy and Nikki as they geared up for battle. "There's nothing that Luis, I, or any other Guardian can say to convince you otherwise."

"It's my fault they're dead," Anna said as tears welled up in her eyes. The image of all the demon hunters who had died while she led the Mexican hell spot haunted her mind.

"Do you think they blame you?" Victoria asked. "I know, deep down, that you know they wouldn't. They may have been harsh, but trust me, they respected the hell out of you."

Izzy, Nikki, and John approached the women,

followed by Aidan. Both demon hunters had dual black battle axes strapped to their backs. The young man carried what seemed to be a black grenade launcher. The aluminum-alloy seventy-four-millimeter weapon had a circular cartridge system for six rounds. A strip of rounds was strapped to his chest, as well as a small black duffle bag.

"You look funny with that weapon," Victoria said with a smile.

"What is it?" Anna asked. "We've never used modern weapons to battle the undead."

"From the Guardians Research and Development team," John said, looking at Victoria.

Anna looked at her sister. "This is what you work on in your spare time?"

"The Judge is a joint effort with Luis," Victoria said, looking at her younger sister. "It's a gas launcher designed for tough monsters—like an Arzkang demon."

"Conventional weapons can't harm this demon," John explained. "Beneath its fur, its hard skin will cause battle axes, swords, and arrowheads to bounce right off."

"So what's with the firepower?" Nikki asked. "You're going to put it to sleep with gas?"

"We can't," Victoria said. "But we developed a solution that will help weaken its molecular structure."

"Since we can't perforate the skin, we created a gaseous form to introduce the venom into its system," John said.

"How long does it take for the gas to do its thing?" Izzy asked.

"A couple of seconds," Victoria said. "But the effect is not permanent. It only gives you a window."

"Of course," Nikki said. "You wouldn't want to make it that easy."

"Okay," Izzy said. "I guess we're ready. Let's head toward our starting point."

The demon hunters led the way while Guardians walked behind them, their steps causing a crunching sound in the snow. Izzy signaled her pet to walk next to her. The wolf obeyed and strolled right next to his demon hunter.

"Thanks for being here with us, Anna," Izzy told her younger sister. "We couldn't do this without you."

"It's the least I can do for how you've helped me," Anna replied.

There was a moment of silence as they continued walking. "Let's stop here," Nikki ordered. She crouched down, signaling for the others to do so as well.

"Now we wait," Izzy said, looking at John. "Anything yet?"

John looked at the device Samantha had given him. "Nothing yet. Any moment now."

"If we do manage to tag these demon hunters, what are we going to do with their unconscious bodies?" Nikki asked.

John smiled at the question. "I have a plan."

"Surely not leaving them in the snow for them to freeze to death," Izzy said.

"I wouldn't do that to our demon hunters," John said, ruffling the duffle bag around his chest. "Obsidian-infused restraints," he said.

"If you haven't noticed, I'm not too thrilled that Guardians have all these measures to control demon hunters," Anna said.

"They're precautions, Anna," Victoria explained. "Yes, the previous Guardian Assembly was very archaic in its methods of wielding and controlling the demon hunters. That has changed now. Our measures are..."

"Less deadly," John stated. "There are journal entries of both demon hunters and Guardians, where magic spells or incantations were used on demon hunters to turn against each other."

"Not to mention free will," Victoria said. "You all have a choice to be here, a choice to wield your powers for the well-being of others or your own."

"You seem to take a lot of precautions when demon hunters turn on the Guardians," Nikki said, looking at John. "You don't seem to have a failsafe measure if a Guardian turns on the demon hunters."

Victoria and John looked at each other before responding. "That is where you come in," John replied.

"You're the failsafe," Victoria said.

Izzy, Nikki, and Anna looked at each other, puzzled at the response.

"The Assembly promotes the vision of what a demon hunter and Guardian should be," John said. "It's up to you and us to uphold that vision, holding ourselves accountable."

"Like you right now, Izzy," Victoria stated. "You've been struggling to battle your sisters all this time. You all know the significance of taking a human life. We're here to help you remain true to your vows."

"You're the heroes of this story," John said. "If we did not help you, you would be the first to hold us accountable and stop us if necessary."

Victoria shook her head. "Unfortunately, power

attracts pathological personalities," the Guardian said. "That happens in all organizations. We are not exempt from that. Today, a few demon hunters have lost their way. Next time, it could be a corrupt Guardian desiring to wield the power you girls have been gifted."

"Remain true to your oath," John said. "That is the only way."

Izzy nodded, looking at her Guardian, piercing him with her green eyes. "I understand."

There was a long moment of silence after that. The group waited silently as Izzy noticed Anna holding her crossbow tightly. "Were Mercedes, Maria, and Blanca close friends?" the green-eyed girl asked.

"We weren't that close," Anna said, looking at the snow-covered ground. "I think they didn't like me very much."

"I doubt that," Nikki said.

Anna looked at the red-headed demon hunter. Nikki smiled, tapping the side of her temple softly. "Your thoughts are skin deep, Anna. We can feel them."

Anna smiled sadly.

"They followed your orders," Izzy commented. "It's hard to do that if there is no level of trust and sisterhood."

"Their last words still ring in my mind," Anna said.

"They called on you," Nikki said. "They trusted you to help them. And when they realized you were too far, they trusted you to bring justice to their deaths."

"And you succeeded in that," Izzy said. "You brought closure to their families. That is something you can take comfort in."

Anna nodded, remembering Sigfried's eyes full of fear right before she tore him apart. "Your sisters can rest," Nikki said. "I, for one, feel better that you're here. You're here battling at our side."

"I'm sure my mom feels the same way," Izzy said, touching her younger sister's shoulder. "One of the ones she chose for The Gathering is part of her rescue."

Anna took a deep breath as she grasped her crossbow tighter. She nodded at her sisters as they continued to wait.

"Do you feel the rogue demon hunters?" Victoria asked.

"Not at this range," Nikki replied. "But that will change once we approach."

"And that is now," John instructed. "The Security feed is down. Move in! We'll follow close behind."

Izzy nodded and signaled for Aidan to sprint forward. She then looked at Nikki and Anna. "Let's do this," she ordered.

The three demon hunters started running toward the compound at top speed, the snow offering little resistance to their agility. It wasn't long before they all felt the aura of a couple of demon hunters. Anna took a point and saw a dark silhouette. She didn't think twice, firing a projectile from her gauntlet, aiming where the neck would be. She heard a soft grunt before the first demon hunter collapsed on the snow-covered ground.

Izzy and Nikki did not break their stride as the mansion's walls appeared before them. Two older demon hunters looked up as they tried to reach for the radio. The projectiles from the gauntlets were already airborne, striking the demon hunters before they could call for help. Two more were down.

Anna reached her sisters as the three of them put their backs against the mansion walls. They heard a woman screech at the back of the mansion. "A wolf in the perimeter! How did he get through?"

Izzy noticed John and Victoria stop beside the demon hunters, unconscious on the ground. She saw her Guardian pull out what seemed to be black zip ties from his duffle bag and hand them out to Victoria. The Guardians then proceeded to tie up the demon hunters by their wrists and ankles. For a few seconds, Izzy felt curious about John's plan to get the rogue demon hunters out. She shook the thought away and focused on the task at hand.

Izzy motioned Nikki and Anna to follow her as they sprinted, covering the back perimeter of the mansion. The brown-haired girl lifted her arm, seeing a rogue demon hunter fend off against Aidan. The small wooden projectile impacted the side of the neck, causing the demon hunter to fall.

Aidan moved fast to the subsequent encounter, and Anna and Nikki followed close behind. Two more demon hunters appeared. Anna and Nikki fired from the gauntlets, but these female warriors were ready and smacked the wooden arrows with their blades.

Anna jumped and connected with a flying kick to the chest of the first woman, sending her flying. The second one was going for her radio before Nikki smashed the device with her metal gauntlet. The rogue demon hunter tried to kick Nikki, but the red-headed demon hunter evaded, moving to the side and striking the woman on the thigh with a hard punch. Nikki looked at Anna and ordered with her thoughts, *I got yours!*

Anna nodded as she aimed her gauntlet at Nikki's opponent. *And I got yours*, she thought back. The projectiles crossed each other in the air as they struck true to each rogue demon hunter.

Izzy whizzed past both her sisters, following her wolf to the next demon hunter a few feet from where she was, her mind fighting against the spell that blocked the area. Her mind found both her mother and Grace. *We're near,* the green-eyed demon hunter thought out. She could feel her mother and sister acknowledge her message, but their minds were focused on their current battle. Demons were being streamlined through a trap door for them to fight. They were running out of time. *Hang in there*, Izzy thought out.

A thirty-year-old dark-haired demon hunter grunted as she felt a projectile pierce her skin as she collapsed on the snow-covered ground.

All of a sudden, Aidan stopped in his tracks and growled at the night. Izzy stopped her run and shivered, feeling the aura that approached. "Glad you could make it, little sister," a girl said with a heavy Slavic accent.

Izzy's reflection appeared before her. The blonde hair and blue eyes were the only visible differences between the two sisters. Isabella composed herself as she saw Leah in the flesh for the very first time. Nikki and Anna reached Izzy and stopped right at her side.

"You girls get inside and get Grace and my mom out," Izzy ordered.

"Why do you think I will let them continue?" Leah asked as she pulled her knife from her back pocket. The blade glinted in the moonlight.

"Because I will make you," Isabella retorted. She whistled at Aidan, prompting the wolf to dart to Leah's right side. The blonde prepared to throw her knife at the wolf before Izzy fired one of her projectiles. Instinctively, Leah blocked the tiny arrow with her knife, giving Aidan a chance to pass by.

Izzy sprang toward Leah, firing another shot. The blonde demon hunter blocked with her knife again just as Nikki and Anna ran past her. Izzy launched a high kick, which Leah blocked easily. She countered with a straight punch, and Izzy dodged, taking a step back.

"You're strong, Isabella," Leah said. She attacked her twin sister, slashing with her blade from left to right. Each deadly swing was at full force. Izzy had a hard time dodging as she moved away from the arcs. The blade sliced part of her black Canada Goose jacket.

"You know this is a waste of time, right?" Izzy asked. "You'll gain nothing from killing me." The brown-haired girl fired another projectile, but Leah sliced the wooden arrow with her knife.

"Who says I want to kill you?" Leah asked, kicking high and aiming at Izzy's face. Izzy blocked, effectively pushing Leah away. "I just want you to go through the same hell I went through," Leah continued.

Leah put her knife away and adopted an unnatural fighting position Izzy barely recognized. The blonde girl crouched as low as she could, with her left leg and arm extended low in the front while her right arm arched back. All the support was on her right leg behind her.

Izzy noticed Victoria and John pass by. John nodded at Izzy before continuing their journey as Leah attacked with a right-hand punch. The speed and power of the blow was something Izzy had never experienced, putting both her arms up and blocking the strike. The immense force struck Izzy's gauntlets, pushing the girl back and leaving a trail in the snow. Leah was not done. She took two steps forward, shifting her body to the left side and spinning—the full force of the kick connected with Izzy's unprotected chest, sending her flying back.

Isabella's back collided with a pine tree, cracking the wood behind her. "Is this your idea of torture?" Izzy asked, putting herself in a defensive stance.

"You still don't realize it, do you?" Leah said. "While you're out here with me, your sisters are failing and dying in there."

Izzy screamed and launched herself forward, toward Leah. She fired left and right haymakers, aiming for the head. Leah blocked the attacks, wincing in pain, feeling the weight of the gauntlets on her arms. Izzy's power could not be denied as her relentless barrage of strikes pushed Leah back. Izzy jumped and connected with a knee to the chest, pushing Leah back, followed by a spin-kick to Leah's temple. Leah rolled with the strike as she spun in the air; she extended her leg and connected with a kick to the face, causing Izzy to scream as she collapsed on the floor.

Both demon hunters kicked up and faced off again. "I'm going to take them from you," Leah said. "I will make them suffer—every last one of them—no mother and father, no sisters, no guardians, even your stupid pet wolf. "

"I won't let you!" Izzy retorted, launching herself at Leah, grabbing her by the shoulders, and smashing her against the mansion wall, cracking it with her sister's body. Leah fired a knee strike, connecting with Isabella's unprotected stomach, knocking the brown-haired girl's wind out of her.

As Izzy staggered, Leah grabbed her by the shoulders and smashed her against the wall. "You're weak, Izzy. You don't have the strength or will to fight me. Your compassion makes you weak. The only true strength comes from hate. And I hate the living hell out of you!"

The blonde demon hunter then threw Izzy onto the snow-covered ground. Izzy tried to crawl away, and Leah just smiled. "I know what you're thinking," Leah said as she stalked her prey. "I know what you're feeling. You can't hide them from me. That doubt in your mind is what gives me power over you. That stupid feeling of compassion—the silly notion that you can stop without killing me. In order to stop me, you have to become me."

"You have no power over me," Izzy said, looking at her sister as she threw snow at her face. Leah instinctively used her arms to take cover, but Izzy was already in action, kicking Leah in the shins, right below the knee. Leah screamed as she fell to her knees. Izzy spun, crouched in the snow, and struck Leah with a spin-kick to the temple, bringing her blonde sister down.

Izzy stood up and grabbed Leah by the shoulders, throwing her against the mansion's wall. The impact cracked the concrete, knocking the air out of Leah's lungs. Izzy lifted her gauntlet and fired two more projectiles, but Leah moved swiftly out of the way as she pulled out her knife and threw it at Izzy.

Izzy lifted her metal gauntlet and the blade bounced off with a clang, falling and sinking into the snow.

Leah threw herself at her sister as they grappled in the snow, rolling from side to side. Izzy tried to gain the advantage by firing one final projectile from her gauntlet. It missed, sinking into the snow.

Izzy fired again, but an audible *click* signaled she was out of ammunition. Leah smiled at the sound as she wriggled her arm free from Izzy's grasp and sunk her fist into her sister's stomach. Izzy felt the air knocked out of her from the blow. Leah was relentless, striking two more times. Unable to block, Izzy took the punches.

Smiling, Leah searched the snow around her until she found her blade. She grabbed it and placed it right under Izzy's throat, causing her opponent to stop moving. "You lose, little sister."

Izzy looked into Leah's rage-filled blue eyes. "Are you sure?" Izzy whispered.

Leah looked perplexed at Izzy's question. "Defiant to the end," Leah said, pressing the blade onto her sister's throat, piercing her skin just enough for a trail of blood to ooze from the tiny cut. "I can leave you here and let you bleed out, with the tormenting thoughts on what I'm going to do to those you love."

"I doubt it," Izzy said with a smile, as she grabbed Leah's arm with her right hand, using her strength to push the blade away from her throat.

Leah looked into Izzy's green eyes, and all she could see was unwavering determination as the girl pushed her arm back.

Leah's smile faded, seeing her sister's strength. She gasped suddenly, feeling a piercing in her leg. She looked down and saw Izzy's left hand holding a small wooden projectile that was now stuck to her thigh. Slowly, Leah's eyes rolled back, and she collapsed on the snow-covered ground.

Izzy took a deep breath as she sat up and looked at her twin sister. Even unconscious, Izzy could see Leah's face contorted. Her sister's inner turmoil could not be hidden, not even in her sleep. "I'm sorry," Izzy whispered.

The brown-haired demon hunter stood up, wiping the blood from her throat as she grabbed Leah's knife. She then proceeded to walk toward the path Nikki and Anna had taken.

*

NIKKI AND ANNA REACHED the mansion's front door, trying to catch their breath. Aidan stood right next to them, serving as an invaluable ally in the incursion. "How many did you take out?" Nikki asked.

"Six," Anna replied. "And you?"

"I think five," Nikki said, seeing Victoria and John trailing behind as they tied up an unconscious demon hunter. Nikki closed her eyes, trying to feel out Izzy's essence. The familiar vibration flowed right back. *I'm coming*, Izzy thought out to Nikki.

Nikki smiled and looked at Anna. "Izzy kicked ass," she said to her younger sister and the wolf standing next to them. "Are you ready for this?"

Anna smiled, prepping her gauntlet. "Let's do this."

Nikki could feel demon hunters at the other side of the door. "Stay low," she ordered.

Anna crouched to the side of the entrance, Aidan

following her lead. The red-headed demon hunter kicked the door open and moved out of the way. Crossbow arrows started flying out the door. "These girls are packing," Nikki said with a smile as she readied her gauntlets.

Anna signaled to Victoria and John to stay back. She rolled in front of the entrance and aimed her gauntlet inside, seeing five older demon hunters with their crossbows reloading. Anna activated her gauntlet, fired her projectiles, and rolled out of the way.

Nikki moved inside, firing her darts, tagging the rogue demon hunters and bringing them down. She looked to the side and saw three of them by a set of computers. The red-headed demon hunter fired her projectiles just as Anna ran and slid, aiming her gauntlet at the opposite side. Three more demon hunters collapsed on the floor of the mansion.

Two large, five-foot-nine women jumped from the side and tried to attack Nikki and Anna. But Aidan was on them, jumping from his hiding place and bringing both demon hunters crashing down. Anna and Nikki fired their projectiles, putting the demon hunters to sleep.

Soon, the only aura from the rogue demon hunters came from below. Nikki and Anna regrouped just as John and Victoria joined them.

Seeing the unconscious demon hunters lying on the floor, John looked around, amazed at what he saw.

"Where is everybody?" Victoria asked.

"They're on the lower level," Samantha said from behind one of the computers.

John, Victoria, Nikki, and Anna approached her as

Izzy entered the mansion. "Where's Mom and Grace?" she asked as she ran up to join them.

Samantha pulled out the black device from her pocket and pressed the button again, re-setting the security feed of the compound.

Izzy looked in horror, watching her Mom and Grace fight for their lives inside the octagon cage. Lifeless demons lay at their feet, but now they were fighting five vampires with no adequate weapons to kill them, as a crowd of spectators watched with gleeful and sadistic looks on their faces.

Samantha changed the camera settings and pointed to the rogue demon hunters, who numbered fifteen.

"That's Sylvie," Sam said as she pointed out the purple-pinkish-haired woman. "Once Grace and Elizabeth finish the vampires, she will pull out the Arzkang demon, using the orb around her neck to control it."

"No more demons for them to fight?" Victoria asked.

Sam pressed a few buttons on the keyboard and showed the cells below. Three demon hunters guarded a solitary vampire. "Neil is the only one left," Sam said.

Samantha then typed in a command key and opened Neil's cell.

"What are you doing?" John exclaimed, not believing what he was seeing. The vampire unleashed his fury on the demon hunter who watched over him. The girls and their Guardians watched in horror as Neil fed off his captors.

"What needs to be done," Sam said calmly. "These demon hunters are beyond redemption, and you know it."

"Let's get in there," Izzy ordered her sisters as they scrambled toward the cellar entrance.

"Neil has fed off the demon hunters," Sam warned. "Their blood has now fed into his powers. If Sabine mopped the floor with you, you have no idea what Neil can do."

Izzy, Nikki, and Anna ran purposefully toward the cellar entrance, while John and Victoria looked at Sam.

"Death is a necessary evil," Sam said. "You Guardians better get that ingrained into your thick skulls."

CHAPTER XVII

Lake Tahoe, Nevada, USA; Feb 9, 8:35 p.m.

SEAN LOOKED AT HIS wife and Grace as they finally destroyed the last vampire locked inside with them. Both demon hunters were exhausted after fighting nonstop for the previous thirty minutes. Both fell to their knees, trying to catch their breath as they looked at each other and smiled.

"They're excellent," Daniel admired as he turned toward Sean. "I'm sure you're proud of them. I bet you want to go inside and help them out."

"That's not exactly in my job description," Sean replied.

Daniel looked surprised. "You are truly cold-blooded," Daniel said. "You know how many years my organization has been trying to get rid of Elizabeth Somiere."

"I guess since the moment she accepted her calling," Sean replied dryly as he saw Elizabeth give him a reassuring look with her green eyes.

"Almost," Daniel said. "It was her graduation day.

She stopped one of our clients from fully embracing his destiny and wiping out of the cursed town of St. Helena. That is when she caught our eyes. Pesky little blonde girl disrupting well-laid plans."

"And affecting your bottom line," Sean said as both demon hunters stood up and looked at the trap door, knowing exactly what would come next. The spectators were screaming at Sylvie, who was trying to calm the crowd down.

"Place your bets in the app," Roxy screamed at the crowd. "Who will walk out of the cage alive? The demon hunters or the Arzkang demon?"

Sean heard a loud *thump* coming from the trap door. The vibrations of its paws shook and rattled the black metal chains around the cage. The older Guardian noticed the orb around Sylvie's neck glow as she summoned the beast to emerge from its cozy cell. Sean took a deep breath, seeing the seven-foot, white-furred beast dwarf the tiny demon hunters locked inside with it. It extended its fingers, releasing its famous claws as it drew what seemed like a grin on its white snout.

The crowd furiously typed on their cell phones, while others were in awe of the beast as Roxy instructed them to double their bets. Sean looked at Sabine, who was close to Sylvie, with two demon hunters guarding her. Sylvie had not left anything to chance.

"The Glenix Orb," Daniel stated, seeing Sean's fixation on the magical object around Sylvie's neck. "It is indeed a priceless gift from me to Hela Corp." The man just smiled as he looked at the demon hunters locked inside with the demon. "My bonus will be considerable with my achievement today. You can thank me personally for your wife's demise. My prize awaits in Los Angeles." Saying this, the man stood up and picked up his coat.

"You're leaving?" Sean asked. "In your moment of triumph?"

"Of course," Daniel said, slipping on his coat and taking out black leather gloves from the pockets. "I see my investment has paid off in spades."

"That's too bad," Sean replied, looking at the two demon hunters guarding him.

"Why is that?" Daniel asked.

"You're going to miss how we're going to burn Hela Corp to the ground," Sean replied.

The Guardian strained against the chains that imprisoned him and extended his arms at full force, breaking the metal and sending shards flying. The Guardian turned the rings in his hands and grabbed the arms of the demon hunters watching over him. The small needles pierced their skin as both women collapsed on the stands.

The rogue demon hunters started running toward Sean just as the cellar door broke open. Nikki, Anna, and Izzy stood tall, looking at the overwhelming odds against them.

Daniel looked at Sean with fear in his eyes, seeing the older Guardian release his hidden power. "Don't worry," Sean said. "My girls don't kill humans. They're pure and will remain like that as long as they keep their vows."

"Kill them!" Daniel ordered Sylvie as he ran away from the stands.

Sylvie nodded and motioned for the Arzkang demon to attack. The white-furred monster roared as it extended its muscular arms and started running toward Elizabeth and Grace. Both demon hunters jumped out of the way, but the beast swung its large arms, connecting with a backhand fist, sending Grace and Elizabeth flying against the black metal cage.

Grace screamed as her body touched the obsidian-infused metal. For a moment, she felt one side of her body go numb as she rolled away. She looked up and saw that the Arzkang demon was upon Elizabeth.

"Mom!" Izzy screamed as she fought and powered through the rogue demon hunters who crowded her, Nikki, and Anna. The brown-haired demon hunter performed a spin-kick, striking two demon hunters in the face. She then moved forward and performed a handless cartwheel, firing projectiles from her gauntlets while upside down, taking down the two women who had rushed her. As Izzy came to her feet, three more demon hunters attacked her. The girl screamed as she rushed her opponents head-on.

Nikki fired one projectile from her gauntlet, striking down one demon hunter while three more surrounded her. She tried firing a second one, but one of the rogue demon hunters had already closed in on the distance. The red-headed demon hunter took on the challengers and struck hard with her gauntlet-covered fists. The older dark-haired woman grunted in pain as she tried to kick the red-headed demon hunter, but the teenager was already moving, striking with her gauntlet across the face. Nikki moved on to the next demon hunter, and she fired a projectile at her first and stunned opponent. The demon hunter spun, performing a butterfly kick, pushing the demon hunters away, providing the space she needed to fire projectiles at her foes.

Anna pushed the taller and older women surrounding her, firing her projectiles and taking down two more demon hunters. A blonde woman grabbed her by the shoulder and tried to punch her in the face, but Anna ducked and rolled to the side, striking the taller woman's leg with her metal gauntlets. The woman screamed in pain, collapsing on her knees as Anna rolled to the side and spun, extending her leg and connecting with the blonde woman's face.

Grace grimaced in pain as she saw her sisters in action. She stood up and shook off the numbness in her left side. She then sprang into action, running as fast as she could and jumping on top of the Arzkang demon. She tried to wrap her arms around its large throat while Elizabeth kicked at the monster's knees— it was like hitting steel. The demon screamed, feeling a nuisance at its feet as it kicked hard. Its large paw found its mark, connecting with Elizabeth's chest. Blood spurted from the blonde demon hunter's mouth as she flew against the metal cage.

"No!" Grace screamed. The monster grabbed Grace's arms and pulled her away from him. The demon hunter had never experienced such power as the beast twirled and flung her back against the metal cage. Her back collided hard against the metal, causing her to scream in pain.

She looked at the stands and saw the human spectators running away. Something was happening. Then she saw Neil, the vampire, jump into the spectator stands and start feeding on the humans. His vampire visage was utterly unleashed as his red eyes glared and looked toward Sylvie. Demon hunters were trying to block his way, but he was laser-focused, tearing the rogue demon hunters apart.

"Grace!" Anna called out.

Grace turned toward her younger sister, who had reached the metal door. "Careful!" Grace warned. "The entire cage is obsidian-infused!"

Anna nodded, pulling her short sword from her back and bringing it across the padlock. Orange and red sparks flew everywhere as the padlock broke. Two rogue demon hunters reached Anna, but the petite demon hunter crouched and struck both in the lower abdomen. She rolled out of between them and fired two of her projectiles, striking both women and dropping them.

Grace saw the door open, but the Arzkang demon was almost upon Elizabeth again. Elizabeth jumped out of the way as the demon punched and slashed with its claws. The claws created amber sparks as they collided with the metal cage.

"Grace!" Elizabeth ordered as she dodged a massive punch from the beast. The fist collided hard with the cage, rattling the entire structure. "Get out of here!"

"I won't leave my Guardian behind," Grace replied, running toward the beast. The raven-haired demon hunter jumped and kicked the beast right on the back. The girl bounced off and rolled to face the white-furred demon, who looked at her with menace in its eyes. It growled as it tried to claw at her, but Grace performed a backflip, evading the beast.

As the Arzkang demon focused on Grace, Elizabeth

had space to move toward the exit. She saw Anna by the door, fending off two rogue demon hunters. "We need weapons in here!"

Anna nodded and called out to her sisters with her mind. *Need weapons now!*

Nikki and Izzy pushed away the demon hunters who surrounded them. "Let's do this," Izzy said, grabbing Nikki's hands and swinging her sister to the side. The red-headed demon hunter extended her legs, butterfly-kicking, connecting with two women and pushing them back. She then pulled on her sister as the brown-haired demon hunter repeated the same move. Both demon hunters moved closer to the cage. Halfway toward the octagon, Izzy and Nikki pulled out one of their battle axes and threw them to Anna.

Instinctively, Anna grabbed both axes mid-air and stepped inside the cage with them, throwing one to Elizabeth. "These will be useless against that beast," Anna said, watching Grace dodge repeatedly, keeping the Arzkang demon at bay. "We've got something that can weaken it, but we must get it out of the cage."

Elizabeth nodded at the younger demon hunter. "Follow my lead." Elizabeth darted to the right while pointing at Anna to head to the left. The blonde demon hunter slid on the octagon and struck at the beast's right Achilles tendon with her axe. The blade bounced off as if it hit solid stone.

The Arzkang demon turned toward the blonde Guardian, only to feel a nip on his left side. The demon looked down and saw tiny Anna throw her axe toward Grace. The beast stomped hard, but the dark-haired demon hunter was too fast and rolled out of the way.

Grace grabbed Anna's axe and rolled toward the side, looking at the exit. *The way is clear!* Grace screamed with her mind, turning toward Elizabeth.

Elizabeth nodded and signaled Anna to make her way toward the exit.

The petite demon hunter obliged and ran just in time to see a dark-skinned demon hunter try to seal the cage door. Anna fired a projectile, and Roxy moved out of the way just in time. But Anna was already airborne. She jumped and double-kicked the door with her tennis shoes, sending the door flying back and striking Roxy in the face, causing her to scream in pain.

Grace helped Anna as Elizabeth reached them with the Arzkang demon on their tail. They exited the cage as quickly as possible, stepping over Roxy, who was nursing her battered face.

Sabine looked bored at the commotion, seeing the humans and demons scatter like cockroaches. The two demon hunters who had been watching over her had scattered to fight Izzy, Nikki, and Grace, or Neil, who was delighting in tasting demon hunter blood. Sean was close behind, fighting the demon hunters who'd tried to control him. The ancient female vampire focused her attention on Sylvie, who looked in disbelief as she saw her empire crumbling down. "You didn't truly expect all of this to turn in your favor, did you?" Sabine asked.

Sylvie glared at Sabine as the orb around her neck glowed with an intense blue light. "You underestimate my power," the purple-pinkish-haired demon hunter said.

Sabine admired the Glenix orb and then looked at the rogue demon hunter. "That is the thing that you lack," the vampire said. She quickly grabbed the orb with her bare hand and yanked it, bringing Sylvie forward.

Sylvie tried to pull away, but Sabine's features morphed into her vampiric demon form. The vampire fired a right-hand punch that struck the demon hunter squarely in the chest, sending her flying back. The force shattered the chain around her neck, leaving Sabine with the orb in her hand.

Every demon hunter stopped fighting, looking at Sylvie on the ground, gasping for air while looking at the vampire who held the Glenix orb in her hand. The Arzkang demon stopped in its tracks as if it had just woken from a long sleep.

Sabine looked at the demon and pointed the Glenix Sphere at the monster. "You're free," the vampire said. The blue glow from the sphere disappeared as if the mystical energy from the object had escaped. Sabine smiled at the Arzkang demon. "Do your worst," she said.

The beast growled, extending its claws and grabbing the obsidian-infused metal cage. The steel bars and chains crumbled like paper in response to the monster's power. The Arzkang demon brought down its arms, tearing the cage apart with bits still hanging from its large paws. The beast roared as it flung its arms, releasing the metal from its hands and sending deadly projectiles toward all the demon hunters.

Elizabeth looked in horror and turned toward her demon hunters. "Get down!" she ordered, throwing herself on the floor. Anna and Grace followed their Guardian's instructions as the deadly metal projectiles flew over their heads.

Izzy and Nikki threw themselves aside, yet the demon hunters they fought weren't quick enough. The metal projectiles spiked their bodies, becoming embedded in their flesh and projecting them against the far wall.

Nikki shut her eyes as she saw the metal projectiles pierce the older demon hunters as if their bodies were made of butter.

Izzy looked in horror at the five lifeless demon hunters skewered and nailed to the concrete wall on the opposite side of the cellar. She looked at the door and saw John and Victoria enter with looks of horror on their faces.

"Stay back!" Izzy ordered her Guardians.

John pushed Victoria to the side and hid behind the door frame. "Did that thing kill five demon hunters in one move?" Victoria asked.

John nodded as he released the safety of his grenade launcher. He stepped through the cellar entrance and fired a single canister at the Arzkang demon. The beast smacked the canister away, sending it to the side.

"Crap," John said as he hid back alongside Victoria.

"Did you hit it?" Victoria asked.

"In a way," John replied. "It swatted the canister as if it were a fly."

Sean looked at the scene and saw the Arzkang demon focus on the human Guardians. He jumped from his location and rounded the damaged cage, picking up discarded black metal chains. He wrapped them around his fists and ran toward the demon, striking with all his might at its lower back. His fists bounced back as he winced, feeling the pain in his hands.

The Arzkang demon now focused on him with a soft growl. It roared at the Guadian and thrust its right hand with its exposed claws. Sean grabbed the large paw and stopped the blow before the claws could pierce his flesh, stopping them a mere inch from his face. His arms strained, holding the beast in place. The older Guardian looked at Elizabeth, Anna, and Grace, who were still on the floor. "Run!" he ordered. "I can't hold it for much longer!"

The demon hunters stood up and regrouped alongside Izzy and Nikki. "John!" Izzy screamed, turning toward her Guardian. "Shoot it now!"

John stepped out one more time and fired a round at the beast. The Arzkang demon grabbed Sean with its other paw as if second nature. The Guardian grunted in pain as the demon squeezed and flung Sean toward the incoming projectile. The projectile exploded into a cloud of smoke as soon as it hit Sean on the chest while he was in the air. The older Guardian crumpled to the ground and coughed as he inhaled the toxic fumes.

"Sean!" Elizabeth screamed, running toward her husband. Izzy followed suit, accompanying her mother.

The unstoppable Arzkang demon roared a war cry while mother and daughter knelt beside Sean while Nikki, Grace, and Anna ran cover for them.

Grace looked at the giant white-furred demon and tried to think of a plan. Her mind drew a blank, seeing the colossal force behind the demon. The bitter taste of fear started to creep in, piercing her soul.

"Hey!" Grace heard Neil scream at her. The demon hunter looked at the vampire, who now had Sylvie in his hands and Sabine standing at his side. Both ancient vampires pierced her with their bloodshot eyes. "Are you going to cower in fear? Was your calling a mistake? Are you going to be the scared little girl you've always been?"

Grace stood up and looked at Anna, whose face was pale, seeing the sheer power of the monster they were facing.

"What are you going to do, little girl?" Neil asked.

Grace took a deep breath as she firmly grasped her battle axe. "Anna!" Grace ordered. "Get the grenade launcher from John!"

The sixteen-year-old girl took a deep breath and started running toward her Guardians.

Nikki looked at her sister. She could feel the raw emotion trying to squash the fear inside her. "Let's take this beast down!" Grace ordered her sister.

Nikki nodded. The red-headed demon hunter then turned toward the ancient vampires, noting a slight smile curl on Neil's lips before dragging Sylvie away. She looked at Izzy, who was kneeling next to her mother while Sean groaned in pain. "Is he okay?" Nikki asked.

"I'm fine," Sean answered, sitting up and gasping for breath.

Izzy nodded at her sister, standing up and grabbing her battle axe. "Just got the air knocked out of him."

John looked at Anna, who rushed at him as she grabbed the grenade launchers from his hands. "We're going to need this," she said.

"Do what you have to do, little sister," Victoria said, standing beside John. Both Guardians saw the sixteen-year-old run back to her sisters while they took in the devastation. Most humans had escaped, but some were hidden behind the seats surrounding the crumbled octagon cage. The girls had neutralized several rogue demon hunters, but others hung lifelessly against the concrete wall where the Arzkang had impaled them. Others lay dead with their blood drained by Neil. The ancient vampires dragged Sylvie back down to the lower-level cells while looking back at the four demon hunters who stood together as they confronted their massive foe.

"You have to fight this thing outside!" John yelled at his demon hunters.

Grace looked at her sisters. "It will be on its turf," she stated.

"We fight better on the outside," Nikki said, looking at Anna and Izzy.

"Let's do it," Izzy said.

Anna turned toward her Guardians. "Get out of the way!" the petite demon hunter ordered. "Large beast incoming."

Nikki and Izzy stepped up front and fired their little projectiles at the beast, aiming for its eyes. The tiny wooden arrows bounced off its red eyeballs as if they were dust. The beast growled at the girls for their impertinence.

Anna fired a canister from the grenade launcher, aiming at the head. The beast smacked it to the side. The Arzkang roared at the girls as it extended its black claws.

"That got its attention," Grace said. "Let's get it out of here."

Anna started running toward the exit, followed by Grace, Izzy, and Nikki. The towering beast roared one last time, moving with breakneck speed after them.

John covered Victoria with his body, only feeling the white-furred beast run past them and stomp up the concrete stairs to the main floor.

Elizabeth helped Sean stand up, seeing the Arzkang demon storm after her demon hunters. "Are you sure you're okay?" she asked her husband.

"I'm fine," Sean said, turning his attention to John and Victoria. He then looked directly into his wife's green eyes. "Go help the girls. They may need you up there. Victoria, John, and I will clean up here."

Elizabeth looked around and saw several dead rogue demon hunters while others slept peacefully. She then saw Roxy sitting next to the collapsed metal cage, nursing her broken face. "Have Roxy give you the names of the ones who didn't make it," Elizabeth instructed. "We have to take care of their families as protocol. And get the ones who are still alive outside."

"We're on it," Sean said while signaling John and Victoria to start dragging the unconscious women out of the facilities.

Elizabeth started to make her way out and then turned toward her husband. "You made a deal with Sabine, didn't you?" she asked.

Sean nodded. "It was the only way to get in and keep our girls safe."

"Your soul is stained enough, Sean," Elizabeth said. "You can't keep doing this."

"I'm a Guardian," Sean said. "You know it's what I do, whether you agree with it or not."

Elizabeth nodded and started running toward the exit after the Arzkang demon.

Sean saw Victoria and John start moving the unconscious demon hunters near the entrance while he walked toward Roxy. His hands still had the black obsidian chains wrapped around them. The dark-skinned demon hunter looked at Sean, not wanting to fight him.

The older Guardian crouched down and looked directly into her dark eyes. He slowly wrapped the black chains around her wrists without her putting up any resistance. "Give me the names of your fallen sisters," Sean ordered. "We'll notify the families."

"Most of them left no one behind," Roxy said. "It made it easier to recruit them."

Sean nodded as he helped Roxy to her feet. "There is always somebody," Sean said. "Despite what they did, we'll preserve their legacy."

Both walked toward Victoria and John, who were now sweating, getting the unconscious bodies ready to be moved. "What will happen to them?" Roxy asked, focusing her attention on girls who still drew breath.

"They'll be offered a choice once again," Victoria replied.

"But Hela Corp is done," John said as he pulled out his phone and started dialing. "Hey," the younger Guardian greeted. "We have about two dozen for transport. What's your ETA?" There was a slight pause at the other end of the line. "We'll meet you outside."

"What about Sylvie?" Roxy asked Sean.

Sean looked down at the cellar door where Sabine and Neil had taken Sylvie. "Get the demon hunters ready for transport," Sean ordered John and Victoria as he helped Roxy sit on the ground. The older Guardian then started making his way to the mansion's lower level.

CHAPTER XVIII

Lake Tahoe, Nevada, USA; Feb 9. 9:00 p.m.

ANNA EMERGED FROM THE mansion, darting fast to the right. She could feel the stomping of the Arzkang demon behind her and her sisters. Izzy and Grace darted left while Nikki continued moving forward, being the main bait. "Shoot it!" Nikki ordered as the white demon emerged, stomping after the red-headed demon hunter.

Anna fired one canister, but the beast ducked out of the way as the projectile flew over its head. Izzy watched in horror as the grenade flew toward her and Grace. With a flick of her arm, she smacked the projectile with her metal gauntlet, sending it to the side. The grenade exploded, releasing a cloud of black smoke.

Nikki turned back, seeing the demon right behind her. She darted left, but the demon anticipated her move and slammed its fist into her stomach. In awe of the beast's power, Nikki gasped for air as she was flung away and her body smashed against a pine tree. The red-headed hunter felt a coppery taste in her mouth as she grunted in pain. "That hurt," Nikki whispered as she collapsed on the snow-covered ground.

"Nikki!" Izzy screamed, running toward the demon. She jumped up just as the beast turned its ugly head, and its red eyes made contact with her. Izzy smashed her metal gauntlet at its face. The brown-haired demon hunter felt pain in her wrist and forearm, but the Arzkang demon did not flinch.

The monster roared and coiled down at supernatural speed, springing back up and connecting with a powerful uppercut that struck Izzy below her jaw. A white flash of pain clouded Izzy's vision as her body arched back, feeling a metallic sensation inside her mouth. The white-furred demon then double-fisted Izzy in the stomach while she was still in the air. The demon hunter grunted in pain as blood spurted from her mouth and her body crashed hard against the snow-covered ground.

The Arzkang demon lifted its foot, ready to stomp on the demon hunter, when it heard the grenade launcher fire again. The beast smacked the projectile out of the air and turned its attention to the remaining demon hunters.

Anna and Grace ran toward the monster on each side with their unsheathed blades, ready to attack. The beast moved to the side as Anna's sword swung and missed. Grace's axe bounced off its body like it just hit a metal object. The beast roared, and with a swift motion, he backhanded both demon hunters across the face. Anna and Grace screamed in pain as they were flung back.

Izzy coughed out blood, staining the white snow to her side. She looked in horror as the Arzkang demon returned its focus to her. It unleashed its giant claws and was about to skewer her when a soft growl caught its attention. Aidan rushed the seven-foot monster and climbed at its back, biting and scratching. That gave Izzy enough time to roll out of the way. "Aidan!" Izzy ordered as she cleaned the blood from her mouth. "Get away from it!"

Unsure of causing damage, Aidan ran up the demon and jumped off its head, landing next to Izzy. The demon hunter turned toward Nikki, who was getting up from the walloping. A strain of blood oozed from the side of her temple and mouth. Anna and Grace were also recovering as they surrounded the beast.

"Suggestions?" Izzy asked her sisters as she measured the formidable monster.

"How many rounds left, Anna?" Grace asked.

"Two more," Anna replied.

"He's too focused," Grace replied. "He can sense the grenade coming every time you shoot at it."

The Arzkang demon attacked the demon hunters, putting all the girls on the defensive. It clawed at Grace and fired a powerful kick at Izzy. Both demon hunters barely dodged.

The beast unleashed a powerful punch aimed at Anna, but she blocked it with her short sword. It struck again, but the petite demon hunter smacked the fist away with her blade. The monster then grabbed snow from the ground and threw it at Anna's eyes. The young demon hunter did not see it coming, as the icy substance clouded her vision. She screamed in pain as the snow stung her eyes.

The Arzkang demon took advantage and extended its claws, ready to strike. Nikki sprang into action, diving and tackling Anna out of the way. The demon's claws lacerated Nikki's back, causing her to scream in pain as she and Anna rolled out of the way.

Grace and Izzy looked in horror at the red stain on Nikki's jacket. "I'm fine," Nikki gasped in pain, trying to reassure her sisters. "It's just a flesh wound."

Anna cleared her eyes and gasped at Nikki's injured back. Her fear immediately turned to rage as she grabbed the grenade launcher and marched toward the beast, aiming at the monster's head. "You die tonight!" She screamed. The demon hunter fired a round at the head, but the beast flicked it away with its paw.

The Arzkang demon moved fast and thrust its claws toward Anna. The demon hunter tried to dodge and move out of the way, but the beast was too fast, and it skewered the demon hunter right on her left clavicle. Anna screamed in agony as the grenade launcher hung from her right hand as the beast lifted the demon hunter off the ground.

"Anna!" Izzy screamed, running toward the demon. She rapidly climbed on its back and smashed both her metal gauntlets against the demon's ears. The beast roared in agony for the first time as it tried to shake the demon hunter from its back.

Both Nikki and Grace screamed at Anna as if their mind focused on a singular thought. "Shoot it now!"

Anna grunted in pain, took a deep breath, lifted the grenade launcher with her right arm, and aimed it at the demon's face, firing the final round. Izzy jumped away from the demon's back as the grenade exploded, engulfing the monster and petite demon hunter in a cloud of smoke.

The Arzkang demon took a deep breath and inhaled the toxic smoke as it fell to one knee. Anna grabbed the claws of the beast that had pierced the left side of her upper chest. She pulled them out, feeling an ounce of weakness from the demon. "Kill it!" Anna screamed as she collapsed on the ground.

Izzy and Grace twirled their axes and struck the demon across the back. The Arzkang arched its back in pain as black blood spurted out. Nikki stood up and swiped her battle axe right across the demon's throat. The blade pierced right through the monster's flesh, causing black blood to gush forth from the jagged gash. Both Izzy and Grace then pulled their axes out and brought them down together against the demon's skull. The head exploded like a melon as the demon fell lifelessly on the ground.

Nikki collapsed on the ground next to Anna, wincing in pain, trying not to think about her lacerated back. She put her hand over Anna's collarbone wound as Izzy and Grace reached them while Aidan stood next to them and nibbled on the dead Arzkang.

"It's just a flesh wound," Nikki whispered to Anna, applying pressure to the demon hunter's shoulder.

"I see that," Anna said, looking at the sky. She closed her eyes, trying to block the pain.

Elizabeth ran up to her demon hunters and knelt right next to them. She looked at Grace and Izzy, who appeared battered but okay. She inspected Nikki's wounds and saw the large wound that the Arzkang had left on her back. The blonde demon hunter removed her jacket and applied pressure to Nikki's wound while Nikki helped Anna.

"You did it," Nikki whispered to her little sister. "You got it."

"Glad I could help," Anna whispered back. "I can now retire in peace,"

Grace and Izzy looked at each other, relieved to see their sisters okay. The sisters physically embraced as apologies flowed between them with their minds. No words were spoken. It was just raw emotion.

Grace was about to say something when she spotted two headlights of a large vehicle approaching. Both Izzy and Grace stood up and got ready, noticing it was a large white bus with black polarized windows, which came to a stop ten feet away from them.

The engine shut off, and the vehicle's door opened. A raven-haired, blue-eyed woman in her mid-thirties stepped out. She wore a black leather jacket, red turtleneck blouse, dress pants, and block heel booties. "Did we miss anything?" she asked.

"Aunt Clara!" Izzy exclaimed, recognizing the woman and running toward her.

"My favorite niece," the woman said as she embraced the girl.

"For now," Elizabeth whispered as she looked at her younger sister. "Late as usual."

"Needed to pick up reinforcements," Clara said as she motioned for the passengers inside the bust to step out.

A forty-year-old man with glasses and gray hair stepped out of the bus. He wore business casual pants and an oversized, puffy black winter jacket.

"Alex," Elizabeth acknowledged the Guardian and her sister's husband. "I'm glad you could make it."

"When Sean calls out help for you, Liz, you know I can't say no," the Guardian replied, acknowledging the younger demon hunters.

Two women stepped out of the bus. The first one seemed to be in her early thirties, with long, curly brownish-blonde hair, sparkling green eyes, and a soft smile. "You and your girls couldn't get into trouble in a warmer climate, Liz?" the woman said. She blew into her hands, trying to keep warm. Her denim jacket, black and red plaid shirt, black blouse, black jeans, and black knee-high boots were not helping with the cold.

"You're such a crybaby, Danny," the woman behind her said in a British accent. "As if there is no snow in Missouri."

"For the last time, Xiomy. I was in Florida when Clara and Alex called," Danny responded, looking at her demon hunter friend. Xiomy's style was similar to Danny's. The only significant difference was her shoulder-length purple hair. In her mid-thirties, Xiomy wore a leather jacket identical to Clara's, a floral blouse, black jeans, and ankle booties.

Nikki grimaced, bravely smiling. "The original Delta squad reunited," she noted. "It would have been cool if you had shown up fifteen minutes earlier."

"Another crybaby," Xiomy said as she approached Nikki and inspected her wounds. With her dark brown eyes, she could see the lacerations slowly sealing up. "You did good, Nicole."

Danny stepped forward and looked at the defeated

demon with the exploded head. "Wow," the blonde demon hunter marveled. "You took out an Arzkang demon. Remember that time in Kansas, Clara?"

"Don't remind me," Clara said as she dropped beside Anna and pulled out a medical kit. She motioned Nikki to move and started patching up the younger demon hunter. "Where's your medic?"

"Inside the mansion," Izzy replied. "Getting the other demon hunters ready for extraction."

"How many are unconscious outside the compound?" Alex asked.

Nikki looked at Izzy for confirmation. "With all the commotion, I kind of lost count," the red-headed demon hunter said.

"I'll count them," Danny said, starting to walk in the cold. "We might as well brace the cold." She then turned toward Xiomy. "Are you coming, Your Royal Highness?"

"Wouldn't want to leave you alone," Xiomy replied, following her sister.

"Some things never change," Elizabeth murmured.

Grace looked at Izzy and spoke with her mind. *Neil is still in the mansion.*

Izzy nodded and looked toward her mother. "We're going back into the mansion to help Dad," Izzy said.

"What about Leah?" Elizabeth asked. "You're going to have Xiomy and Danny pick her up?"

Izzy turned toward Nikki and then toward Grace. "This is more important," Izzy replied.

Nikki strained as she got back up. "You two ain't going without me," Nikki said.

"Let's finish this," Grace said.

"Good luck, girls," Anna said while Clara continued to patch her wound. "Grace. I hope you get the answers you seek."

Grace nodded as she turned her attention toward Elizabeth. "Are you coming?"

Elizabeth looked the raven-haired demon hunter straight in the eyes. "I've got to stay with Anna," she replied. "Be careful. Neil and Sabine are not vampires you want to face in your current conditions."

"We're not fighting," Grace said as she walked toward the mansion, followed by her sisters. "We're just going to talk."

Lake Tahoe, Nevada, USA; Feb 9, 9:05 p.m.

SEAN SLOWLY MADE HIS way down the stairwell. When he got to the bottom, he saw three dead demon hunters lying on the floor. Their faces were pale, and their lifeless eyes stared into nothingness. Two small orifices could be seen on the sides of their necks.

At the end of the hall, Sabine and Neil waited while Sylvie knelt in front of them. "I'm glad you could join us," Sabine said. "Do you think your girls can take on the Arzkang alone?"

"They will," Sean said. "It is a great training exercise for what is to come."

"You read the Tome," Neil noted. "That's perfect. All the vampires and demons your girls have faced pale in comparison to what they will face two years from now."

"They need the practice," Sean said as he looked at Sylvie.

"You're having second thoughts about our arrangement?" Sabine asked.

"Not really," Sean replied. "Death is a necessary evil." Neil pulled on Sylvie's purple-pinkish hair as the vampire looked into her eyes. "Your stupid antics created a huge roadblock in our plans," the vampire said. "How many demon hunters did you serve Anderson on a silver platter?"

Sylvie remained silent. Sabine smiled at the rogue demon hunter's bravado. The elder vampire peered into her mind and extracted the number. "Fifty-seven," Sabine marveled. "And their families, too." She then turned toward Sean. "As well as their Guardians. Your records will confirm that.

"You betrayed the code," Neil said, addressing the demon hunter. "Do you have any last words to justify your traitorous actions?"

"The Guardians betrayed us," Sylvie spat out. "With this false sense of hope by cutting down our freedoms. We can rule the world, yet you make us waste our time on this earth, fighting an endless battle defending these faceless innocents."

"I'm sorry that is how you see the world," Sean said. "The weight of responsibility matches the strength of power you must carry. That's the price we all must pay."

"The power is wasted on you if you don't wield it with purpose," Neil said.

"We wield it for our purpose!" Sylvie spat out. "We answer to ourselves and no one else."

"I would agree with you," Sabine said, to Neil's surprise. "But you crossed the line when you went after demon hunters who remained faithful to their calling.

You betrayed and caused the death of innocent girls and their Guardians who had a sense of purpose in this world. You sold your power for a bowl of lentils. The price of power is responsibility, and you squandered it."

"That's why we strip you of your power today," Neil said. He knelt and sank his sharp fangs into Sylvie's neck. Sylvie gasped as the vampire sucked her life-giving force. Slowly, her strength faded until her eyes stared into nothingness. Neil stood up and dropped Sylvie's lifeless body on the ground while he wiped the blood from his lips. He could feel the strength in his vampire body enhanced by the demon hunter blood he had just ingested.

"This concludes our arrangement," Sabine said to Sean.

"One last thing," Sean stated, blocking the only exit.

"Really?" Neil asked. "I just drank from half a dozen demon hunters. Do you think your feeble former demon strength can stop both of us?"

"You'd be surprised by what I'm capable of," Sean said with a stone-cold look.

Neil felt doubt creep into his dead heart, seeing the Guardian blocking the door.

"I know you're trying to help," Sean said. "Stop with the riddles. We're fighting the same battle. You two alone can't deal with what's coming. We have the numbers and the will. Share with us what you know."

"It's in the Tome," Sabine replied.

"It is not in the Tome!" Sean snapped.

"Then you're reading it wrong," Neil stated. "All the answers you need are there."

"Sean," Sabine called out, returning her facial

features to human form. "Knowledge also comes with a price. You, Elizabeth, and your demon hunters must go through the trials. If you don't, the price Xianquan and Anhe paid will be for nothing."

Neil's face morphed back to his human form as he adjusted his suit. "Read it again!" the ancient vampire ordered. "Read it until you figure out what will come to pass."

The trio heard footsteps coming down. Sean looked behind him and saw Izzy, Grace, and Nikki come running down. They looked horrified, seeing the dead demon hunters lying on the floor of the cell.

"Your Guardian was too late," Sabine said with a smile, pointing at Sylvie's dead body as she saw the look of dread in the teenager's eyes. "Besides, he wouldn't have been a match if he made it in time."

Neil stared directly into Grace's dark eyes. "You prevailed against the Arzkang demon. I congratulate you."

Grace stepped toward the vampire, staring upward while Nikki and Izzy stood at her side. Neil towered over all three demon hunters as he looked down upon them. The elder vampire saw something change in Grace. Something inside was different.

"Tell me why," Grace whispered.

Neil looked down at Grace. For a fraction of a second, Nikki noticed a slight glimmer of what could be described as a paternal look in Neil's eyes. But it was soon gone. "Your mother and father believed that death was a necessary evil," the vampire said.

"Sabine already said that," Grace challenged. "I want a direct answer from you. Why?"

"You're smart, Grace," Neil said. "You never leave anything to chance, just like your mom and dad. They would be proud of you."

Time seemed to stop at that moment as Grace felt a surge of energy within her body. She felt Izzy and Nikki behind her, feeding her energy to her body like a new ability within her had been unleashed. Grace swung her right fist, aiming at Neil's face. The lightning-fast blow struck the vampire hard and sent him flying to the side. Neil's body cracked the concrete wall behind him as he collapsed against the floor in a heap.

Neil rubbed his face and looked at Grace, who glared at him. Nikki saw the vampire's bewilderment as a small smile curled on his lips. The red-headed demon hunter caught a glimpse of pride in his eyes before it disappeared.

Sabine smiled at what she had just witnessed. She gave Neil a knowing look as he stood up. "I'm glad I killed these demon hunters before you did that," the male vampire said, cleaning up his suit. "You could've killed me with that punch."

Grace moved fast and fired another punch, but Neil grabbed her little fist this time and stopped the blow with his hand. He slightly crushed Grace's hand, causing her to wince in pain, but her eyes were ever defiant. "Never repeat the same attack twice in a row," Neil stated with a serious look. With supernatural reflexes, he grabbed Grace's shoulders and shoved her with force to the opposite side of the wall.

Grace's body cracked the wall behind her as she gasped in pain. Izzy and Nikki were about to attack when Sabine stepped in and stopped them. "This is not your fight," the female vampire said.

"The hell it isn't," Izzy responded.

"You fight one, you fight us three," Nikki stated.

"It's okay, Sabine," Neil said as he looked at Sean. "I think the lesson is over for now." The vampire adjusted his suit and made his way out of the cellar.

Sabine turned toward Grace, who stood up and had a defiant look in her eyes. "Keep training," the female vampire said. She then started walking out before looking back at Sean. "This concludes our business arrangement."

Sean nodded and signaled the demon hunters to stand down. Izzy looked surprised at Sabine's last words. "Dad? What did she mean?"

Sean walked over toward Grace and looked at his demon hunter. "I have a lead," he said to her.

Grace looked into his dark eyes and hugged him. Sean patted the young girl on the back as he turned toward Nikki and Izzy. "Take note of the demon hunters here," he ordered. "Leave their bodies."

"What are we going to do with his place?" Nikki asked.

*

TWENTY MINUTES LATER, NIKKI, Izzy, Grace, and Anna looked at the mansion, seeing it ablaze with all the fallen sisters inside. Aidan stood by them as a protective guardian. "I guess that answers my question," Nikki said.

Anna sighed, looking at the girls. "You sure know how to make your sister feel welcome."

"We try our best," Izzy replied, looking at her

younger sister. "Thanks for giving us a hand."

"That's what sisters are for," Anna said, looking at Grace. "We watch each other's backs."

"Yeah," Grace said, looking at Izzy and Nikki. "That's what family is for."

"Are you still retiring after this?" Nikki asked Anna. "Just two more years."

"I spoke to my sister," Anna said. "I will help the new girl take over in Mexico and be there as a consulting force. But my leadership time is done."

"From what we saw, you held your own in your town," Izzy said. "But if that's how you feel, we're behind your decision."

Behind the demon hunters, Sean and Elizabeth silently looked at the fire that consumed the mansion. "Did you get all the names?" Sean asked his wife.

"Roxy provided them," Elizabeth said. "We'll cross reference them to our records and inform their next of kin."

Clara approached the couple, with Danny and Xiomy behind her, as did Victoria and John. "We rounded the perimeter and put all the demon hunters inside the bus," Clara informed. "We will transport them back to Ireland using our portal in California."

"Good," Elizabeth said. "How is Leah?"

Clara shook her head. "We didn't find her."

"What?" Elizabeth asked. "What do you mean you didn't find her?"

Izzy walked toward the group with Anna, Nikki, and Grace behind her. "I fought her a hundred yards from here. I used the dart that John had prepped. She's supposed to be there."

"We checked twice," John stated. "No sign of her."

"Although we did see some tire marks in the area," Danny said.

"A guest of Sylvie might have picked her up?" Xiomy suggested.

Elizabeth looked at Izzy and then at Sean with a defeated look. "Damn!" the blonde Guardian exclaimed.

"If she's still out there, she will look for us," Sean said to Elizabeth. "And we'll be ready.

"We lost her again," Elizabeth whispered.

"And we'll find her," Sean reassured his wife. He then turned his attention to Izzy. "We'll find her."

The group stayed silent for a moment, contemplating their next steps. Sean looked at John and Victoria. "I'll take your rental," Sean told his younger counterpart. "We'll head back to St. Helena with the girls. You take Anna and Victoria and ride with the rest of the demon hunters to handle the loose ends."

"Got it," John replied.

Sean turned toward the young demon hunters. "Say goodbye, girls," the older Guardian ordered. "We ride in five minutes."

The demon hunters nodded as they all hugged Anna. "I need to make a trip to Mexico," Grace said. "Not fair that these two went and I didn't."

"Ring me up," Anna replied. "Maybe you can handle the spice better than your sisters."

Grace smiled, looking at Izzy and Nikki, who both had a sheepish look on their face. "I'm sure I will."

Izzy, Grace, and Nikki then started walking toward the black SUV, followed by Elizabeth.

Sean looked at Anna walking with Victoria toward

the bus. He remained with John, Clara, Danny, and Xiomy. "Thanks for making this trip," Sean said. "We needed the extra hands on this one."

"Don't mention it," Clara said. "We were due for a Delta Squad reunion."

"Clara said something about the end of the world coming in two years' time," Xiomy said. "Worse than New York?"

"That's what it looks like," Sean said.

"I have two kids, Sean," Danny said. "We did our time for this world."

"I know," Sean said. "But if we fail, there will be no world for you to live in after."

Danny took a deep breath, thinking about what Sean had said. "Listen," Sean said. "You won't be on the front lines, but we need your expertise, especially if this happens on multiple fronts."

Danny and Xiomy looked at each other, nodding. "What do you need from us?" Xiomy asked.

"Right now," Sean started. "I need you to help Clara with this batch of demon hunters. If anyone can talk sense into them, it is the original Delta squad. Get them ready to fight on our side. Guide the younger girls."

"That's a tall order," Danny said, "especially if they're not open to changing their ways."

"Help them," Sean pleaded.

Xiomy understood what Sean was saying. "We'll do our best."

"That's all I ask," Sean said. "Again, thank you."

Clara and the demon hunters walked away toward the bus, leaving John and Sean alone.

"I got confirmation on who was behind the issues

in Mexico," Sean said.

"You're sure?" John asked.

"Confirmed," Sean replied. "Are you ready to do this? There's no turning back after this."

John nodded. "There hasn't been a return point since Angie died."

"She's gone, John," Sean said. "This won't bring her back."

"I know," John said, turning his attention to the demon hunters in the SUV. "It's not only because of Angie. I'll do it because no other demon hunter should suffer the same fate as she did."

Sean nodded. "I'll explain your absence to the girls these next two weeks. Take your time."

"Will do," John replied, shaking Sean's hand. "It's our job as Guardians. Our responsibility."

The young Guardian walked away toward the bus while Sean looked on.

EPILOGUE

St. Helena, California, USA: Feb 26, 3:00 p.m.

IZZY LOOKED AT THE stopwatch in her hand as the seconds ticked away. She then looked up, seeing Nikki run full speed around the school track in her black and white shirt and pants, leaving all the student joggers trailing behind. "Easy," Izzy whispered to herself.

Nikki crossed the finish line right in front of her sister. "Time?" the red-headed girl called out loud.

"Three seconds better," Izzy replied. "Best one yet."

"Let me go for another lap," Nikki replied.

"Can you take it easy?" Izzy asked. "The others are starting to stare."

"They're aware of our talents," Nikki replied. "This is normal for them."

"Not when you beat the fastest guy here by ten seconds," Izzy replied. "Tone it down. We have to lay low, remember?"

Nikki scoffed as she picked up her varsity school jacket. Izzy returned to the stands where Grace, Jaime,

Bryan, and her boyfriend Stephen were studying. "Where were we?" the girl asked, with Nikki soon joining her.

"Trig," Stephen replied, handing her a set of papers.

Looking at the math, Izzy frowned as she handed some papers to Nikki, who also looked disgusted. "Can I just continue running?" she asked.

"Hey," Grace scolded. "You want to get into the Air Force Academy; sit down and do what I tell you. Your dad can only get you in so far."

Nikki sat down, grumbling, and grabbed a piece of a half-eaten sandwich and a number two pencil. She looked at the problems worksheet and started doing the exercises. After the trip to Mexico and Nevada, she had finally caught up with schoolwork, but she still felt it was a chore.

Several minutes transpired before Grace dropped her pencil and looked at the timer on her cell phone. "Time," she exclaimed.

"You're too fast!" Bryan complained half-jokingly. "Give us a minute to catch up."

"I did," Grace said. "That is why I called TIME."

"Have I mentioned that I hate your girlfriend?" Jaime said to Bryan.

"You're not the only one," Nikki said, frowning at her work.

Stephen peered over Izzy's shoulder and saw her numbers. "Not bad," he said. "We got the same."

"We could both be wrong," Izzy said, giving Grace her answer sheet.

Grace grabbed all the answer sheets from her friends and sisters and looked over them. "This is pretty good, Rogers," the dark-haired teen said.

"Really?" Nikki asked.

"I hate to say it, but I can't lie on the math," Grace replied.

"What about us?" Stephen asked as he hugged Izzy.

"You did okay," Grace said.

"Just okay?" Izzy asked as she grabbed her answer sheet from Grace's hand. "I'm the only one who opened the books while we were traveling, and I did just okay."

"Math is just not your thing," Grace replied as she let Bryan hug her.

Izzy scoffed as she sank into Stephen's arms, seeing a group of football players approach the group.

"Hey, guys," one of the boys greeted. The seventeen-year-old, six-foot-two-inch young man had short black hair, dark skin, and dark brown eyes. His black varsity jacket had the letter 'C' stitched on his chest. Always confident, there was a sense of nervousness in his greeting as he stepped away from his pack of friends. "How is the studying coming along?"

"Hey, Charlie," Stephen greeted. "Some are doing better than others."

"What's up, fearless Captain?" Grace asked with a smile drawn on her face.

"Oh," Charlie said, getting a little bit nervous. "I just wanted to ask Nikki a question."

Nikki looked surprised as Izzy and Grace just smiled mischievously at her sister. "Me?" Nikki asked.

"I wanted to ask you if you would go to the Spring formal with me," the boy said.

Nikki's cheeks turned bright red, matching the color of her hair. "Ummm," Nikki started, looking at her sisters for support. "We were planning to attend as a group."

"Yeah," Jaime said. "But we all have dates. You are the only one who was going stag."

"Ummm," Nikki said again, as if she had forgotten the English language. In her mind, she heard both her sisters scream at her. *Say yes! Please do it for the plot.*

"Okay," Nikki blurted out.

"Great," Charlie said. "Do you mind if I tag with your squad, or do you want to meet at the dance?"

"Ummm," Nikki said.

"What my sister is trying to say is that you can meet us at our place," Grace said.

"Great," Charlie said. "Talk to you later." Saying that, the boy walked away.

"You can speak now," Izzy said to her sister. "The big bad boy is gone."

Nikki's face looked like a strawberry. "Was that as bad as I think it was?"

"Totally," Jaimie said.

"One hundred percent," Bryan said.

"Tough thinking of a worst-case scenario," Stephen said.

Nikki sank her face into her hands while Izzy rubbed her back. "What the hell happened to me?" she asked herself. "I've taken on demon trolls, hell gargoyles, and master vampires. And I folded like a paper napkin."

"To be fair, he did seem nervous," Izzy said.

"Yeah," Jaimie said. "I don't think I've ever seen Charlie ask a girl out and feel that his voice would crack."

Grace giggled. "You folded like a wet towel."

Nikki grabbed an eraser and threw it at her sister, who caught it instinctively.

Izzy smiled, seeing the banter between her sisters, when her cell phone vibrated once. She picked it up and read the message. "Mom is just around the corner," she informed the group.

Grace and Nikki nodded as they started packing their books and school supplies. Stephen helped Izzy with her things. "Any news yet on your sister?"

Jaime and Bryan looked up as Izzy looked at her boyfriend. "Not yet," Izzy replied. "She's alive, though. She keeps knocking at my mind at night. And she still likes to throw nightmares at me. But I've gotten used to it."

"A natural to call for attention," Grace said.

"She has her reasons," Izzy said softly. Then she smiled at Stephen. "We'll find her. Mom and Dad are on it."

"Speaking of your mom, she's here," Nikki said, looking at the SUV pulling into the parking lot.

The sisters picked up their gear, said their goodbyes to their friends, and started making their way toward Elizabeth.

"I still can't believe you told them about Leah," Grace commented.

"They would have found out eventually," Izzy said with a shrug. "I might as well prepare them for her."

"I noticed how you didn't mention the part about you and Leah being born in limbo," Nikki said. "Both of you being conceived on a day that doesn't exist."

Izzy glared at Nikki. "There is no easy way to bring that into a conversation."

"We're aware," Grace said. "It still confuses me to this day, and I had an exclusive on that nugget of information."

There was a brief silence before Nikki spoke up. "You

know that it's not your fault you got separated, right?"

Izzy stopped and looked at her sister. "I'm fully aware of that. Call it destiny or stupid fate. Fifty percent chance it could have been me stuck in that hellish place and then land in Eastern Europe."

"If that had been the case, I guess you would be pretty resentful to your sister and parents who had a life of privilege," Grace said. "While she battled her way through hell and back."

"Any theories on why you got separated?" Nikki asked.

"Who knows," Izzy replied. "John mentioned something about balance, which I find idiotic."

"Well," Grace said with a shrug, "You're Catholic. A purpose will reveal itself to you on all this. Isn't that what you believe?"

Izzy continued walking towards her mother followed by her sisters. "I hate that you keep throwing that in my face."

As they reached the SUV, the blonde Guardian called out to her daughter. "Izzy, I've got news for Grace. Can you ride in the back?"

Grace, Nikki, and Izzy looked at each other. They silently obeyed as Elizabeth started the vehicle's engine.

"Is it about the Tome?" Grace asked as she jumped into the front seat of the car.

"Yes," Elizabeth said. She slowly pulled away from the parking spot and started driving back home. "We got word from John in Mexico."

"When is he coming back?" Izzy asked. "It's been more than two weeks now."

"He's been closing some loose ends," Elizabeth said, looking in the rearview mirror at her daughter.

She then turned toward Grace. "With the help of Luis and Victoria, we got some information from the Tome."

"What is it?" Grace asked.

"It seems that the book's pages were magically sealed," Elizabeth said. "No one could read them without breaking the curse that bound them."

"But the pages were readable when my parents found the book," Grace said. "They scanned it."

"Yes," Elizabeth said. "Somehow, your parents found a way to break the seal of the pages. Once they did that, they made notations in it."

"They wrote in the book?" Nikki asked. "Why?"

"John found out that a few pages had blank spaces to write responses to specific questions," Elizabeth said. "For example, when will the event be? Where? How to stop it? What is needed?

"And Grace's parents provided the answers to those questions?" Izzy asked.

"Yes," Elizabeth said, turning toward Grace. Her face was filled with dread. She parked the car next to their coffee shop and searched for the right words for what she was about to say. "Each question was linked to a curse that wreaked havoc on anyone who broke it by answering it."

"How?" Grace asked.

"Physically," Elizabeth said. "When your parents answered the questions, their bodies took the full brunt of the curses."

"They were dying?" Grace asked as her eyes started to tear up.

Elizabeth nodded. "The longer they waited, the more painful their inevitable death would be." The blonde Guardian paused for a second. "Williams and Lewis looked up the curses and the spells to break them. No one could break them. It was impossible. That's the point of them." Elizabeth took another pause, seeing Grace's eyes. "But your parents found a way. They were the only ones with the magical understanding to perform the ritual."

"Okay," Nikki said. "But how does that explain the ancient ones getting involved? They wrote the thing."

"Sean suspects that Neil and Sabine did not have all the answers," Elizabeth said. "They found a way to get the Tome to Grace's parents, hoping they could break the code."

"That doesn't explain why Neil killed them," Izzy said.

"To spare them," Grace concluded.

Elizabeth sighed as she looked at her demon hunter. "We contemplated that scenario."

Grace took a deep breath, closing her eyes. Tears slowly crawled down her cheeks. "Did my parents fill in the blanks?" she asked. "Did they get the answers needed to stop this?"

"They did," Elizabeth said. "John, Victoria, and Luis are processing the information as we speak."

Anna, Balish, and Raymond, LLP; Los Angeles; February 26, 9:30 p.m.

DANIEL ANDERSON STEPPED OUT of his office building in LA, dressed in a tailored black tuxedo. He was calm and collected as he entered a black polarized limousine waiting for him. The faceless driver closed the door as soon as the man entered, then slowly walked toward the vehicle's driver's seat and drove away.

Daniel pulled out his cell phone and dialed one of his contacts as he poured himself a glass of Macallan whiskey. "Let's go over it again," Daniel said over the phone. "Shred all documentation from Hela Corp. There is no need for them again. Also, cancel my eleven o'clock tomorrow and move my two to four." The man hung up and took a deep breath before sipping his drink. He looked outside the window and watched the street lights of downtown Los Angeles, clearing his mind.

Suddenly, the limousine took an unexpected left turn, going in the opposite direction of the benefit he had scheduled. "Driver!" Daniel called out, pressing the intercom button. The separator door remained closed, and there was no answer. "Driver!" Daniel stated. "You're going the wrong way."

The limousine stopped at a red light, and the doors unlocked themselves. Daniel looked surprised as the right door opened, and a young man in his early twenties entered the vehicle. He was dressed in a black trench coat and a white dress shirt. His brown hair was neatly combed, and his eyeglasses covered his brown eyes. "It's chilly out there," the young man said as the limousine doors locked and the vehicle pulled away.

Daniel frowned at the intruder and took another sip of his drink. "A Guardian, I assume," Daniel said.

"John Simmons," John said, making himself comfortable as he looked directly into Daniel's eyes.

"The Guardians and I have no business to discuss," Daniel said.

"We're not discussing anything on this ride, Mr. Anderson," John said.

Daniel looked bored. He took another drink and

stared directly into John's soul as he crossed his legs. "Look, boy," the man said. "You seem new to this game. So, let me make the rules absolutely clear. You can't touch me. I am a human—a living and breathing human being. Touching me goes against everything you and your Guardians preach to your little girls. So stop wasting my time and get out."

"You murdered several demon hunters," John said. "I just wanted to ask why. What skin do you have in this game? They're innocent, fighting for those who can't fight for themselves. Why do this?"

Daniel laughed as he poured himself another drink. "You're hilarious," he said. He took another sip and dangled his glass. "No one is innocent, no matter how much you preach to your little girls. But to answer your question, I do it because I can. I get paid to do this, and I get paid well. I have no idea why interested parties want so many of your demon hunters dead. And it's not my job to care."

"You have no remorse at all?" John asked with a serious tone. "You will continue doing this no matter what lives you take. No matter how many families you shatter. You will continue murdering innocent girls so that you can get paid?"

"You girls knew the risks," Daniel said. "In this line of work, that is your destiny. I just point the correct foes in the right direction." Daniel smiled as his drink dangled in his hand.

"Okay," John said, nodding his head. "You're right about a lot of things. Especially the part about our girls not tainting their hands in killing human beings. Not even if they deserve it. Not even if they're as despicable as you."

John paused as he looked at Daniel's smiling face. "Our girls are above that. They're heroes in this dark world, and their souls should remain pure when dealing with rancid beings such as yourself."

Daniel continued smiling as the glass dangled from his hand. "Our girls give their lives willingly for those in need. There is no greater calling to that. So yes, Mr. Anderson. Our girls will not take your life."

A drop of sweat streamed down Daniel's forehead. "You want to know something interesting about our organization?" John asked, looking at the limousine's ceiling. "In ancient times, The Guardians considered the demon hunters their puppets. They were their attack dogs to do their bidding, staining the demon hunter's purpose. It wasn't until very recently that there was a change in administration. I learned early on—they don't work for the Guardians. The Guardians work for their demon hunters."

Daniel's smile remained frozen, as his body was paralyzed, with the drink still dangling from his hand. John leaned toward the man with a white handkerchief and took the drink from his paralyzed hand. "We stain our souls so that they remain pure to the horrors of taking a human life," John said.

The young Guardian put the glass next to the whiskey bottle and sat back across Daniel. "You took Angie's life," John said. "You took her life and in the process shattered mine."

Daniel's eyes were full of fear while his crooked smile remained. "You took the lives of countless girls who were doing everything to protect all that is good and beautiful in this world. You shattered the lives of their loved ones. A father and mother who won't be able to hug their daughter. A brother who won't be able to play with their sister. A friend whose heart will be forever empty because you considered it was in your interest to do so."

The limousine stopped in a dark alley. The doors from the front opened and closed. Soon, the passenger doors opened, and Victoria and Luis looked in. "We're here," Luis said.

"These are Victoria and Luis," John stated to Daniel. "The Guardians in Mexico had to deliver the devastating news to countless family members. They wanted to be here for this moment."

Daniel's eyes started to water as he was unable to close them. "The paralyzing agent is only that," John said. "No poison. Just frozen—a side effect of the drink you took. But your nervous system will remain active. The pain sensors are active, so you will feel what happens next."

The young Guardian stepped out of the limousine as Victoria and Luis spilled blood around the vehicle while leaving the doors open. "There is a nest nearby," John said, looking down the alley. "The vampires around here are not very bright, and I'm sure they have never turned anyone. They're just interested in a meal."

John looked back at Daniel Anderson one last time. "Goodbye, Mr. Anderson."

John, Victoria, and Luis headed toward a parked black SUV outside the alley. John jumped in the back seat while Luis took the driver's seat and Victoria got in on the passenger side. Luis started the engine and drove off from the scene.

John pulled out a tablet and monitored the camera feed he left behind on the limousine, seeing Daniel's paralyzed body. It didn't take long before three vampires jumped inside the vehicle and started feeding.

John's phone started ringing, and the Guardian saw it was Sean calling. "Hello," John answered.

"Is it done?" Sean asked.

"It's done," John replied.

"Good," Sean said. "Have Victoria and Luis drop you off at St. Helena. We've got work to do."

John hung up the phone and looked at his friend in the front of the SUV. "Can you take me to St. Helena?"

"On our way," Luis replied.

John looked outside the window and stared at the lights. He took a deep breath, letting himself think of Angela one more time. "I'm sorry," John whispered as the SUV drove into the night.